DARKNESS SHIFTING

Tides of Darkness
Book One

Printed in the United States of America.

First Printing, 2016
ISBN: 978-0692728338

Editor: Julie Hutchings

Cover Concept:
James Hicks
Sarah Fox
Laura Oliva

Cover Design:
Vania Stoyanova

This book is a work of fiction. References to real people, events, establishments, organizations, or locations are intended only to provide a sense of authenticity, and are used fictitiously. All other characters, and all incidents and dialogue, are drawn from the author's imagination and are not to be construed as real.

This book is dedicated to my Sweet Mama,
who gave me the keys to the universe by teaching me to read.

For My awesome

cousin

DARKNESS SHIFTING

Alan

Tides of Darkness
Book One

Much love

Sarah L. Blair

Chapter 1

She smelled it before she saw it.

Like always, the stink of the crime scene crept ahead of the gory view. Sidney Lake knew this one was bad; the meaty smell of torn flesh, the copper scent of blood, mixed with the tinge of electricity buzzing from the third rail of the subway tracks below, the putrid smell of an opened bowel swirled with the filth of scavenging rats.

It all made her very glad she hadn't had time for breakfast. She'd rolled out of bed, thrown her trench coat over jeans and a black sweater, slipped on her favorite black steel-toed boots, and come straight down.

"Sorry about the late hour," Dr. Tom Fellows said.

New York City's Medical Examiner lifted the yellow caution tape marking off the crime scene to let Sidney under.

"It's not late anymore. It's early." She grabbed the paper cup of coffee out of his hand and took a slug. It was cold and sour. She gagged. "Ugh. How long have you been down here, anyway?"

"Too long." The medical examiner took his cup back, finished the last swig, and tossed it in a wire trash can.

Tom would have made a good linebacker thirty years ago, if he'd been taller. Instead, he'd chosen the lab over sports. Now his shoulders had a curve to them that never went away. A result of decades of being hunched over a table dissecting cadavers.

"What have you got?" Sidney asked.

"I was hoping you could tell me," Tom said.

He removed his glasses, rubbed his eyes, and perched them on his nose again as they made their way down the long connecting corridor toward a part of the subway most New Yorkers never bothered taking the time to see: the abandoned City Hall Station. It was the first subway stop opened to the public in 1904, legendary for its intricate mosaics and architecture.

"You're the medical examiner. I thought identifying bodies was part of your job description."

The fluorescent lighting bounced off the white tiles and she figured it was no wonder Tom had lost track of time. The stark and seemingly endless tunnel reminded her of the hallways at the morgue where she was used to watching Dr. Fellows work. Except the Office of the Chief Medical Examiner didn't have graffitied ads for one-time use toothbrushes and torn up movie posters plastered in the hallways.

Tom gave her a lopsided grin. "Wouldn't have called you in for any run-of-the-mill homicide, would I? The weird stuff is your jurisdiction."

Sidney opened her mouth to tell Tom exactly where he could put his weird cases this early in the morning, but they reached the platform and she saw the source of the awful stench.

Blood coated the tiles as if someone had hurled cans of paint at the walls. She swallowed back a gag and took a deep breath in through her mouth, filling her lungs slowly, and out through her nose, forcing the stink away.

"The amount of blood one body contains." She shook her head. "It's amazing."

Tom nodded, allowing her to take a moment while her mind tried to make sense of the mess in front of her. It was always hard to process the bits and pieces at first, but once she picked out something familiar in the middle of the carnage, it all fell into place.

Her brain told her this was a cadaver, but it was like none she'd ever laid eyes on before. There was a leg over here, half a rib cage over there, and the head was... well, the head was something else entirely.

They moved around the curve of the short platform where a man she'd never met crouched by the other half of the rib cage scribbling notes on a clipboard.

"Agent Lake, I'd like you to meet my new assistant." Tom swept his arm wide to make the introduction. "This is Dr. Jackson Banks."

Whenever Tom called her in to view a scene, he'd already sent off the first responders, done the photos, and gathered the evidence. All that was left for Sidney to do was figure out what type of creature they dealing with and how to stop it. She hadn't expected anyone new to be let into their exclusive circle. Hell, their investigation team was so private it didn't even have a name.

They called themselves Agents or Detectives depending on the situation, and they were only official in as much as they were certified private investigators. They didn't have jurisdiction because they were above jurisdiction. They were like the Men In Black, except they weren't dealing with aliens. They didn't have the space-age technology for all the fun gadgets and weapons either.

As disgusting, and frightening as the job could be sometimes, it was also thrilling and she was grateful to have it. She wasn't sure where she would be if her boss Mitchell Harris hadn't pulled her off the self-destructive path she was heading down six years ago and given her something meaningful to focus on. She'd wanted an escape from reality, from thinking about the awful way her parents met their end, from the nightmares that still haunted her. At least this was a more effective way of fighting the darkness than taking whatever pills she could get her hands on and drinking her way through all the hottest clubs in town.

"Call me Banks." The man stood, clipboard in hand, shoe covers soggy with blood, drawing her out of her thoughts. His hands were enveloped in cerulean blue neoprene gloves, so he shrugged an apology rather than offering to shake. He gave a half-smile; embarrassed by the informality. "Jack is fine, too. Everybody called my father Dr. Banks."

There was a drawl in his words that made her think of wide, shady porches and sweet tea in sweaty glasses. His graham cracker hair had gone too long without a trim. He was well-built and, unlike Tom, would have fit right on top of the homecoming float next to the prom queen.

His smile spread into a straight-toothed American grin, easy and contagious. Sidney started to smile but stopped herself. They were at a crime-scene. This was a job. She needed to be professional.

"I'm Lake," she said.

"Pleasure," Banks said, and glanced at the pile of shredded flesh between them with a shrug. "Well, considering."

"A maintenance train operator spotted the body here on the platform right after 2:00 a.m.," Tom said. "Nobody saw or heard anything, but there was enough time between trains for this to take place."

"You're finished photographing?" Sidney used the covered band she always kept on her wrist to pull her long, mahogany hair up into a messy bun on top of her head. She slipped on the shoe protectors over her well-worn boots and traded Tom her black trench coat for a pair of gloves.

"All yours," he said.

She worked her fingers into the gloves and crouched next to the body. It was hard to tell exactly what was what. She noted the ragged marks at the edge of the wounds, and raised her eyebrows.

"This was done by hand?"

"That's my guess," Banks said. "Some of the severed edges are cleaner than others, but most of the damage happened by ripping or tearing. If you have a look at this, though, it explains some of the wounding. Whatever caused this damage was similar in nature to the victim."

He lifted John Doe's arm. Sidney squinted, despite the bright lights that had been brought in to illuminate the scene. At the end of the arm were five fingers of a man's hand with thick black fingernails that narrowed and curved slightly at the ends.

"Are those claws?" She raised her eyebrows.

"That was our conclusion." Tom stood by, watching.

"That's not all," Banks said. He reached over to the head of the body. The flesh at the neck was torn nearly all the way through, and the weight of the skull pulled back gave her a good view inside the esophagus.

Sidney grimaced, and made note of the jagged skin around the edges. "This was done by hand too?"

Banks gave a single nod. She wasn't sure she wanted to think about what could be powerful enough to yank someone's head off.

"And check this out." Banks slid his hand under the skull and lifted it up. The thing stared right at her. Its limp tongue stretched out long between extremely sharp canines. Thick hair covered the entire face, not only along the jawline, which jutted out much farther than what was normal for the shape of a human skull. The one eye that remained intact was rolled back into the head. On either side of the cranium stood tall pointed ears.

Sidney stared into the face of a wolf.

"Is it what we think it is?" Banks was a little too excited about the find. He used the tips of his first two fingers to tilt the head down a little more to give her a better view.

"No." She shook her head and stood up. "Werewolves are extinct."

It was a sentence she repeated to herself so many times in the middle of the night, she'd lost count. Every time she woke up sweaty and shaking, she whispered those words to herself in the dark. Now she was on this

6

filthy abandoned subway platform face-to-face with one of the creatures right out of her nightmares.

The gloves stuck to her palms, making it hard to yank them off.

"Come on," Banks insisted. "This may as well be straight out of the *Wolfman*."

"Hollywood special effects aren't generally what we go on when identifying these types of things," she said as she stuffed the gloves into a red jug marked *Biohazard*. "Werewolves never even made it to America. They were hunted into extinction hundreds of years ago. There's no such thing as werewolves. Not anymore."

"Then what is it?" Banks asked, his drawl too genteel for such a gory scene.

Sidney wished she had an answer to give him, but she didn't. There were things she'd witnessed on this job that she never could have imagined would be possible. Witches and sorcerers were the most common thing they dealt with. Poltergeists and ghosts, sure. They even came across an occasional gargoyle or leprechaun every now and then. But not this. Not werewolves.

"We'll get it loaded up and back to the lab," Tom said. "Maybe we'll find something new once we get it out on the table."

He returned her coat but she didn't put it back on. A thin sheen of sweat covered the nape of her neck.

Banks' forehead creased deeply and his lower lip jutted out the tiniest bit. She couldn't tell if he was concentrating on a new theory or disappointed his first one hadn't worked out.

"Nice to meet you," she said.

"Be seeing you around, I'm sure," he said, and went back to study the scene in front of him.

Tom escorted her back up the tunnel, even though she insisted she could go it alone.

"Let me know what you find out at the lab," she said.

"You'll be my first call."

"We should get together for another cookout soon. It'd be nice to see you over something other than a dead body," Sidney said.

Tom chuckled, "A ribeye is still technically a piece of dead meat."

"But so much more appetizing," Sidney smiled.

"It's a good idea. Banks is new in town, I'm sure Carla would like to take him under her wing."

"She's good at that. Make it happen." Sidney gave him a light punch on the shoulder. "Stay safe."

"You too."

She turned and shuffled up the stairs along with a crowd flooding the walkway from the Number Six train. She flinched as her eyes adjusted to the full daylight above ground.

Lush green grass carpeted City Hall Park. Daffodils waved happily in flowerbeds around the edge of the path. Tiny green buds dotted all the branches on the trees overhead. Lawyers in bold power ties carried expensive leather cases towards the courthouse down the block. Students cut through the park on the way to early classes at the university over on Park Row. Tourists hurried across the street to walk the Brooklyn Bridge.

Not one of them knew what was down there in the subway tunnel. They were all too busy and self-involved to guess what lay in the darkness beyond the platform. Sidney and her fellow agents had to keep it that way.

Chapter 2

The stink of the crime scene stuck to Sidney like perfume sprayed by an overzealous Macy's sales associate. She wanted to go home and take a long, hot bath, but she was already downtown only a few blocks away from the office. She opted to go grab that coffee she'd skipped in her hurry to get out the door.

She cut through the park to her favorite little coffee spot. A tiny hut in the middle of the sidewalk, painted green and crammed full of newspapers and magazines, pastries, bottled water, and all the other various and sundry items necessary for a respite from the rush of life, an island oasis in the middle of the bustling city. After the unnerving crime scene, the sight of her favorite vendor behind the counter was a comfort.

"Morning, Jai." She waved while he handed a receipt to a man in a brushed silk suit. Lawyer, she guessed. The man pushed out the door without even so much as a thanks, leaving her as the only customer in the shop.

"Hey there, pretty lady."

Jai's straight, jet black hair lay neatly across his forehead. He wore a white button up under a navy blue t-shirt with the Yankees logo on it. It was pretty much his uniform.

"What's going on today?" Jai made himself busy during the lull by refilling the donut case with all shapes and flavors of fried dough.

"Oh, you know, the usual." She checked her image in the shiny side of the donut case, smoothed a finger over her eyebrows, and made a mental note to stop by the salon for a wax. Shrugging back into her coat, she switched her impromptu bun to a high ponytail. "How's the coffee coming?"

"Brewing fresh. Be right up." He came out from behind the counter and snapped the plastic tie around a bunch of newspapers with a pocket knife, then rearranged the stack to a new pile. The headline on the *Times* caught her attention:

CONGRESS PASSES BILL, AWARDS LAKE INDUSTRIES CONTRACT

Below the headline two men shook hands in a full-color photo. The piercing turquoise eyes and familiar smug smile from the man on the right raised her heart rate. She picked up the paper and read the beginning of the article.

Chairman of Lake Industries, Alexander Lake (pictured above, right), was in Washington D.C. yesterday, shaking hands with the U.S. Defense Secretary, Richard Skeller (above, left). Lake Industries, a research and development firm known mostly for its genetic research, has partnered with the U.S. Army Research Institute for Behavioral and Social Sciences (ARI) and will be using the newly awarded 1.2 Billion Dollar grant to fund a new division of military research.

"Here you go, pretty lady." Jai offered her a steaming cup. "With half-and-half, right? Your favorite."

She tossed the paper back on the stack and took the cup. "Thanks."

"Everything okay?" he asked. "You look like you saw a ghost."

11

"Technical term for that is *spectral apparition*," a familiar voice said behind her.

Jai raised an eyebrow. "You would know, Mr. *Ghosts Gone Wild.*"

Her partner, Graham Williams, pressed his hand to his chest at the reference to his former television show. "Ouch."

He was the all-in-one brother and best friend she'd never had, and they gave each other constant hell. Sarcasm and insults were their preferred method of communication. It was perfect for her, really; he had her back no matter what, and she never had to get too personal.

"Low blow, Jai," Sidney warned. Just because she teased her partner constantly didn't mean anyone else had the right.

"Morning, Lake. Mmm, jelly. Come to Papa." Williams took the high road, pretending the other man had just become a spectral apparition. He wiggled his fingers at an oozing donut as if he could bring it forth from the case by sheer will power alone. It reminded her of other oozing things and she turned, leaving Williams to finish the transaction.

Outside, her partner sucked in a noisy breath as they cut back through the park towards Park Row.

"What a great morning, huh?" Williams took a big bite out of his jelly donut and spoke with his mouth full. "These flowers, gorgeous."

She took a good look at her partner. His dark unruly hair stuck out on one side and his beige trench coat hung from his lanky frame like it was still on a hanger. The tie he wore, a navy background with royal blue plaid, and a bright turquoise vine running throughout, hung crooked around his neck. "What's with the tie?"

"What about it? It's vintage."

"Vintage clown?"

"Be nice. It's early," he said.

"You're in a cheery mood. Did you get laid or something?"

"Sure did." Williams shoved the last half of the donut in his mouth and licked his fingers off one at a time. "Megan was feelin' frisky. I took advantage. Sue me."

"So that's why you weren't at the crime scene."

"No. Today's Friday, remember? I take the girls to school every Friday. This is not a new thing."

"I think you were avoiding it."

"Was not."

Sidney shrugged. "Admit it. You're a wuss when things get gory."

"I did thirteen riveting episodes of that stupid show and thirty seconds of me barfing is all anybody remembers. Am I *ever* going to live that down?"

"Not as long as the Internet exists." Sidney bumped his shoulder with her own. "Besides, I was referring to that time with the sushi. You still owe me for those shoes."

"You're never going to let that drop, are you? Whatever you saw today can't be any worse than what those hexed koalas did on that cargo ship. I didn't barf then and that was the grossest thing ever."

"This was worse."

"No way. Nothing can be worse than devil koalas."

"Nefertiri's Curse was worse than the devil koalas. Remember how those research students were—"

"No. Don't even." Williams shuddered. "So what are we dealing with now? It seriously can't be as nasty as flesh melting Mummy curses."

Sidney wasn't concerned about being overheard. The street grew quiet as they made their way down toward the waterfront in the shadow of the Brooklyn Bridge. The traffic on the ramp above made it difficult for anyone to hear anyway. Still, she waited until after they passed the narrow dog run before she said anything in case the older woman flipping through *Cosmo* felt like being nosy while her tiny Yorkie sniffed around.

"New Guy thinks it's a werewolf."

"They're extinct, right?" Williams stopped short at the corner. "Wait, what new guy?"

"Tom got a new assistant. About damn time. I was starting to think he'd moved into the morgue. Maybe this way he can come up for some fresh air once in awhile." She took a few steps into the crosswalk. "And yeah, they're supposed to be extinct."

"A lot of things aren't supposed to exist, but they do." Williams caught up to her and they crossed the street together. "Is he cool?"

"The new guy? He's okay, I guess. Kind of hard to get a feel for someone when you meet them over a shredded hunk of torso."

"Ugh. Gross."

A narrow four-story red brick walk-up stood on the next corner. The ground floor contained an eclectic little bar called the Cowgirl Sea-Horse. Antler chandeliers hung from the ceiling draped with fish netting and colorful paper chains. With great food and cold booze on the menu, it was a nice little spot to hang out and even nicer that they had a deal with the owners. The agents went about their business on the top floor and no one asked any questions.

Williams opened the side door with his key card and they went in. The place was empty this time of morning, but the kitchen staff would be arriving soon to prep for the day. The door clicked shut behind them and they went straight through the kitchen to the staircase that led up to their office.

"We should bring the Banks guy here," Sidney said. "He had a Southern accent. Maybe he'll like the shrimp and grits."

"Or the chicken fried chicken," Williams said. "Not to stereotype or anything. But for the simple reason that it's freakin' awesome."

"You eat that junk almost every day. When's the last time you had your cholesterol checked?"

"What? It comes with collard greens. That's healthy."

Sidney opened the office door and entered the loft area. It wasn't a huge space, but it was plenty of room for their little group. The original hardwood floors were still there from the days when huge ships sailed into port at the end of the street and horses clip-clopped heavy wagons across the cobblestones.

Their space rose above the surrounding buildings, so natural light filled the room. A glass wall hung with

Venetian blinds partitioned off the chief's office from the rest of the space.

This morning his door stood open and he was already behind his desk.

"Morning, Chief," Williams said, on the way to his computer.

Sidney stopped and leaned in the doorway. "You're here early."

The chief glanced up. His collar was unbuttoned and his sleeves rolled to his elbows.

"Or did you never leave?"

He rubbed his hand over his bald head and sat back in his chair. "I hear we had a cold one this morning."

"Couple blocks from here." She went into his office and placed her coffee on the edge of the desk next to his nameplate. The black carved granite read: Chief Mitchell Harris.

She narrowed her eyes. "Where were you between midnight and 2 a.m.?"

He tossed a ballpoint on his desk and stood. She had to tilt her head back a little to see his face.

He lowered his voice, giving it that gruff sound that made her ache for cool sheets and warm skin. "Going to arrest me?"

"Lucky for you, I left my handcuffs at home."

A smile twitched across his mouth. He scratched the stubble on his jaw as cover, then took a toothbrush out of the top drawer and grabbed yesterday's red and black striped tie from the edge of his desk. Sidney hid her disappointment when he directed the conversation back to business. "Williams went to the scene with you?"

"He was conveniently late." She followed him to the bathroom. "You know he has a weak constitution."

"It's FRIDAY," Williams yelled across the empty room. "Kids. School. My turn. Not new."

They both ignored him.

"What were you able to determine?" the chief asked.

"It can't be what it looks like."

"What's it look like?"

"Werewolf."

Sidney didn't say anything else, allowing a moment to let the information sink in while he freshened up. There were plenty of nights when Mitch had been the one to hold her and tell her the ugly things in her dreams weren't real. All she had to do was look at him to know they were both recalling her screams of terror in the middle of the night. He turned off the water and wiped his face with a paper towel from the dispenser.

"What's Tom's opinion?"

"Hasn't formed one yet."

Mitch turned up his collar and tied his tie. When he finished the knot, she folded the collar down. She caught the edge of his worn-off cologne, a mix of chocolate and oranges. The rope of worry that bound her up loosened a little.

He ran his hands along her upper arms. "You're shaking."

Sidney tossed a quick glance out the door and saw Williams engrossed with something on his computer screen.

"Haven't finished my coffee yet." She gave Mitch a brave smile. His eyes were the same gray color as the shadows the bridge cast over the street outside. "I'm fine."

"You always forget, I can tell when you're lying." His hands dropped away, leaving her arms cold. He checked his appearance again in the mirror, then pulled an electric razor out of the cabinet.

"Hey, photos are up," Williams called out.

The chief crossed the room and leaned over Williams' shoulder. The flat screen monitor showed the photos from the crime scene in high resolution.

Sidney took her time in joining them. She still had the stink on her clothes, she didn't need to relive the visuals. She also refused to let this case get to her. The last thing she wanted was for the chief, or anyone else for that matter, thinking she was too scared to do her job.

The chief squinted at the picture.

"Wow. Definitely a werewolf," Williams said.

Sidney stayed behind her partner, and paid close attention to the chief's reaction instead. He squinted as he studied the photos, and if she didn't know any better, she would have said his skin paled a few shades. But he couldn't have been an FBI agent for twenty-five years only to get squeamish at something like this.

"Werewolves haven't been anything more than a fairy tale for centuries." The chief straightened up, but the edges of his mouth were set in a tight line. Sidney could tell when he was lying too.

"Then what the hell do you call that?" Williams gestured to the screen.

"There's no point jumping to conclusions until we get a report from Tom," the chief said. "Lake, my office."

She followed him into his office and he shut the door against Williams' open-mouthed stare. Her partner hated being excluded from anything.

"I can put you on something else if you're not comfortable with this." He moved behind his desk but didn't sit down.

"It's all right. I can handle it."

He tapped the pen on the desk for a few seconds while he watched her. "Peters is tracking down a possible revenant. You could give him a hand."

"No. I want this case." It grated on her nerves when he pulled the overprotective card.

He sank down in his chair, silent. Finally, he met her gaze again. His eyes were tired, and for the first time ever, she saw the shadow of age on his face. It scared her. She pushed the thought away and pretended it hadn't crossed her mind.

"This hits too close to home and you know it." Sidney opened her mouth to protest, but he cut her off. "I'm sorry, Sidney. If I'd known what we were dealing with, I would never have sent you down there this morning."

"I told you, I'm fine."

"Liar."

Sidney straightened her shoulders. "I can do this."

The lines at the edges of his eyes deepened. He pinned her with his dark gray stare while he considered her words. Finally, he gave a curt nod toward the door. "Get Williams."

She called in her partner and the chief addressed them both. "Where are you guys on that missing chimera? His wife's called twice this week."

"No leads. It's like he just disappeared into thin air," Sidney said.

"Nobody disappears into thin air. There's always an explanation."

"That wife of his is pretty annoying. You sure he didn't go out for milk and not come back?" Williams asked.

The chief threw his pen at Williams who ducked, causing it to hit the glass wall with a *thunk*. "You two track down your friend Renny. The way he gets around, he might have seen or heard something about this incident last night. I'll give Dimitrius a call. Maybe he can give us some insight on what these things might be."

"You got it, Chief," Williams said.

"And be careful," Mitch warned.

"Yes, sir."

She followed her partner out, leaving the sound of the electric razor buzzing behind them.

Chapter 3

The afternoon sun played hide-and-seek with the pedestrians of Canal Street. It emerged from behind a cloud and brightened the street long enough for them to glance up with hopeful faces before disappearing again. The agents didn't have a specific way of getting in touch with Renny, he always seemed to know when they were looking for him. If they waited in one spot long enough he usually showed up.

They decided to grab lunch from a food truck and hang out in the Jeep for a stakeout.

"I love how casual the chief is about calling up one of the most powerful dudes in the world. Like they're BFFs." Williams spoke with his mouth full.

"No biggie," he continued. "I'm on a first name basis with the Queen of England. She likes it when I call her Betsy. Bono and I are buds too, but I wouldn't want to bug him."

Sidney didn't respond.

He elbowed her. "Oh, come on, that's funny."

"Huh? Yeah, good one." Sidney stared down at her food, not able to summon an appetite.

Mitch was right, and it annoyed her when he was right. She shouldn't be anywhere near this case. Somewhere in the FBI archives was an unresolved file containing photos of her parents in a similar state as that victim in the subway this morning, minus the fangs and fur. Torn to pieces in their own bedroom one night with no explanation other than Sidney's recurring nightmares. In the past three years since Mitch had

21

recruited her to the agency, she'd seen a lot of scary shit, but none of it left the blood chilled in her veins like this did.

"What's with you today? It's shawarma. You love shawarma. Why are you staring at it like it might snarf you down?"

The idea of being eaten made her fold the foil over her pita and hand it over. "You want it?"

He took it and started in. "Is it the body this morning? Because that shizz is going to give me nightmares and my parents weren't even—"

She cut him off with a sharp stare.

"So, is Renny a creepy dude or what?" He changed the subject. "There's something off about him, right? Do you think he lives in the subway? Maybe he's part Mole Man."

"You think everyone's a Mole Man." Somewhere amongst the queasiness of fear was an undertow of excitement tugging at the edge of her conscience. After twelve long years of wondering, maybe this was finally her chance to uncover the truth about what happened to her parents.

"I forgot to tell you." Williams swallowed the last bite of her food before he continued. "Megan wants us to double next week. There's some guy she wants to introduce you to. A friend of a cousin or something. I wasn't really listening."

"No, thanks." Sidney took a swig of her bottled water.

"Please? She won't get off my back about it."

"Not happening."

"This one's some kind of doctor. Megan says it's perfect. He'd work. You'd work. You guys would never actually have to see each other."

She gave in to a smile. That sounded like something Megan would say. The leggy redhead never had trouble getting a date in her life. Williams was a total dork. They were an adorable cliché, the supermodel falling for the nerd. Together, with their two little girls, they were the perfect portrait of Upper West Side bliss.

It wasn't as if Sidney had a hard time getting a date for herself. More like, she never wanted one. Giving up clubbing meant giving up on fucking whoever she happened to wind up with at the end of the night. Just like the drugs and drinking, random dicks were no longer an escape route. She definitely didn't want to hook up with any of Megan's long lost frat boyfriends.

Now it was important to her to get to know someone before she got serious with them. The catch was that throwing herself into the job made getting to know any outsiders nearly impossible. Her occasional flings with the chief were enough to satisfy her. And he was mature enough that they could keep things professional without the mess of a relationship getting in the way.

It was nice to have someone she could trust and have fun in bed with. Love meant loss. The death of her parents had taught her that. Falling in love, having any kind of serious relationship with anyone was a risk too big for Sidney to take.

"At least tell her I asked, so she doesn't think I forgot." Williams leaned forward and squinted through the bug streaked windshield. "Hey, is that Renny?"

23

She sat up a little and spotted a familiar, greasy head of hair bobbing through the crowd. "Let's go."

She got out of the car and kicked her door shut.

Williams followed.

She maintained focus on the maroon jacket flapping in the light breeze. Renny kept his head down, but his nervous gaze darted from side to side like tiny black beetles in his eye sockets. She stayed in his direct path, hoping she could intercept him before he was even aware of her presence.

The man had a tendency to be skittish.

Almost as soon as the thought flitted through her mind, he lifted his face and saw her. Renny froze in the middle of the sidewalk. He held his hands up in front of him, palms out toward Sidney like a traffic cop signaling her to stop. He turned on the heel of his worn-out sneakers and headed in the opposite direction.

Out of her peripheral vision, she made note of Williams, working his way up to the corner in case Renny decided to run for it. She jogged to catch up with Renny and fell in step beside him.

"No, no. I have no time. No time for talking." Renny had a thick accent, something Eastern European.

"We'll make it quick. Have you eaten?"

The small man curled further inside his Members Only jacket as if he could disappear. It smelled like it hadn't been in a washing machine since 1982.

He licked his lips in response to her question, but kept his head down and stuck to his determined path like he was on a tether. "I have nothing to say."

"Are you hungry? I haven't eaten," she said.

"Is tempting offer." His black eyes flicked past her. She felt Williams at her elbow.

"Hi, Renny," Williams said.

Renny sank back into himself, like the frightened turtles the vendors sold in neon plastic boxes to tourists. "No. No. Busy day today. Thank you, maybe next time."

He sped up and dodged around a group of teenagers in matching yellow shirts taking pictures of fish heads on ice.

"Renny, wait." She turned and smacked Williams on the arm. "You scared him."

"No way. Not my fault he's a total nutter."

"Where did he go?" She stood on tiptoe straining to see over the never ending flow of people, but the head of stringy hair didn't resurface. "You let him get away."

"*I* let him get away?"

Sidney turned in a slow circle, scanning the crowd.

"There." Williams pointed toward a side street and took off down the alley.

She followed in his wake for half a block before she nearly collided with a woman carrying a basket of cabbages, and had to dodge a delivery truck backing out of an alley.

By the time she skidded around the corner onto Mott Street, she'd lost sight of Williams, but caught a glimpse of Renny, who disappeared into a store with knock-off handbags hanging in the front window. She chased him through the racks of t-shirts and out through an emergency door in the back.

"Renny, stop!" She tumbled into the alley after him. He slid on some forgotten take-out containers and slammed into the brick wall, but turned and kept running. Williams yelled from the other end of the alley, already out of breath. She kept up the chase.

Their informant climbed up a mountain of trash bags then grabbed the bottom rung of a fire-escape ladder. A loud clank reverberated down the alley as the ladder loosened from its holding. It was too late, Sidney was already in midair trying to catch his legs. She lost her balance and grabbed on to the frightened man. The rusty ladder gave way and they tumbled to the ground.

Luckily, they had a nice squishy pile of trash to land in. One of the black bags tore open, when Renny tried to move his foot out of Sidney's face. Fish guts and other discarded pieces from the market spilled out onto the pavement. There was no way to avoid rolling in the slimy mess.

"Thanks a lot, Renny." She pulled a tentacle out of her hair and scrunched up her face.

Williams jogged up to them, hand on his side, breathing as if he'd just crossed the finish line of the New York Marathon. He bent at the waist trying to catch his breath and caught a whiff of Sidney instead.

"This is way worse than that time you were covered in goblin—"

"Don't even." Sidney rolled off of the trash heap. "You swore you'd never bring that up."

He shoved his nose into the crook of his arm. "What? So he had kind of a crush on you. It was cute."

"It wasn't cute. He ruined my blue dress." She held out her hand and he pulled her to her feet.

"I don't have to be here for this conversation."
Renny climbed up and tried to sneak off.

"Not so fast, buster." Williams caught his jacket.

"Come on Renny." Sidney loosened Williams' grip
on him and picked a squiggly tentacle off the already
filthy velour. "Wouldn't you rather eat some food instead
of swim in it? How about a nice Reuben?"

Chapter 4

They chose a deli over on Lafayette.

It was past the lunch rush so the place was empty except for a family of tourists.

Sidney and Renny grabbed a table in the back corner, while Williams ordered and paid for the food. The family picked up and headed out in a rush, leaving their empty soda cans and sandwich paper on the table.

Sidney didn't want to pressure Renny, so she got up and threw the trash in the can next to the table just for something to do. New Yorkers were efficient, not rude. Williams brought the sandwich back and pulled up a chair from the next table sitting in it backwards, arms propped on the back.

Their informant dug into the sandwich as if it was his first and last meal put together. Wiggly bits of sauerkraut dangled from the side, reminding her of things she'd picked out of her hair back in the alley.

"Ever thought about entering the hot dog eating championship?" Williams asked.

She booted him under the table.

"What?" Williams rubbed his shin. "You spend a lot of the time in the subway, don't you? Ever seen any Mole Men down there?"

Renny stopped chewing for a second before he shook his head and went back to stuff another bite in his mouth. He made it obvious he was only there to eat. It was typical for him to be skittish, but this was extreme even for him.

"There was a body found last night on the City Hall platform." Sidney kept her voice low so the barrel of a man trying to listen in from behind the counter couldn't catch what they were saying. "Know anything about it?"

Renny kept chewing.

"We wouldn't be here if it wasn't important," she said.

"What do you know about werewolves, Ren?" Williams asked.

Renny stopped chewing. "That is not my name."

"He's just trying to be friendly." She gave her partner a hard stare.

"I know nothing about what you ask. No one has seen the werewolves in centuries." Renny finished his sandwich and took a gulp of soda. "But, I will tell you. There is fear. The darkness is dangerous."

"Dangerous how?" she asked.

"Is not easy to explain. There is something. The darkness whispers."

Williams turned his head toward Sidney and mouthed the word, *crazy*, behind his hand where Renny couldn't see.

She made a mental note to punch him in the throat later and turned her attention back to the informant. "Is there anything else you can think of? Maybe something a little more specific?"

"The monsters are afraid."

"What could possibly be bad enough to make the monsters afraid?" Williams asked.

The man crumpled up his sandwich wrapper into a tiny ball and twisted it in his hands. He looked past

Williams for a moment before he turned his attention directly on his face.

"You are not good enough for her," Renny said.

"Wait. What?" Williams asked.

The anxious man stood up, grabbed his soda can, and tossed his trash in the bin on the way out.

Williams frowned. "That dude really doesn't like me."

"Wonder why?" Sidney didn't bother hiding the sarcasm as she watched Renny melt into the crowd. Of all people, she knew what it was like to live in fear of the darkness. She wished there was more she could do for Renny, but whenever she offered more than food or a cup of coffee he tended to disappear even quicker.

Williams' cell phone rang before he could form any snide remarks of his own. He answered and motioned that he would take the call outside. Instead of following, she went down the back hall in search of a bathroom.

A handwritten sign taped to a door read: *Customer Only!* She took a wild guess and tried it.

Calling it a closet would be generous. Of all the tricks she'd learned at crime scenes to block out the stench of the dead and decaying, she still couldn't manage to suppress the overwhelming smell of stale urine.

She twisted the only knob on the sink. The faucet spit out something closer to the color of weak tea than water.

"Seriously?" Sidney stared.

Someone banged on the door. "Lake, you in there?"

"Hang on," she called out.

It was either this or smell like walking calamari all day. She pulled her ponytail holder out of her hair and ducked her head under the water. The shock of the cold on her scalp felt worse than walking through a ghost. Spectral Apparition. Whatever.

Gritting her teeth, she scrubbed the fishy bits out of her hair with one hand while she tried to keep the long tendrils from actually touching the sink with the other.

More banging.

"Settle down," Sidney shouted.

She shut the tap off and wrung out her hair, then dabbed at the other spots on her shirt and jeans. She scrubbed a paper towel over her neck and arms with soap that had been watered down to extend its pitiful life.

Williams banged again. "Hurry up. Got a situation."

She grabbed her jacket and opened the door hard.

"Ow! What the—oh, Lake. Wow. Oh, man," he said. His hands shot up to cover a laugh. But not fast enough.

"Don't even." She gave him the evil eye and combed through her hair with her fingers in an attempt to make herself remotely presentable.

Williams snapped his mouth shut. He pointed to his phone and raised his eyebrows.

"Okay, who called?"

"Chief." Williams waited until they were outside to give details. "There's a demon in an office building uptown."

"Demon? I thought Peters was after a revenant."

"Was, yeah."

Sidney stopped short. "*Was?*"

Williams tugged the sleeve of her jacket, urging her to continue down the sidewalk.

"Is he okay?" she asked.

Peters was one of the older agents on the team. He always told the best stories on the nights they spent drinking at the Cowgirl.

He'd been there. Done that.

"He's alive."

"What happened?" she insisted. They reached the car and her partner went around to the driver's side. He stared at her over the roof.

"He just retired."

Chapter 5

"Shit." Sidney stared at the tangle of cops, firetrucks, ambulances, and buzz of people up ahead. It was like an anthill erupted right in the middle of Madison Avenue. "Did they evacuate the entire building?"

Her cell phone rang. The caller-ID said it was the chief and she answered, "Almost there."

"Traffic's a mess. I'm stuck below Grand Central," the chief said. "Get to Peters. Make sure he's all right. Don't do anything else until I get there."

"Okay."

"I mean it, Lake."

"It's fine." She hung up and directed Williams to the corner. "Stop here. We'll never get through this."

She yanked the parking pass out of the glove box and hung it on the rearview mirror. The tag allowed them to park wherever they needed without getting towed. They got out of the car and pushed through the crowd. It was amazing how far a trench coat and striding with a purpose could get them behind a police line. Sidney found over the few years she'd been with the Agency that people who were scared wouldn't question someone who looked official. They had to flash their IDs to get through the door of the shiny office building, but the officer waved them in with barely a glance. He was probably glad he wasn't the one being asked to go inside.

They found Peters in the empty cafeteria, tucked into a half-moon booth in the back corner, hypnotized by the contents of a styrofoam cup on the table in front of him. His knee bounced like a jackhammer and his brown leather jacket creaked when he scratched his forehead with his thumb. A cloud of cigarette smoke hung in the air above him.

"Six years I've gone without one of these." He made a disgusted face before he sucked on the cigarette again, then closed his eyes and blew out slowly. Salt-and-pepper hair brushed the his collar as he shook his head back and forth.

Sidney sank into the booth across from him. Williams propped himself against the wall.

"In all my years," Peters told them in his Brooklyn accent, "I ain't never seen one manifest like this."

She watched his deeply creased face. He seemed older than his fifty-some-odd years; so different from the chief who was nearly the same age. Decades of tobacco use and seeing things no human could even imagine had taken a visible toll on Peters.

He glanced around the cafeteria to make sure they were alone. He kept his voice low out of habit, or because he was afraid the demon might overhear.

"I thought it was a revenant at first. It's that solid. But it was determined, focused. I realized too late it was a demon. It's got six board members trapped up on the thirty-seventh floor."

She reached out and placed her hand over his, covering an old scar that looked like melted wax, but it was soft as well-worn suede.

"It's my fault. I froze up." He shook his head again and dropped the butt of his cigarette in the dregs of the coffee. He dug in the pack for a new one. "All I could think about was Angi's graduation next month. She's got *Summa Cum Laude*. Can you imagine? A kid of mine that smart?"

"That's fantastic." She extricated the new cigarette from between his fingers and pushed the pack away. "The chief will be here any minute."

"No time. If they're going to have any chance at all you have to move. Now."

Sidney tossed a look to Williams. He lifted one shoulder and let it fall. It was an unspoken rule that Peters was second-in-command after the chief. She scooted out of the booth. Sure, Mitch might get angry, but there were six people up there who might end up dead if they didn't handle it.

"Take these." Peters gave her two plastic bottles of water, just like the ones in the cooler next to the cash register.

"Holy water?" Williams asked.

He confirmed with a nod. "Might come in handy."

"Thanks." She tucked one in her own pocket and her partner took the other.

The lobby was classic Madison Avenue, covered in marble and shiny metal with potted palms in the corner to give the illusion of life.

There was a keycard entry with a turnstile between the main door and the elevators. Williams maneuvered himself over the bars then turned to help Sidney. He held his hand out to nothing but air.

She glanced at the disabled access gate as it swung closed.

"Smartass," he said.

Sidney found the bank of elevators that led to the thirty-seventh floor and pressed the 'UP' button. The doors opened with a muffled sound, and they stepped into the elevator car.

Polished bronze walls surrounded them on all sides, distorting her image. The early morning was catching up with her, but she couldn't afford to feel as deflated as the elevator made her look. With a sigh she put her hair up and reached around her neck to pull out the silver cross she always wore. She closed her fist around it, feeling a sense of calm ease the fear that vibrated through her body.

A smell of rotten eggs drifted into the elevator compartment as they neared their destination.

Sidney scrunched her nose.

"She who smelt it." Williams made a face.

"Wasn't me." She shook her head.

The doors opened on their floor and the smell of sulfur nearly suffocated her. She tried breathing through her mouth, but then she tasted it and fought the urge to spit.

The outer office of Fox and Henning Financial had a plain reception desk and a peace lily that was too big to be real. The lights were off in the main lobby, leaving nothing but the red glow of the EXIT sign by the stairwell. The two partners exchanged a look.

"What do you think?" Williams whispered.

"Too quiet," she whispered back, and pointed to an engraved directory on the wall. They found the direction for the board room and headed down the hall to the left.

After passing a long line of deserted offices, another arrow labeled on the wall directed them to the right.

Dead end.

Two tall doors barred the way in front of them. They gave each other a silent nod. Williams reached up to knock, but Sidney put her hand on his arm.

She pressed her ear against the wood and listened to the muffled sounds inside, counting at least three different voices. She turned and nodded to let him know this was the right place.

"How we gonna do this? Open Sesame?" Williams asked quietly.

"Too loud," Sidney whispered.

"Genie In a Bottle."

"We don't have a flash-bang."

"Texas Hold 'Em?"

"Fine. But I'm not saying it."

"Why do I always—"

Sidney glared.

"Fine."

She held up three fingers and counted them down. When she made a fist, he put his hand on the doorknob to open it, but jumped back.

"*Sonofabitch.*" He hissed and tucked his hand against his chest.

She pulled out the holy water. "Let me see."

He held out his open palm and she poured the water over his hand. It sounded like water dancing in a skillet of hot oil.

"Ow, that stings!"

"Wuss." She poured a little more over the door handle. There was a more violent sizzle as the cold holy water broke the power of the curse.

"Ready?" she asked. Williams shook his hand off, then squeezed his fist open and shut a few times to test it out. The skin was red and blistered, but he nodded that he was ready.

"Let's do this."

She counted down again and opened the door. Her partner took one step in and one step to the right and yelled, "Reach for the sky!"

She followed, and took a step to the left, allowing the door to close behind her.

Sidney blinked a few times until her eyes adjusted to the daylight pouring in through the massive wall of windows. A glossy executive table with high backed leather chairs spaced evenly around it took up the middle of the room. At the opposite end, four middle-aged men raised their hands in the air.

Two more men were on the floor between the wall of windows and the table. The first was splayed out on his back. His feet were towards the door and he had a significant paunch, so she couldn't make out his face. The second man, the youngest out of all of them, kneeled over him.

The demon stood at the table across from the four men.

Peters was right. It was the most clearly manifested she'd ever seen. It took the form of a walking corpse. The skin had a slight bluish-gray tinge and the texture of foam rubber. It reminded her of an automaton in one of the haunted house attractions that opened around Halloween.

Silently, it faced them.

"My name is Agent Lake." She spoke to the board members in a voice that was much stronger than she felt. "This is my partner, Agent Williams."

The demon bared its teeth and growled, in an angry tiger warning. The hairs on her neck stood at attention. In the space of a blink the head twisted and changed. The nose and ears elongated, and the eyes flashed bright yellow while the pupils turned to black serpentine slits. The vision was gone as quickly as it had come.

"Great," Williams said. The tone of his voice let Sidney know exactly how not-great it really was. Her heart felt like it was about to jump out of her chest and make a run for it with or without her.

She made eye contact with the younger man kneeling at his co-worker's side. His eyes were a light, soft blue, and he was closer to her age than the rest of the men in the room, she wondered if maybe he was an intern right out of college.

"He okay?" she asked.

"He's breathing," the intern said.

The demon leaped on top of the table. The four men sank low in their chairs.

"I didn't invite you," the demon hissed. A pressure crushed Sidney's chest, like an elephant stepped on her. Williams gasped beside her and she knew he felt the same thing.

She shut her eyes and willed her arm to move. It was numb and stiff, like the time she'd been removing wallpaper in the bathroom and accidentally hit the uncovered light socket with the metal scraper blade.

All she could manage was a whisper, but she said the first scripture that came to mind. "And the Word became flesh and dwelt among us, and we beheld His glory, glory as of the only begotten from the Father, full of grace and truth."

Then Williams recited The 23rd Psalm and she joined in. As they finished together, her voice strengthened and her breath came easier. Somehow she was able to move her arm enough to wrap her fingers around her cross. The silver warmed in her palm and the pressure on her chest released.

Williams fell to his knees, coughing. Sidney sagged against the door. She reached into her pocket and felt for the holy water. She wouldn't dare use it until the time was right, but simply knowing it was there reassured her.

She caught her partner's eye and pointed to her pocket. He checked his own and nodded.

"Which one of you conjured this thing?" she asked the men at the table. "Who did it?"

"Conjure? Ha!" The demon's laugh sounded like shattering glass. Ignoring the demon angered it, but giving it attention and showing it fear only made it stronger. There was no way to win.

A seam opened down the front of the entity on the table. The skin drooped and fell away like a wilted banana peel. Something huge rose up out of it, the color of true black. It sucked in all of the available light as it drifted upward.

As it reached the ceiling it took the vague form of a human; two arms, two legs, one head. The eyes returned and blinked vertically like a snake. A hundred tiny yellow daggers filled the mouth. The fingers—if they could be called that—ended in razor-like claws. They reminded her of the ancient dinosaur fossils she'd seen at the Museum of Natural History.

"Over here," the young man with blue eyes said. The man on the floor moved his lips but no sound came out.

She uttered another prayer and dashed across the room.

"Prayers are useless without faith to back them up." The demon's wicked laugh filled the whole room.

Before she could even blink, the air grew thick and she felt like she was trying to breathe through a pillow. Her skin crawled as if thousands of tiny pixies skittered across her flesh. Her ears filled with a humming, and she tasted metal.

Mitch hadn't asked her to join the team because she was any kind of a wuss who would freeze up when things got tough. He'd chosen her because he'd seen something she wasn't able to see in herself. She pushed past the onslaught of magic and squeezed the cross around her neck.

"Come on, Williams. We're not going to let a measly demon kick our asses, are we?"

He gasped. "No way."

The assault released. She fell on her hands and knees beside the board member. Sweat beaded up on his forehead. His eyes remained half-closed and unfocused. His breath came in short rasps.

"Call it off. You have to send it back." The hum grew so loud she could hardly hear her own voice to know whether or not she was screaming. "Banish it!"

The man convulsed on the floor. Sidney turned his head to the side and thick foam oozed out of his mouth onto the carpet. His head went loose in her hands, and a sound came out of him as if being forced through a straw.

"What's your name?" she asked the young man.

"Edward." He glanced above her head.

It was too late.

The demon dissolved and swirled around him; Edward completely disappeared within the blackness. A short scream ended with an abrupt and sickening crunch. Blood sprayed across Sidney's face. Edward fell to the floor, his chest opened wide and empty, like a victim from a cult alien film.

The pure darkness hovered over her in an ugly storm cloud.

"You smell… delicious." The thing breathed the full stench of sulfur across her face. Sidney shut her eyes and turned her head away as a long line of thick saliva dripped closer.

A weight between her shoulders pushed her to the floor. Her cheek stung as it rubbed against the berber carpet. The bottle of water crushed under her, making her only line of defense completely useless.

Thick claws tore through her jacket into her flesh and there was a quiet *pop* accompanied by excruciating pain. She sucked in a breath, preparing for her arm to tear away from her body.

"You can't have my arm, asshole," she ground the words through gritted teeth. "Get off me!"

The thing seized up on top of her as if electrocuted. It screamed a sound so deafening and miserable that she screamed too. The enormous conference table shuddered and cracked right down the middle with a bang like lightning splitting a tree.

The demon twisted and writhed in the air above her, still screaming—the sound of a thousand violins playing all the wrong notes.

It dissolved into a billow of black smoke.

Sidney blinked up at the ceiling in a daze.

"Lake?" Williams' face entered her vision. "What the hell were you doing?"

"More than you were." Her arm was numb, and she glanced over to make sure it was still there. The second she moved, the pain rushed in.

"If it wasn't for me you'd be that dude." He grimaced at Edward's corpse on the floor, and looked back at her when she didn't answer.

"Hey, Sidney?" Things were always bad when he used her first name. "I don't think your hand is supposed to be turned around like that."

"Move." She pushed him aside with her good arm as she rolled over and lost the few bites of lunch she'd eaten.

Williams scooted behind her to avoid the mess.

"Yeah, I don't think that's good either. We should go." He tucked his arms under hers and lifted her up.

She bit her lip to keep from screaming. Every tiny movement was agonizing. He held her uninjured arm around his neck and practically dragged her back to the elevator bay.

The four executives waited for the car to come up. One of them had a wet spot on the front of his pants. Silent tears made tracks down another's cheeks. All four were pale and shaking. None could speak.

She glanced down at her torn jacket. Blood dripped from her limp fingertips onto the pristine carpet.

The elevator doors opened. They all stepped in. Williams was the only one with presence of mind to push the button.

The doors closed them inside the elevator car. With the four extra men it seemed much smaller than on the way up. Or, maybe it was Sidney's vision narrowing.

She stared at her reflection again. It was even more blurred than before, and this time dark spots floated across her image.

"Come on, Lake." Her partner tucked his arm around her waist. "Almost there."

The downward motion of the elevator made her stomach roll. Sidney swallowed hard, trying to keep her eyes open. She leaned into Williams, letting him hold her up. As soon as the doors slid open and the rest of the men exited, he scooped her up in his arms. A scream echoed across the marble lobby. It might have come from her own mouth, but she couldn't be sure.

The trip back to the cafeteria was a smear of nothing; the same sensation as highway hypnosis—one second they stepped out of the elevators, the next they

44

pushed through the door to the cafeteria. She knew something should have come in between, but couldn't think of what it might be.

Williams lay her out across the table. Her legs hung off the edge, her feet rested on the seat of the booth. Peters and Williams stared down at her. Strong hands cradled her head.

Williams looked her in the eye. "Sorry, Partner, this is gonna suck."

"Hang in there, Sid." She tracked the sound of the voice and found the chief's strong, square chin hovering above her head.

"Get her up," Peters said.

"You sure it's a good idea?" The chief didn't even finish his sentence before Williams wrapped his arms around her and pulled her up into a sitting position. The room spun like she'd been lifted into a tornado.

"Not good," she groaned.

Williams tucked one arm around her neck and one low around her waist, and held her up against his chest.

The men got her out of her coat and Peters ripped away the shredded sleeve of her sweater, exposing her arm. Long ragged marks ran down her shoulder to her elbow.

"Is that my bone?" she asked.

"Don't look," the chief told her. He squeezed her left hand while Peters took hold of her right arm. She sucked in a sharp breath.

"No screaming in my ear," Williams warned.

"Ready?" It sounded like Peters. "One, two—" He rotated the joint back into place. It was over before she even knew it was happening. The pain signals registered in her brain and she cried out, but Williams pressed her face into his shirt to muffle the sound.

"Sorry, Lake. That was the easy part."

She glanced over in time to see Peters with more holy water.

"No. No, wait. I'm fine. Really."

"You could lose your arm." Peters gave her a sorry frown. She knew he didn't want to hurt her. She also enjoyed having her arm where it was.

"Trust me, it's better if you don't watch. Williams you're good right there. Chief, keep her arm steady."

She turned her head against Williams' shoulder. The chief wrapped one hand around her arm above her wrist, and the other below her elbow. His hands were so big they practically covered her entire forearm. Peters tilted the bottle over her shoulder and water sluiced through the wounds.

There was only the sound of the water splashing on the floor as it washed over her arm. It felt cool and wonderful. The pain lifted away with the thin waft of steam that rose off her skin.

Sidney relaxed against Williams with a sigh of relief.

"Something's not right," Peters said.

Sidney lifted her head. All three men stared at her.

"What?" she asked. "Why did you stop?"

Peters poured more water over the wound. The water mixed with her blood and formed a pink puddle under the table.

"That doesn't hurt?"

"No."

"I barely even touched that door handle and I felt like my hand would melt off when you poured the water on it." Williams showed Sidney his hand. It was bright red, like a sunburn. "Still stings."

"Did you regurgitate anything?" Peters asked.

"My lunch," Sidney said.

"Nothing black or oily?"

She shook her head.

Peters' shoulders sagged and he put the lid back on the jug. "The evil didn't get in."

"How is that possible?" the chief asked.

"Beats the hell outta me." Peters put his hands on his hips and stared at Sidney. "But how often do we see shit in this line of work we can't explain?"

"Like, every five minutes," Williams said.

"You two get things tied up here," the chief said. "Tell the press it was a gas leak. You know the drill."

Sidney slid off the table and her knees wobbled. He put his hand under her good elbow to steady her. "Come on, let's get you home."

Chapter 6

Sidney was too tired to open her eyes. Instead she listened to the regular rhythm of wiper blades swiping across the windshield and a sharp blast of a horn here and there from impatient cab drivers.

First she felt Mitch's stare, then his fingers curled her hair behind her ear. It was only for a second, but it made her ache for more. She turned her head to the left, hoping to catch the brush of his hand on her cheek, but she wasn't quick enough.

Sidney opened her eyes in time to see Mitch return his hand to the steering wheel as the tide of cars surged forward.

"How you doing over there?" he asked.

She lifted her shoulder without thinking and regretted it. A windbreaker printed with the bright yellow letters FBI covered her body, trapping her arms under the seat belt. The twinkling lights of Park Avenue stretched out beyond the rain dotted window. It wasn't full dark yet, but the tall buildings cast a false twilight over the wide avenue that made the brake lights of the yellow cabs seem brighter.

"What I wouldn't give for some pea soup right about now," she said.

Mitch smiled, but she could tell by the way his thumbs turned white around the steering wheel, he wasn't happy.

The light changed. They made a left onto 46th and crossed Lexington. He pulled up at the curb in front of her building and shut the engine off. She tried to free herself before he made it around, but his windbreaker was wrapped around her like a strait jacket.

Mitch opened her door and leaned across her to unbuckle the seatbelt. She caught a whiff of his worn off cologne, a citrusy sweet scent of oranges and chocolate. The prickle of his five o'clock shadow teased her cheek. He must have noticed the hitch in her breath because he stopped with his hands on either side of her and stared into her eyes. So close, all she had to do was lean forward a little….

"Come on. I'll walk you up." He pulled back to help her out onto the curb.

"Thanks for the ride." She handed him his jacket. "I'll be fine."

He shut the car door and the double *beep* of the lock told her there would be no argument. While Sidney felt her empty pockets, trying to remember what she'd done with her keys, Mitch was right there, opening the outside door to the entrance of the four-story walk-up with his own set.

The smell of boiled artichokes drifted down into the narrow stairwell from Mrs. Oliva's apartment on the second floor. After six years, Sidney was used to the stale air in the unvented center of the building. It smelled no different than the day she moved in when she was eighteen.

The antique elevator probably hadn't worked in her entire lifetime so she bypassed it, taking the garish red staircase that wound its way up the inside of the building. Climbing this staircase always made her feel like she was living in an Alfred Hitchcock film. Of course, it wasn't unusual for her days to play out like a horror movie. Today had been rated 'R' for sure.

After all that happened, it was nice to feel the strength and warmth of Mitch's hand splayed across her back, steadying her as she climbed to the third floor. She leaned against the wall and let him unlock her door.

"Maybe it's better if you don't come in." The day had left her raw and needy. She didn't trust herself to be professional right now.

He flicked the light on and held the door open, tilting his head inside.

She followed him, unable to decide if he was angry or disappointed with her. Maybe both. It definitely wasn't the first time he'd brought her home injured and taken care of her. He had to be getting tired of the routine.

Sidney wanted something different, something more, but she didn't know how to ask for it. The nights she spent in his bed were always the most restful. She felt safe with him, and that brought its own set of problems. She didn't want a man or anyone else to make her feel safe, she wanted to feel safe with herself.

She shut and locked the door behind them.

Her apartment was two spaces merged into one, covering the entire third level. A galley kitchen, barely big enough to walk through, connected the wide open living room and front bathroom with her bedroom and a second bathroom toward the back of the building. The window in her back bathroom let out onto the roof of the restaurant below, giving her access to a small patio with a spectacular view of the Chrysler Building.

Mitch disappeared into the back. A second later, water turned on, but she was too numb to follow him. She was too numb to do anything except stand there and stare at the shadows under her desk by the window.

It reminded her of how the demon had absorbed all the light in the room, like it was swallowing it down. She shivered where she stood and kept her eyes on the print of her favorite painting by John William Waterhouse, a red-haired lady and her knight called *Lamia*.

Mitch's hands circled her waist. She sucked in a sharp breath and curled her fingers into fists.

"Only me." With a reassuring squeeze, he led her through the apartment into the back bathroom and the cast iron claw foot tub filling with steaming water.

"I slept with the lights on for a month after I met a demon," he said, while he undressed her like a rag doll. He slowed down, careful as he pulled her camisole over her arm to check her injury. Sidney risked a glance. It looked like an excited three-year-old had gone wild with a red marker.

There were other scars from other battles here and there across her body, some worse than others, but none as bad as the newest one.

"It tore that guy's heart out of his chest like it was nothing," Sidney said. "My whole arm should look like the back of Peters' hand, but it doesn't."

"It's like he said, some things don't have an explanation. You can't question everything in this line of work or you'll end up on permanent vacation in a padded cell."

"But—"

"You'll feel better after your bath."

He rattled the bars on the window to make sure it was locked tight while she climbed into the tub and sank under the bubble-filled water. The ache melted out of her muscles immediately.

"You staying?" She rested her head against the back of the tub.

It took him a few seconds to turn around and she wondered if he'd even heard. He came back and turned the water off, then picked up her clothes from the floor.

"Want me to?"

It was too quiet with the water off. The question hung in the air like the steam over the tub.

Now that he was here, the answer was yes, and that was the biggest reason she wished he'd left her at the door. Mitch was twice her age, and her boss. Wanting him to strip down and join her in the tub was messed up, but she couldn't help it. She didn't need to pay a therapist thousands of dollars to tell her that.

She lifted her eyes to his. "Maybe you could check under the beds."

His shoulders eased down. "Don't worry, Jean-Luc Gaspard killed the Boogey Man in Amsterdam, 1932."

The Boogey Man was the least of her worries, and they both knew it. The image of that creature in the subway came back to her. The ears and the fur, that long tongue and the mouth full of huge sharp teeth, reminded her too much of what stalked through her nightmares.

"But there are other things."

"I know."

❀ ❀ ❀

Sidney dried off and dressed in a plain long-sleeved t-shirt and some black yoga pants. She twisted her damp hair up in a knot. The smell of food led her to the table in the front room.

"Chinese?"

"Just arrived." He unpacked little white boxes from a brown paper bag and set them out on the table. His dress shirt and tie hung over the back of the chair, and she took a moment to appreciate the cut of his arms in his white undershirt.

He had wide shoulders tapering down into a narrow waist. It helped that he kept up his fitness level from his FBI days, jogging laps around the park most mornings. Occasionally they ran together, but Sidney preferred the solitude of swimming, with nothing but her heartbeat and breath to keep her company.

"Feel better?" he asked.

"The bath was nice." She opened a box and made a face.

He paused in his unpacking. "I thought Lo Mein was your favorite."

That man's open chest and all the torn bits previously connecting his heart to his body flashed through her mind. She swallowed hard. "Not today."

Mitch opened two more boxes and offered them to her. "Beef and broccoli or sesame chicken?"

"Vegetarian is a good plan for now." She grabbed the beef and broccoli then sat down, using the chopsticks to pick out the tiny green trees.

He set a white pill on the table next to a glass of water. Sidney paused, glanced up at him. He knew full-well about the lifestyle he'd rescued her from. The battle had been short, thanks to him.

"Extra-strength ibuprofen."

She relaxed, sliding the pill back across the table. "Thanks, I don't need it."

"You should eat some protein."

"I'm not hungry." She shoved her chopsticks in the container and cracked open her fortune cookie. The advice on the piece of paper made her snort out a sardonic laugh, "It's time for you to explore new interests."

He smiled a little. "Knitting?"

"Yeah. Funny." They spent a few moments in silence while Mitch ate. She rested her head back against the wall and shut her eyes. "What if they're not extinct?"

He finished chewing and swallowed. "They are."

"Renny says there's something out there even the monsters are afraid of." She opened her eyes and stared him down. "What if this is worse than we think?"

"I spoke with Dimitrius. He assures me the werewolves are extinct."

"But what if he's wrong?"

Mitch set his chopsticks down and gathered the boxes. "Then we'll cross that bridge if we come to it."

"What if we're already there?"

He lowered his chin, his jaw ticked. Once. Twice. "I trust Dimitrius."

He put the boxes back into the bag and took it to the kitchen.

Sidney followed.

He opened the refrigerator, threw out a few old containers, and put the bag inside.

"Mitch, what if whatever killed my parents is back?"

The refrigerator door shut with a muted thud. He grabbed one of the leftover napkins and rubbed a spot on the laminate countertop. "That's the thing about a run-in with a demon. It messes with your head, brings all your fears and doubts to the surface. It feeds off the ugly in your life and throws it back in your face. Give it a couple days, it'll wear off."

"You think I'm paranoid?"

"No, I think that due to demonic influences, you're making connections where there are none."

"Hold on, you said it yourself this morning. You were ready to pull me off this case. Now I'm making connections where there are none?"

"What I'm saying is that we shouldn't jump to conclusions without more information."

"Yeah, okay." She went back into the front room and picked up pillows from the couch, rearranging them for something to do. Mitch followed her only as far as the edge of the kitchen.

He crossed his arms over his chest and leaned against the doorway. "I know you need closure, Sid. But at some point, you're going to have to move on."

She froze with some files from the coffee table in her hand.

"In this line of work, you've got to be able to accept there are things you might not ever get answers to. Strange things happen. Unexplainable things. You have so much going for you, here and now. You can't get where you need to be if you're too busy dwelling in the past."

The night she'd first met Mitch, when he'd introduced himself to her at the MET during some charity fundraiser, her grandfather had spoken almost the exact same words, ordering her to stop dwelling in the past. She glared at him now, determined not to let him see how much his words hurt.

The difference was that he was okay with not knowing and she wasn't. Maybe she didn't want to know all the gory details, but whatever had torn her parents to pieces in their bed while she slept down the hall was still out there. If only she knew that the monster was locked up or dead, she might have an easier time sleeping at night.

"Why did you even ask me to join the agency in the first place?" she wondered.

His eyes darted to the floor before coming back up to meet hers. "I told you before, you've got what it takes to be great at this. Tenacity. Bravery. You're strong in a way most people only dream about."

A knot blossomed in her throat. She wanted to believe in herself the way he believed in her, but after days like today, it wasn't easy.

"Unfortunately, those same strengths can get you into trouble when you don't have the experience to back them up. That's what you're lacking. You've got to listen to me, Sidney. You have to trust me. I promised that I'd protect you when I brought you into this, and I can't do that if you don't follow my lead."

"You promised?" She frowned. "Who?"

"Myself." He rubbed his head with a sigh. "You."

"No, you don't get to pin that on me." She shook her head. "I didn't ask you to make any promises on my behalf. I can—"

"Take care of yourself? Yeah, you sure did a great job with that today." His words stung worse than a bite from a pissed-off pixie.

"Well, you've certainly fulfilled your chivalry quota for the night." She tossed the folder on the desk and it landed with a slap. "Why don't you go home and polish your armor."

The second the words left her mouth, she wished they hadn't. The way he refused to meet her eyes made her regret it even more. She turned around and hefted up the window, then stayed there facing the street so he wouldn't see her cringe as pain shot through her newly repositioned joint.

The cool night air floated in with the sounds of the city. Noisy laughter drifted up from a group of people waiting on a table downstairs. A cab honked over on Lexington. A street sweeper hummed by.

The hardwood floor groaned against Mitch's footsteps as he came into the room. Sidney glanced up at his reflection in the window, but didn't turn around.

"It's been a long day for both of us." He picked up his windbreaker, shirt, and tie. "Your keys and phone are here on the table. I checked the closets and under the bed. All clear."

She shut her eyes. There was a hollowness in her chest, same as if the demon had reached in and ripped her heart out.

"Thanks."

"Call if you—" he cut himself short. "Get some rest."

She remained in her place by the window until the door shut, then she crossed the room and peeked through the peephole. He stood there, waiting. She turned all the locks and listened until his footsteps faded down the stairs.

Turning to lean back against the door, she scanned the front room. Despite every light blazing, the apartment suddenly felt empty. No, void.

She took her phone, tempted to call and ask him to come back. It would be nice to have a warm, strong body to curl herself around in bed tonight. There would be no sleep for her otherwise.

Instead, she grabbed the remote and turned on the TV simply to feel like she wasn't alone. The evening news anchors were too cheery for her mood, but just as she was about to change the channel a pre-recorded scene of a press conference outside the White House rolled. Her grandfather's full head of crisp, white hair ruffled in the sunny breeze right behind the President.

She grabbed the remote and turned up the volume.

"...*Chairman and founder of Lake Industries, Alexander Lake was in Washington today for more talks centered around a new research and development grant awarded to the company in conjunction with the United States Army.*"

The next clip showed her grandfather walking through the White House Rose Garden, smiling and shaking hands with the President. Sidney clicked over to a show about moonshiners, and wrapped up under her thick throw blanket, suddenly shivering.

Her grandfather had never been the sunny, playful sort like she imagined other grandfathers to be. He'd never used his thumb to pretend he was stealing her nose. He never bounced her on his knee, or told her stories of trudging to school in the snow uphill both ways. Distant, was the nicest word she could choose to describe him. Cold, calculating, megalomaniacal were probably the most accurate.

After her parents were killed, he was all she had. There had been no words of comfort, let alone hugs or any kind of reassurance that she was safe in her own home. Instead, he'd continued on with business as usual, then shipped her off to boarding school in the fall. In school, she kept to herself and refused to form anything other than she shallowest of relationships. Of course, she fit right in with her classmates. The only difference was that their parents chose to be absent from their lives on purpose. She wasn't really sure who had it worse.

Mitch and Williams were the closest she'd been with anyone in over twelve years. Every day she woke up wondering if that was going to be the day when the other shoe would drop and she'd lose them, too. She stared at her phone again, thinking that was the real reason she'd let Mitch leave tonight. It was easier to keep him at a distance. Safer.

She jumped when the phone rang in her hand. It took her a second to decide whether or not to even look at it. As if thinking the thought she'd just had might have brought tragedy forth into reality, but she checked the caller ID with a rush of relief, then answered.

"Hey, Tom. What's up?" She didn't even bother trying to hide the tiredness in her voice.

"I've got the vic from this morning out on the table." The Medical Examiner's breath came loud over the phone.

"You okay?" Sidney sat up a little.

"It's amazing."

"Amazing, how?" She'd fallen for Tom's brand of amazing before. The last time he'd been this excited, she found herself getting an intimate lesson on the reproductive organs of a merman.

"It's, uh, well—" Tom was never someone who was at a loss for words. "It's a little unusual."

Sidney let the blanket fall from her shoulders as she stood up. "This isn't the same as that vampire you thought you found, is it? Because those teeth were implants."

"No, no, no. You'll want to see this."

"All right." She could never say no to Tom's enthusiasm. Besides, a night in the morgue was way better than spending a night alone with her own personal demons. "On my way."

Chapter 7

The cab dropped Sidney off in front of the building with the turquoise tiles on First Avenue. It housed the country's original forensics lab, the Office of the Chief Medical Examiner, otherwise known as the OCME. During the day, the place was a bustling scene of doctors, police officers, detectives, lab techs, interns, and lawyers.

Sidney liked it better after hours when Tom brought out the weird stuff. It was quiet, like now, and they didn't have to worry about being interrupted. Roy, the usual guard, wasn't at his desk when she walked in, but everybody had to take a break to pee sometimes.

Tom was expecting her, so she continued on to the elevator. The long hallway leading to the labs reminded her of *The Shining*. Every time she came she expected some kid on a Big Wheel to roll around the corner from the hallway leading out to the loading dock.

A loud bang like a car crash startled her from her thoughts. The swinging door leading to Tom's autopsy suite bumped open. Something slid to the floor with a heavy smack.

Sidney instinctively crouched to the floor against the wall, making herself as small as possible.

Tom lay halfway out the door, his glasses tilted at an unnatural angle, hand splayed out over his head. His eyes were open. Unblinking.

She almost screamed but caught herself at the last second, so it came out as a choked whisper, "Tom!"

Voices came from inside the autopsy suite and Tom's body slid out of sight. Sidney took out her phone to call Mitch. She fumbled and dropped it with a clatter on the polished floor. She cursed silently, while she glanced back and forth between the door and her phone. She hit the speed-dial for Mitch, but the call failed.

Just as she was ready to make a run for the loading dock to catch a stronger signal, the doors banged open again and two men exited, carrying a body bag between them.

They were big guys. All muscle. Dressed in black. Close cropped hair.

She froze, hoping maybe, if she was still enough and small enough, they'd go on without noticing her.

The phone buzzed in her hand.

The man in the back zeroed in on her.

All she had was keys and phone, no weapon. Damage could be done with her keys, but that meant offering herself up for close contact. Not a smart idea.

An unnatural growl rolled out from the man's throat.

"No. We have orders," his partner said.

Something in his eyes seemed familiar. Sidney couldn't place what kind of creature she was looking at, but it wasn't human. It made her feel like she was the prey and this man wanted to eat her.

A popping, tearing sound, stopped her breath in her throat.

The man's fingers grew into long, sharp claws. His nose and jaw jutted out of his face with a crack while his canines protruded down over his lips. Clothes ripped and fell to the floor, as he came down to stand on all-fours in front of her.

It was right out of her nightmares.

All those years of dreams, and here the thing was, stalking toward her.

Sidney squeezed her eyes shut, and prayed she was dreaming. She waited to feel Mitch shake her, to wake her up.

Hot breath blew against her face.

Her hair stuck to the tears on her cheeks.

The phone buzzed again and this time it didn't stop.

She jerked, just as the thing lunged. It smacked into the wall with a thud.

Fight or flight instincts kicked in. She sprang to her feet and dashed for the autopsy suite. Out of the corner of her eye she saw a second pile of clothes in the floor next to the forgotten body bag.

The other man was gone.

She pushed through the door of the autopsy suite, and her feet went out from under her. Lights popped in her vision. It took a second to realize she was in the pool of Tom's blood.

She jerked her foot away from the second monster, barely avoiding its snapping jaws.

A pair of shears lay on the floor near an overturned tray. She grabbed them and brought them up as the thing pounced.

It impaled itself in the soft spot under its ribcage. A whoosh of air left its lungs, and it choked. Sidney turned her head, narrowly avoiding the sharp canines. Heavy paws pinned her injured shoulder to the ground.

She let out a scream from behind gritted teeth.

Jaws chomped down next to her ear.

She twisted the shears and the thing threw its head back, writhing and howling.

It rolled onto the floor. She yanked out the shears with both hands, then jabbed into its neck, twisted, and pulled out again.

Blood erupted from the wound, squirting out intermittently like a lawn sprinkler.

The other creature snuffled at Tom's body.

"Get off him!" she screamed.

It lifted its head and growled. Goosebumps rose on her arms. She dashed behind an autopsy table.

It leaped.

She ducked and rolled under. The shears slipped from her trembling, blood-soaked hand. The thing tumbled over the top of the table, skidding into the cabinets.

Sidney smashed the door of the fire-extinguisher with her elbow and grabbed the tank. The sting of glass radiated up her arm.

The other creature snarled, scrambling to its feet. She brought the butt of the tank down on its head. It whimpered and went still.

She lifted again and smashed down harder.

The skull collapsed with a final crunch.

Sidney let out a shaking breath. Heavy paws threw her forward and her head met with the edge of the counter. The room danced around her as she slid to the floor. Her arm throbbed with the same pain she'd felt earlier from the dislocated shoulder. It hung limp and useless at her side.

A growl rumbled in her ear right before wet, hot jaws clamped down.

The pain she expected didn't come. Squeezing pressure, but no pain.

Sidney reached out for something, anything, to help get the thing off her.

She closed down on a large shard from the fire extinguisher case. The glass cut into her own palm, but it didn't matter. She thrust it into the creature's eye.

It opened its mouth to yelp, freeing her shoulder.

She shoved the glass inside its mouth as it opened for another bite, wedging its jaws open.

She spotted the electric saw Tom used to cut open skulls for his autopsies. The creature banged and thrashed into the overturned table, trying to free itself.

Sidney climbed to her feet and grabbed the saw. The loud buzz caught the creature's attention. It growled and they locked eyes. Blood dripped out of its mouth.

She backed it into the corner against the cabinets and brought the saw down on its head. Blood sprayed her face, but she didn't dare close her eyes until it collapsed.

It had managed to recover before, she wasn't taking any chances of it happening again. She didn't stop until she'd cut through the neck completely. She did the same to the other creature and turned the saw off.

Sudden silence rang in her ears.

She sank down and rested her cheek on the floor.

Cold seeped in, spreading out and up from where her skin touched the tiles.

Mitch's voice ordered her to keep her eyes open. But she was so tired.

It was easier to let them close, just so she could rest for awhile.

Chapter 8

"Don't be ridiculous. There's no such thing as werewolves."

Sidney's grandfather sat in the big chair behind his desk in the library. The glow from the fire illuminated the heavy crystal tumbler he drank from, sending sparkles across the opposite wall. "The police are still investigating what happened to your parents, but there are certainly no such creatures on the list of suspects."

"I know what I saw," she insisted.

"What you think you saw is a figment of your imagination," Alexander Lake said. She could tell by his tone that he was losing his patience with her 'stories.' "Doctor Gardner says it's perfectly normal for your mind to create fantastic scenarios about such an occurrence. But that's all this is. A fantasy. There are no monsters creeping around your room."

"It was real. It had huge green eyes."

"The better to see you with, my dear?" A smile played across his thin lips.

"Why don't you believe me?"

"Because you're speaking nonsense." He turned his attention back to the papers on his desk. "We're finished here."

Sidney stayed, not wanting to face that long dark hallway again. The fire was warm and inviting. All she wanted was to curl up in one of the big chairs and go to sleep there.

She was afraid to say the next words out loud, but even more afraid not to; they came in a broken whisper, "I don't want to be alone."

"Go to bed, Sidney."

Her worst fears confirmed, she turned and left the room, holding her breath as she stepped into the hallway. She stopped *short when she saw that her parents' bedroom door was open. It had been closed a few minutes ago when she'd tiptoed to the library to talk to her grandfather.*

She stood in the hallway, swaying back and forth with indecision. Going back into the library wasn't an option. Finally, she got up the courage to put one foot in front of the other and dashed past.

A low growl leaked out from the darkness.

All she saw was a pair of huge green eyes before the thing knocked her into the wall. Its breath blew hot and wet on her face and powerful jaws clamped down on her shoulder.

❀ ❀ ❀

"It's a dream. You're safe."

Sidney clawed at the air. The sweet scent of citrus and chocolate brought her back to her senses. Mitch's face filled her vision. He grabbed her wrists to hold them still.

"It's me," he said.

Sidney dug her fingernails into her palms, breathing hard.

"You're okay. I'm here. You're safe," he told her.

A monitor beeped quietly near her head. She wore a thin hospital gown. An IV pricked the back of her left hand.

It was hard to swallow. Her mouth was dry like she'd tried to eat the stuffing out of her pillow. She wanted to speak, there were so many questions, but the words wouldn't come out.

Mitch reached over and put a straw to her lips. The cool water she sucked down tasted like it came from the

Spring of Life itself. After two big gulps he snatched it away.

"Slow down. Take it easy. They're trying to lower your fever. Could be an infection from the bite."

"More." Her voice didn't sound right. It was raw and scratchy, like she hadn't spoken in days. She wasn't sure what he was talking about. Her nightmares were so much more vivid now. Like her dreams and reality had collided. She had no idea what was real anymore.

"Small sips."

Another few gulps went down.

Pain shot through her legs, worse than any cramp she'd ever gotten swimming. It was as if her muscles were pulling apart and knitting back together at the same time. She screamed and writhed as the spasms made their way up her body, spreading through to her very fingertips.

The monitors went wild, beeping and screeching. Sidney grabbed Mitch's hand and held on. The nurse rushed in and punched buttons on the monitor until it went silent, then added a shot of something into the IV line.

Sidney whimpered.

"I know, honey. This will help you relax," the nurse said. She smoothed her hand over Sidney's forehead. Her touch was so cool and gentle. Sidney closed her eyes as a different kind of warmth spread through her body.

"We'll get these ice packs changed out. It's a good sign she woke up. Was she able to speak?"

Sidney couldn't stay awake long enough to hear Mitch's response.

❖ ❖ ❖

An earthy scent of cool moss and freshly turned earth hit her nose. For a second she wondered if she'd been buried alive.

"She needs to be in the water. It will help."

"How do you know that?"

The second voice belonged to Mitch.

"No time to explain. You have to trust me."

That was a new voice. Something British, but she couldn't place the region.

The door clicked shut and there was nothing but the soft steady beep of the monitor near her head.

"Hey." Mitch squeezed her hand.

Sidney turned her head toward his voice. A small silver cross hung around his neck. She reached out and touched it with the tip of her finger.

He glanced down as if he'd forgotten it was there.

"I saved it for you." He removed it from his neck and placed it back around hers.

Her lips formed the words to tell him thank you, but there was no sound behind it.

"It's all right. You don't have to say anything."

"Tom?" she rasped.

He glanced to a place on the bed somewhere near her feet, and that was all she needed to know.

"They shot him." Tears filled her eyes and she couldn't get the words out fast enough, even though her throat was less than cooperative. "They shot him and they turned into wolves."

"Don't worry about that now." Mitch caught her tears with his finger. "One thing at a time. You need to get well."

"They're real, Mitch. I *know* what I saw. My parents—" She tried to sit up, but he covered her forehead with his palm. He didn't need to apply any force, the weight of his hand was enough to keep her still. "They're back. You believe me, don't you?"

"Look who's awake. Good to see your eyes, honey." The nurse came in the room loud and overly cheerful. "How about we try a nice bath?"

Mitch kissed her hand again. "We'll talk about it later."

Chapter 9

The bed bounced and Sidney jerked her eyes open to see a small gym bag by her feet. Her hand was free of the IV and the monitors were silent.

"Hey, Sleeping Beauty." Williams' voice boomed in the small room.

She glared at him, certain that if she was still hooked up to the heart monitor, it'd be going wild right about now. "Don't sneak up on me like that."

He paused, worry tugging his eyebrows together. "Sorry, Sidney I—"

"Don't get mushy on me." She eased up into a sitting position, testing out the idea of being fully upright for the first time in... she wasn't actually sure how long.

Williams sat his lanky frame in the chair, propping his feet up on the bed. He smelled like jelly donuts. "You look like you've had a busy Spring Break in Cabo."

A solid round of verbal sparring was just what she needed to feel normal again. She took in his sweater vest and ridiculously colorful tie. "You look like a clown threw up on a librarian."

He twiddled his thumbs in his lap. "That's the best you've got?"

"You're going to bust my chops right now?" She peeked in the bag. "What's this?"

"Chief packed it for you."

Clothes and shoes, a hairbrush, toothbrush, everything she needed was tossed inside. The smell of her own clothes mingled with Mitch's scent and all she wanted to do was curl up in his arms.

"Where is he?"

She glanced over and caught Williams staring at her, eyes slightly narrowed, like she was a fruit fly and this was Freshman Biology.

"Hey! Williams!" She waved her hand around in front of his face. "Do I need to get my Nargle repellant?"

"What? Nothing." He played innocent. "Need help with anything?"

"I think I can dress myself, weirdo."

Sidney climbed out of bed. She grabbed the bag in one hand, and used the other hand to hold her gown closed in the back.

"No peeking," she said.

"Gross."

She shut the bathroom door and freshened up using the toiletries Mitch had thrown in. It was the same toothpaste she usually used, but it tasted different. Each ingredient stood out on its own. She checked the back of the tube; she was able to pick out the difference between the peppermint and the *xylitol*, whatever that was.

She tested her shoulder, rotating her arm around as best she could in the small space. It didn't feel loose; it didn't feel like anything. In fact, her range of motion was better than it was before.

Quickly, she pulled off the hospital gown to look at her scars.

They were faded.

She checked each one. They were still there, but barely visible, as if they'd been scrubbed away. Even the marks the demon had made were hardly more than a memory.

She swiped her hand across the mirror, removing the condensation, and leaned in for a closer look at her shoulder. Faded indentions in the shape of teeth marked the skin next to her collarbone.

Her knees went weak, she grabbed the edges of the sink to keep herself upright. After the ordeal she'd been through, there was no way she should be healed so soon.

An upbeat rhythm tapped on the door.

"Sidney? Everything okay?" Williams asked. There he was, using her first name again.

"Fine." She hoped her voice didn't sound as weak as it did to her own ears. "I'll be out in a minute."

While she got dressed, she sucked in long slow breaths in an attempt to calm herself. It was half a lifetime ago that her parents were killed. She'd spent every day since then wondering if she was crazy.

Now the creatures inside her head were a reality.

For the first time in her life, she wished her grandfather was right.

❉ ❉ ❉

The elevator doors opened to that long hallway leading to the autopsy suites.

Williams walked out. Sidney couldn't.

He held his hand out to stop the doors from closing. "Gotta do it sometime, Lake. Better get it over with quick, like a band-aid."

"Yeah. You're right." She stepped out into the hallway.

"Hang on, what's that? I'm what?" He cupped his hand behind his ear and leaned in.

"Shut up." His humor brought her back to herself a little, helping her feel like this was any other trip to the lab. Even if she wouldn't admit it to him, she was grateful.

Following Williams through the door of the autopsy suite was one of the most difficult things she'd ever had to do. She stepped wide over the place Tom had fallen and edged around the floor tiles where his blood had pooled.

There was no need. Everything was spotless. Even more so than before.

It was all as if nothing had happened. Once more, Sidney found herself questioning her sanity.

Banks and the chief stood on either side of a table with a cadaver opened up between them. Light from a bright lamp illuminated the trunk of a man's body. On the table where the head should be sat a stainless steel bowl filled with bits of bone and shapeless brain matter.

She was expecting to see the creatures, not two human bodies.

"Gross. What happened to this guy?" Williams asked.

The chief glanced at her while Williams and Banks were focused on the cadaver. The edges of his eyes tightened with concern and he offered his hand to her as she approached.

It would be easy to slip in beside him, to let his fingers spread across the middle of her back where his hand fit so perfectly between her shoulder blades, like it was made to go there.

Accepting any kind of comfort now would be too much. Sidney had to keep it together, if only to prove to herself she could. There would be time for a breakdown later. But not here. Not now. They had a job to do. So, she averted her gaze to the body and went over to join Banks on his side of the table.

"It was blunt force trauma to the skull. Something big. Heavy," Banks said.

"Fire extinguisher," Sidney said. All three men stared at her. She shrugged. "He got a little hot-headed."

"Lake, you suck. Leave all joking to the professionals," Williams said.

Banks flashed that easygoing smile at her. Tension eased out of the chief's shoulders, but the worried creases at the corners of his eyes remained.

"What else can you tell us about the body?" He used that deep authoritative tone Sidney liked to call his "FBI voice," the one that always got everybody to shut up and listen.

"On first glance, it seems normal. All of the typical organs are there. All in the right place," Banks said. "However, when I examined the tissue cells under the microscope I found an unidentifiable pathogen."

"Pathogen?" Williams asked.

Sidney gave him a look.

"Like I'm supposed to know what he's saying? I cheated off Megan in college. How do you think we met?"

"It's some kind of virus I've never seen before," Banks explained.

Sidney turned to him. "Would this virus make it possible for a person to change form into something else?"

Banks considered it and nodded. "It's possible. A virus injects its own genetic code into the host cells. The genes are reverse transcribed into the host's DNA which can cause the victim's cells to behave abnormally. It's likely the virus mutated these cells. I looked over the notes Dr. Fellows… left, and he found similar results in the victim from the subway platform."

"If it's the same virus, why do these guys look human and the Doe from the subway is… the way he is?" she asked.

Banks shook his head. "There could be several different explanations. It'll take me awhile to narrow it down."

The chief's phone rang. He checked the Caller ID.

"That's Dimitrius. I have to take this." He went out to the hall.

Banks turned to Sidney. "How are you feeling?"

"Fine." She gave him an awkward smile. She'd never much cared to be the center of attention. "Good as new."

"Better than this dude." Williams moseyed over to the victim from the subway. He pulled the sheet away from the grotesque face and Sidney turned back to Banks.

"Any idea on cause of death?" she asked.

"I compared his wounds with yours and they didn't match up. It wasn't either one of these guys."

"Damn it." Sidney sank down onto a stool. "Like we need more monsters out there."

Williams and Banks both stared at her.

"What?" she asked.

Banks scratched his shaggy hair, then tossed a glance to Williams.

"I kind of feel like I'm missing something here," Sidney said.

"Maybe we should wait until the chief gets back." Williams wouldn't meet her gaze and it pissed her off.

"If you have something to say, Williams, say it." She was scared, and that made her angry. Fear meant weakness. The last thing she needed to feel right now was weak.

Banks spoke up. "I tested your blood when your temperature spiked. You're carrying the same virus."

Sidney glanced over at the pointed ears and furry muzzle of their John Doe from the platform. "What does that mean?"

With every breath she caught a myriad of new scents. The meaty smell of the cadaver opened up on the table. The agar for taking sample cultures. Vanilla and coffee on Banks' breath. A fresh coat of wax on the polished floor. The salty stink of Williams' fear.

"One of those things bit you, Lake." Her partner's shoulders sagged, like the life had drained right out of him. "What do you think it means?"

It was increasingly difficult to maintain a professional façade. She rubbed her palms on her jeans and took in a few slow breaths, same as she'd done upstairs. It made things worse.

She laughed a little and shook her head.

"No way. It doesn't work like that." The small room was too crowded all of a sudden, with Banks and Williams standing over her. The smells smothered her, made it hard to concentrate. "That only happens in the movies. This is real life."

She looked to Banks for help, but he seemed as stunned and confused as she felt.

"I'm not one of the monsters," Sidney said.

"But you may not be *you* anymore," Williams said.

She wanted to hit him.

He was right.

It wasn't a habit of hers to go around hitting people for making a valid point, no matter how much it felt like a slap across her own face to hear it. Still, Williams was the last person she expected to turn on her like this. He was the eternal optimist, always looking for the upside of things, finding the silver lining in the bleakest of situations.

The chief came back in. "What's wrong?"

They all stood there, unmoving.

"What happened?" he insisted.

"Lake was bitten. What if she gets all furry and grows sharp pointy teeth like that dude?" Williams pointed to the John Doe at the end.

"Don't be ridiculous," Mitch said. "This isn't *The Wolf Man*."

"How do we know Hollywood didn't accidentally get it right?" Williams asked.

Mitch's hand came to rest on her back, the same place those claws had dug in. His touch was gentle, warm and solid, the very opposite of how Sidney felt at the moment.

"It's a little early to be jumping to conclusions," he said. "Lake and I are going to see Dimitrius. He has experience with this sort of thing. Go home, Williams. Banks, we appreciate your help, let us know if you find out anything else."

They left Williams with his head hung like a lost puppy and Sidney wasn't sorry.

They were partners. He should have her back now more than ever. Instead, he kept watching her like she might go all Bela Lugosi any second.

Hell, maybe she would, but usually Williams was a Glass Half Full kind of guy. Right now she needed his goofy platitudes of optimism, not his fear. Because, God knew, she was already frightened enough as it was.

Chapter 10

Neither of them spoke as Mitch sped down the FDR. A party boat cruised along the East River, flashing multicolored lights in rhythm across the black water. Sidney envied the people on it. They got to party and live their lives without knowing what really crept around in the darkness, beyond the reach of those pretty lights. Mitch had given her the chance to protect them from those living nightmares. Yet, here she was, on the verge of becoming one of those very monsters she worked so hard to keep at bay.

"Don't let him get to you," Mitch said, his voice low. He was angry. But, at her, or Williams, or the Universe, she couldn't tell.

"How can I not? He's right."

"You could never be a monster, Sid."

"You don't know that. You weren't there." Sidney turned in her seat to face him. "I stabbed that thing in the neck with a pair of scissors. I smashed their heads in with a fire extinguisher. Those brains were in that bowl because of what *I* did."

"You do what you have to do in this job. You know that," he said.

"It felt… satisfying." Sidney's voice wavered. "Like instinct took over."

"Right. Survival instinct."

She wove her fingers together, making a ball in her lap. It had all happened so fast, it was difficult to remember, but bits and pieces of the fight came back to her. Simply thinking about the crunching sound of the skull caused her hands to shake. The flesh and bone had collapsed so easily.

Easier than crushing a paper cup.

That's what scared her most.

It shouldn't be that simple to dash someone's brains across the floor.

She hadn't even hesitated.

"I'd be more worried if you weren't upset," he told her. "Taking another life makes a person question everything."

"I shouldn't be mad at Williams. He has every right to be scared. He has a family to look out for. What if I turn into one of those things for real and tear him up?"

"We'll cross that bridge if we come to it."

"You and your bridges." She shook her head. "I don't want to spend my life locked up in a cage, constantly wondering when I might hurt someone. I don't want to end up as some kind of science experiment. I can't live like that. Promise you won't let me live like that."

He was quiet while he drove.

"Promise me," she begged.

He took their exit and pulled over first chance he got. As soon as the car was in park, he leaned over and covered her lips with his own.

It startled her at first, but his tongue parted her lips and soon enough she melted under his touch. He kissed her until her eyelids were too heavy to open. He kissed her long enough for her to forget they'd ever taken a break. He kissed her until she was ready to climb across the console into his lap, professionalism be damned.

Then, he pulled back, but only enough to breathe.

"We don't know what's going to happen."

His lips tickled when he spoke against her cheek.

"When I saw you laying there on the floor… I thought that was it."

He kissed her forehead.

"I thought you were really gone."

He kissed the soft spot behind her ear.

"Thought it was all my fault for bringing you into this in the first place."

His lips lingered on the teeth marks at her collarbone.

"I will *not* promise to destroy you."

He rested his forehead on her shoulder. She curled her fingertips around the back of his neck, and lay her cheek against his head.

Her words wavered as she fought back tears. "I don't want to be a monster."

Mitch lifted his head and swiped her cheeks with his thumb as he stared into her eyes.

"It takes a lot more than claws and fur to make someone a monster."

Chapter 11

After taking a moment to recover, Mitch drove them down to Centre Street and pulled up in front of a building that took up the entire block. High columns and a filigreed iron gate for a door made it seem more like the police headquarters it had once been, rather than any kind of living space. Sidney studied the stone carved lions guarding the entrance stretched out on their bellies like lazy dogs, more bored and sleepy than intimidating.

"Need a minute?" He kept the car running as a valet approached.

She stared up at the building. "How about a century?"

She didn't have the luxury of either one. The valet opened her door and she stepped out. Mitch joined her a second later. He adjusted his jacket, all business again.

A petite blonde greeted them with a smile too big to be real. Dressed in a little black blazer with matching pencil skirt and crisp white blouse, she reminded Sidney of a flight attendant.

"Mr. Harris, pleased to see you again." The woman spoke with a British accent and shook the chief's hand. Sidney smelled soap and a hint of the starch that made the woman's collar stand as straight as she did.

"And you must be Ms. Lake." Her grasp was firm, as if she was used to shaking hands with extraordinarily strong people. Sidney resisted the urge to squeeze back as tight as she could.

"We apologize for the short notice," the chief said as they followed the woman inside.

"It's quite all right. Mr. Dimitrius is eager to speak with you." The assistant walked with quick, tiny steps. Even in her shiny black pumps she was shorter than Sidney who was five-foot-six in her bare feet. "May I get you anything to drink? Wine, soda, water perhaps?"

Sidney followed the chief's lead and asked for water as they made their way up the steps into the building.

The lobby was nothing but pure decadence. Freshly polished crystal chandeliers sparkled overhead and made the space feel like a luxury hotel with plush furniture arranged in a comfortable waiting area.

The elevators were kept in the antique style to match the rest of the building. Their hostess pressed her thumb to a scanner next to the letters PH to take them up to the Penthouse. A green light blinked and the elevator lifted. Sidney expected the sound of chains and the feeling of being jerked upward that came with most elevators in buildings like this. There was nothing but a quiet hum and a smooth, fast ride to the top.

She noticed that same earthy scent from the hospital when they stepped off the elevator. It reminded her of the smell in the park from the fresh flower beds. Her skin tingled and the hair on the back of her neck stood up. She'd felt magic before. Whatever this was hit her senses in an entirely different way.

They entered a low-lit room with a ceiling so high it almost disappeared into darkness. Directly underneath the huge dome was a large circular table made from rough hewn wood. Maybe it had been polished and gleaming at one time, but it was worn down in certain places. It didn't seem to fit in with the rest of the luxurious décor.

A real wood fire in an enormous fireplace made the room slightly over-warm and hard to breathe in; or perhaps that was Sidney's own uneasiness.

The sword on the wall over the mantel could just as easily come out of the weapons wing of the MET. Stained and tattered leather wrapped the hilt, but the blade was polished so that it almost glowed with the light from the fire.

Old and new. Filthy and polished. Worn and sharp. The weapon was a veritable contradiction of itself. Sidney could hardly take her eyes off of it.

"Is there anything else I can do to make you comfortable?" The assistant smiled.

"No, thank you," the chief said.

"Mr. Dimitrius will be with you in a moment." The door closed behind her without a sound.

Sidney felt exposed here, in the middle of all this space. Then again, that's probably what this room was meant to do, make a person feel small. Intimidated.

The smell she'd noticed when they stepped off the elevator grew stronger. That same mossy sweetness was there, along with the bitter metallic smell of sharpened steel, and musk of polished leather.

It was awful, and yet, strangely intoxicating.

"Do you smell that?" Sidney whispered.

A door at the back of the room next to the fireplace opened before Mitch could answer. The man who emerged wasn't quite as tall as Mitch, but as soon as he stepped through the door, his presence seemed to expand to fill the enormous space.

Sidney didn't need to be introduced. It was very clear who this man was.

At first glance, his shoulder length hair was jet black, but when he stepped into the light it picked up gold and orange tones from the fire and she saw that it was actually a very dark brown. It reminded her of pure chocolate falling in loose waves around his square face, ending in stark contrast with the edge of his pristine, white collar.

His eyes were the same dark liquid brown as his hair. She could tell the second she met his gaze that this man didn't feel the need to impress anyone. His deep set eyes were soft, holding a hint of amusement, as if he didn't have to think about what she might do or say because he already knew.

"I apologize for the wait. Mitchell, it's good to see you again." The voice that came out of his mouth was unexpected and familiar at the same time. It sounded British, but it was more rugged than the Queen's English.

In all her years at boarding school in the UK, she hadn't heard anything like it. It held lilting notes of Welsh, but there were gruff hints of a Highland brogue in there as well. She recalled hearing it at one point in the hospital, but she didn't remember actually meeting him.

The men shook hands as if they'd been pals in grade school.

Sidney stayed behind Mitch, not wanting to draw attention to herself. She could see Dimitrius better up close and noticed that his nose had the smallest rise along the middle of the bridge; it hadn't healed properly after a break. A slight cleft cut through his chin. He had a ragged scar at the edge of his hairline, and another one on the left side of his neck below his ear that disappeared under the back of his collar.

The top two buttons of his shirt had been left undone, as if he intended to draw her gaze downward. He wasn't wearing an undershirt, so it was easy to see the outline of his well-toned chest. A tarnished silver pendant rested right below the dip of his collarbone, tied to his neck with a narrow leather strap. It was some kind of old coin or a stamped crest.

Now that he was even closer, the scent evolved into something more distinct; Sidney picked out the smell of horses, sweat, blood, even the smoky flavor of fire and pitch.

Battle.

He smelled like a warrior.

"Ms. Lake, at last we meet." That voice again, softer and gentler than what a battle-hardened warrior should sound like. She wanted to curl up and listen to him read page after page of Internet search results. "I've heard wonderful things about you."

"I'm sure the chief was exaggerating." It was like being sucked into a whirlpool and Mitch had suddenly become her safety net. Knowing he was right there with the line of his body pressed against hers made her feel more grounded.

"On the contrary…." Dimitrius gave her an unabashed head-to-toe assessment. He offered his hand. She didn't want to take it, but she couldn't be rude.

She returned the handshake much more firmly than she'd done with his assistant. It was the same grip she used to make Williams go weak in the knees and beg for mercy when she was mad at him.

It had no effect whatsoever on Dimitrius. Instead, she felt what could only be described as electricity, an actual current running between them where their skin touched. His eyes narrowed, and she wondered if he felt it too.

"He hasn't done you justice at all," he said. "Dimitrius Arturus Roman, at your service."

He leaned forward at the waist and raised her hand toward his mouth, keeping his eyes locked on hers. A whisper of something brushed across her fingers, like an invisible string wrapping around her hand, curling its way up her wrist. She felt his pulse in her palm, saw it throbbing at his neck millimeters from the edge of the scar. She wanted to lick her tongue over it to find out if he tasted as good as he smelled.

That last thought brought her back to herself. She jerked her hand away before he could touch his lips to her skin. It all happened in an instant. Dimitrius stood there, tilted forward holding nothing but air.

Her breath came so fast it sounded like she'd been running. She tucked her hand behind her back and rubbed it on her jeans.

Dimitrius gave a short nod and stood up straight. "Perhaps we would all be a bit more comfortable in my office. This way."

As soon as Dimitrius had his back turned, Sidney grabbed Mitch's hand. He leaned over to speak directly into her ear, while they followed the mysterious man.

"Ow."

He shook his hand out of her vice grip. Four red crescent marks appeared on his skin where her short fingernails had dug into him.

He spoke through his teeth. "What's wrong with you?"

"Sorry," she mouthed the word back at him. There was nothing more she could say, as they'd caught up to Dimitrius in his office.

"Ms. Lake, I understand you had quite a harrowing experience. I am grateful you have come to speak with me about it, despite this being a fresh trauma." Dimitrius gestured to the couch. "Please, do sit down."

Sidney took a seat on the leather couch next to Mitch as close as she could get without climbing into his lap. He must have sensed her uneasiness because he tucked his arm around her and pulled her in even closer, something he never did in public.

The line between their personal and work relationship had always been very distinct, something they were both careful never to cross. The fact that he was doing it now made her wonder exactly how well he knew this man.

"May I offer you something a bit stronger than water?" Dimitrius stood next to a wet bar behind his desk. He removed the stopper from a small crystal decanter etched with an elaborate flourish and poured a few ounces of something dark and red into a fluted wine glass. For a second, she wondered if it really was liquor.

"No," Sidney said a little louder than she meant to.

"Not tonight, thank you," Mitch said, giving her a look.

"You do not care for Port?" Dimitrius held up the decanter. "This comes from my private collection."

It had been a rough few days. All she wanted was a hot bath and to go finish what Mitch had started in the car. Instead, she was here in some stranger's office being offered a nightcap. She trusted Mitch without question, but this was just flat out weird, even for him.

"Sorry, I'm confused." Sidney glanced back and forth between the two men. "Why exactly are we here?"

Mitch looked to the other man for words.

Dimitrius made himself comfortable in a club chair on the other side of the coffee table. The worn spots on the chair matched up with the way he sat —leaning slightly to the left with his elbow on the arm of the chair— it was obvious he sat there often, and the chair was very, very old.

He fixed his dark eyes on her and took a sip of his wine. "Ms. Lake, when you are ready, I would like very much to hear about these creatures you encountered."

Sidney's patience was running out, and she also didn't like the way she kept losing her train of thought when she looked into his eyes. She focused on the stitching of the chair instead. "I'm not clear on what you have to do with all this."

Mitch shifted beside her. "I didn't get the chance to explain things."

"Explain *what*?" Sidney's eyebrows rose as her patience waned.

"I have something I'd like you to see," Dimitrius said. Placing his glass on the table, he went to the bookcase which filled the back wall of the office and scanned the shelves.

Mitch pressed his lips against her ear and whispered, "Relax. He's on our side."

Sidney glared at him.

"Trust me." Mitch drew a circle with his thumb over and over on the back of her hand.

Dimitrius set a heavy book on the coffee table with a thud. The binding was done in red leather with an intricate gold leaf design. The cover didn't have a title, but there was a gold imprint on the spine.

"A.D. 90?" she questioned.

"The date, yes. All of my personal journals are now arranged in chronological order," Dimitrius said. "I had this archive done up for easy reference."

Sidney watched Dimitrius flip through the book. Photos of ancient handwritten documents filled the top half of each page. Below the photos, three different translations of text were typed out, but he flipped through so fast it was impossible to tell what they were. She couldn't imagine how long it must have taken to compile the information.

The bookshelves held similar volumes, all in order. It was a scholar's wet dream. He found the place he was searching for and slid the book closer to her so she could get a better view. The musty pages mixed with his earthy scent, stirring things deep within her. "Ms. Lake, is this the same type of creature you encountered in the morgue?"

Sidney's heart did a backflip inside her chest. A charcoal drawing of a wolf stared at her from the page. It was the same wolf that stalked through her dreams. The only thing missing was the bright green in the eyes.

"Who drew this?" she asked.

"I did. These are the creatures my men and I fought against. The werewolves we hunted into extinction."

Sidney pulled her gaze away from the drawing and stared at Dimitrius. "I don't understand. This book is labeled A.D. 90. How could these be your drawings? What *are* you?"

Dimitrius sank back into his chair. He sipped his Port and stared into his glass with a bitter smile. "Ms. Lake, I've been asking myself that very same question for nearly two-thousand years."

Chapter 12

"Maybe you should start from the beginning," Mitch said.

Dimitrius smiled, "Like a fairy-tale you mean? Once upon a time, in a land far away and all that?"

"Just tell her like you told me."

Sidney gritted her teeth. It irritated her to be talked over like she wasn't even there. Mitch squeezed her hand in silent apology.

"Right," Dimitrius said. "It's a bit of a long story, but one you'll find interesting, I hope."

"I'm listening," Sidney said.

"I was born to a Roman General during the time the Empire occupied the Celtic Isles." Dimitrius sipped his wine and sank back into his chair. "The Romans built a settlement around an area filled with natural hot springs which still exists today as the city of Bath."

"I used to visit there when I was in boarding school," Sidney said.

"Ah, so you are familiar with the patron goddess of the baths, *Sulis Minerva*?"

Sidney nodded. "The Romans wrote wishes or curses on pieces of lead and tossed them into the water, with the hope she would make them come true."

"Yes, the original temple at the spring was constructed by the local people in her honor, as thanks for her protection from a great evil. You see, Ms. Lake, the world has changed enormously in two-thousand years. People used to believe in magic, because magic was an every day experience. It still is. You know this because you see it in your job. However, it's not common for everyone anymore.

"Since the Age of Reason, the human experience of the supernatural world has been waning. Now science rules. For many people, if something cannot be easily explained by facts and data, it must be attributed to a dream or a bit of imagination gone wild," Dimitrius said.

It was the same thing her grandfather had always said, her imagination was out of control. Sidney felt as if the words Dimitrius spoke went straight into her gut, like he'd shot an arrow of truth into her. Ever since her parents were killed, she'd known there were things out there that couldn't be explained away with simple reason.

"So, what does this ancient goddess have to do with what you are?"

"Sulis made me what I am," Dimitrius said.

"You tossed a wish into the water?" Sidney asked.

Dimitrius grinned and Sidney's heart fluttered faster than a water sprite's wings. "It was a bit more complex than that."

"Tell her about the Saxons," Mitch said.

"Of course," Dimitrius said. "Werewolves were real creatures once. Rare, but very real. They hunted and killed only for food when they were in wolf form. Occasionally, a traveler or drunken villager ventured out at the wrong time and came under attack. It was almost unheard of for a victim to remain alive through the complete change. Because of this, the numbers were kept small. Almost nothing.

"Soon after I advanced in my father's place as General, a raiding army of Saxons invaded the land. They were camping in the woods near the Wye Valley. I believe now the area is known as the Forest of Dean. Unaware of the local legends, the leader went off into the woods to relieve himself one night and came face-to-face with a werewolf.

"But he wasn't the most feared leader of a vicious tribe of Saxons for nothing. He fought valiantly and killed the beast. His hungry men feasted on the meat."

Sidney scrunched up her nose. "Ew, seriously?"

Dimitrius nodded. "Thus, the vicious army of raiding Saxons became an even more vicious army of werewolves. They devoured entire villages, sparing no one, leaving more evil creatures in their wake. Since traditional means of fighting proved useless against these particular man-wolves, more drastic measures had to be taken. Sulis created her own army."

"Wait, you're talking about her like she was an actual person."

"She was as real as you are sitting before me right now."

"I know it sounds kind of crazy," Mitch said.

"Kind of?" Sidney could hardly believe what she was hearing.

Mitch shrugged. "But that doesn't mean it isn't true."

"Right. Whatever." Sidney squeezed her eyes shut for a second. "When you say *created*, what exactly does that mean? How are you here?"

"There are particular lines of energy, called *ley* lines, believed to run through the Earth," Dimitrius explained. "Certain points along these lines have powerful magic associated with them. The Ancients were in touch with this power and knew where the strongest points were located. They built monuments and places for ritual centered around them."

"Like Stonehenge," Mitch said.

"Exactly. The place Sulis performed the ritual to change us was at Glastonbury."

"The Tor?" Sidney asked.

"You know it?"

"We took a school trip there once. I—" Sidney cut herself off when a sudden memory jumped into her mind. Something she hadn't thought of in years.

"You what, Ms. Lake?"

"It's nothing." She definitely didn't want to think about it now. Her head was too full of other things. She didn't have room in it for ghosts—Spectral Apparitions—she corrected herself.

"Go ahead, it could be important," Mitch urged.

Sidney stared at the ceiling for a second while she tried to put her memory into words. "We were at the Chalice Well. I leaned over to look into one of the pools and I thought I saw someone look back at me. I mean, it was my reflection, but… it wasn't. My friend had to grab my arm to keep me from falling in."

Dimitrius scratched his jaw with his thumb, his eyes softened as he stared into his wine glass and a smile played across his mouth. "Sulis has been known to reveal herself in the water."

"Okay…." Sidney shook her head, trying to sort things out in her brain. "So, anyway, back to you. This ancient goddess Sulis, performed a ritual on top of a magical hill in England turning you into a supernatural super-soldier so you could destroy an army of Saxon werewolves."

"That might be the way one would pitch the story to a Hollywood film producer, but yes. That's the long and short of it."

She stood and paced back and forth between the desk and the sitting area, just to work off some of her nervous energy. There was a weird feeling in the pit of her stomach she couldn't get rid of, a tingle across her skin like static gathering in the air before an electrical storm.

"You okay, Sid?"

"Fine." Sidney hugged herself. "I'm fine. He can kill these things and they'll be extinct for real this time. No big deal. That's why we're here. Isn't it?"

"Ms. Lake," Dimitrius leaned forward and pointed to the picture in the book. "Is this the creature that attacked you?"

"Yes." Sidney shook her head. "No. It's the same, but different."

The two men stared at her for a moment. Mitch was the first to speak. "Different how?"

"Those things that killed Tom were more… human. Their heads were shaped differently. Their hands didn't really change into paws either, more like, big hands with claws at the end."

"Could they be some kind of hybrid?" Mitch asked Dimitrius.

Dimitrius held out his hands, palms up. The universal sign for, *who knows?*

"You don't know what these things are?" Sidney asked. This man was supposed to have the answers.

"Evolution is a strange thing." Dimitrius picked up his wine glass again. "Perhaps you have encountered a new species entirely. The body discovered in the subway would seem to suggest such. A sort of 'missing link', if you will."

"But if these aren't werewolves, then what are they?" Mitch shrugged. "Shifters?"

"Fine. Shifters." Sidney continued pacing. "Your werewolves, the Saxon-wolves, what happened if they bit someone?"

"Nine times out of ten, the person did not survive the attack itself. The werewolves didn't hunt for sport, they hunted out of instinct for food. I don't mean to be so crude, but usually there wasn't enough left of a victim to change into a werewolf."

The words didn't make Sidney feel any better. "But what about those who *did* survive?"

Dimitrius tilted his head back and swallowed the last of his wine. A drop remained on his bottom lip and he dipped his tongue out to catch it. Sidney shivered.

"The transformation would be complete within twenty-four hours. You were bitten four nights ago."

"Four nights?" Sidney gaped at him.

"Today's Tuesday," Mitch said.

Sidney sat down again. Three full days she couldn't account for. It threw her mind off balance. Mitch took her hand again and she wove her fingers with his.

"The change would have occurred by now if it was going to happen."

Sidney was so relieved she wanted to cry, but she didn't dare. Not here. Not in front of this stranger. She took in a long slow breath to soothe her raw nerves.

It was a mistake. Mitch's citrusy sweetness mixed with the smoky flavor of Dimitrius and set her senses completely on edge. The room was suddenly too hot and too small.

"Your grandfather has been in the news lately, Ms. Lake." Dimitrius stood and pulled another book from the shelf.

The subject change was so abrupt, it threw Sidney completely off guard.

"What do you know about my grandfather?"

"A great deal, in fact." Dimitrius came around the table and placed the book directly in front of Sidney.

His nearness was too much. When he leaned over and opened the book, she almost reached out to grab his hand. She wanted to mold her body against his, draw in his scent and his warmth, taste the salt on his skin. Instead, she leaned against Mitch, squeezed his hand, and the feeling eased a little.

The book contained a handwritten list. Page after page of names. Dimitrius flipped through until he reached the last page with writing on it, though there were many more pages left empty.

He touched the last name on the list.

Sidney Marie Lake.

Her head grew light as all of the blood drained out of it and pooled deep in her chest, making it hard to breathe as she noted the names above hers.

Henry Alexander Lake.

Alexander Roosevelt Lake.

Vivian Marie Astor Lake.

"My father? Grandfather? Why do you have my family tree written down?"

"You are a direct descendant of the goddess Sulis Minerva. No one in your family has heard this truth in over seventy years," Dimitrius said. "You cannot change into a werewolf, because the magic in your veins prevents it."

Mitch leaned forward and examined the book.

She turned to him. "Did you know about this?"

He shook his head, and his forehead creased deeply as he looked to Dimitrius.

"Why choose Sidney?" he asked.

"Not a choice. Fate," Dimitrius said. "She's the first female to appear in the bloodline in three generations. The Thirteenth Daughter of Sulis."

"I'm not sure I like the way that sounds," Sidney said.

"It's a very good thing, I promise."

"Why is it important that I'm a woman?"

"The blood of Sulis manifests itself within the males of the line differently. They carry with them a certain charisma, a power to sway people to their will. They exude a peculiar kind of confidence which inspires trust and faith. When used for good, it's a wonderful thing. When used for evil, it can be extremely dangerous."

Sidney thought about her grandfather and how everyone seemed to adore him. He had the trust of some of the most powerful people in the country, even the world. But, his charismatic personality had never quite rubbed off on her. Maybe this explained how she was able to see the cold, unforgiving nature that others always seemed to miss.

"Ms. Lake, you are able to wield the power of Sulis in a much more practical way," Dimitrius continued. "From my past experience, the magic responds on an elemental level to the females of the line. It is why Sulis was considered a goddess in a time when people believed in such things."

"No way. I am not a—" She let out a heavy breath, unable to even say it aloud.

"You're surrounded by the supernatural every day. We all are," Dimitrius said. "Most people in this city go about their lives, completely unaware of what's around them. You see it. You experience it on a daily basis, because you know in your heart of hearts that it's real."

"Just because I know it's real doesn't mean I was ever supposed to… to cross over or whatever and become part of it." Sidney stood and took up her pacing again. "I always thought I was a human protecting other humans from this. Now, you're saying I'm something completely different. I'm… some kind of deity?"

She'd been preparing herself for turning furry, not sprouting wings, or whatever it was goddesses got. Her mind reeled as she tried to wrap her brain around the news.

Dimitrius poured himself more wine. "Your great-grandmother Vivian was a dear friend. She understood and believed just as you will."

"Wait, I'm not your great-granddaughter or something, am I? If the next news out of your mouth is that we're related somehow...."

"We are not related by blood in any way," Dimitrius said. "Magic is unpredictable. It requires balance. When one thing is given, something else must be taken away. We could have everlasting life, but never procreate."

She shook her head, taking a moment to let the news filter through her brain, to comprehend what it all meant. Then she came around the desk.

"You were wrong about the werewolves. They do exist." She narrowed her eyes and pointed at him. "How can I believe anything you say about being a... about having magic blood? How can I really be sure I won't change into one of these things?"

"Sidney," Mitch warned.

Dimitrius lifted his hand slightly, to let him know he was not concerned.

"It is the truth, and somewhere deep with in you, you know it. Whether you want to admit it to yourself or not. You vanquished a demon and killed two of these shifter creatures, all in one day. What human could do that and survive to stand before me as you do now?"

The wine glass exploded on the floor as she smacked it out of his hand. She pulled back, ready to knock that flippant smile off his mouth too, but found her wrist caught in his rock solid grip. He didn't squeeze tight enough to hurt, merely prevent her from hitting him.

With her free hand, she snatched up the first weapon she spotted on the blotter, a mother-of-pearl letter opener. One quick turn and Dimitrius had her up against the desk. The full length of his body pressed against hers while she held the pointed tip of the letter opener just under the cleft in his square Roman chin.

They both froze.

"You prove my point quite well," he said, barely loud enough for her to hear, like a secret between them.

Sidney smelled the wine on his breath, the leather strap tied around his neck, the sweet scent of earth permeating his very pores.

She stared at the scar on his neck again. Her wrist burned like fire where their skin touched. His body was as solid as the Oak desk he pinned her against. His hair fell forward and she wanted to run her fingers through it, touch it, wrap her fist around it and yank his mouth down to hers so she could find out if he tasted as good as he smelled.

Instead, she tightened her grip on the letter opener.

His gaze remained locked to hers. He leaned closer, placing the fingers of his free hand on the desk, but he paused as if he could only go so far.

The tip of the letter opener sank into his flesh. A single drop of blood ran a trail down the pearlescent blade. It was a silent dare.

She could tell by the look in his eyes that he wanted her to snake her tongue out and taste him. Sidney threw the opener on the desk and jammed the heel of her hand into his nose instead.

Chapter 13

"We're leaving," Sidney said. She went for the door and nearly collided with the assistant as she rushed through from the other side.

"Sir?" The calm, cool flight-attendant façade was gone.

"I'm all right. Let her go," Dimitrius commanded. He covered his nose, blood running out between his fingers.

Sidney pushed past the woman, back into the room with the circular table. Mitch came after her. He didn't catch up until she was already at the elevator.

"What the hell was that?"

She didn't answer his question. All she wanted was to get out. She searched for the down button, but there wasn't one. There weren't any buttons at all. She pounded the wall in frustration. Pain radiated up her arm.

"Fuck!" she screamed.

"Take it easy." There was his FBI voice again. The one used to negotiate with terrorists or people ready to jump off a building. Sidney wasn't sure which one she was at the moment.

Maybe both.

"How do you get out of here?" She continued down the hall, tugging on locked doors, in hope of finding a stairwell. That smell of fresh earth she'd come across when she stepped off the elevator smothered her now. "I can't breathe."

"Hey, look at me. You're fine." Mitch took her hand in his.

"Don't touch me." She jerked away. "How do we get out?"

The assistant came out into the hall. She stuck a keycard into a sensor on the wall and the elevator doors opened. "This will take you downstairs."

Sidney practically dove into the elevator.

Mitch paused at the door. He spoke in a low voice she probably wasn't supposed to hear, but she did. "Tell him I'm sorry. I've never seen her like this before."

"Of course." She nodded, then gave a glance to Sidney; if it was possible to flay someone's skin off with a simple look, she was sure this woman could pull it off.

The elevator doors shut. They were alone.

Mitch took a breath in and opened his mouth.

"Don't," she said.

"Sid—"

"No."

"But if—"

"NO."

She shut her eyes and leaned back against the wall of the elevator. Dimitrius' scent was stuck to her, same as the stink from the crime scene had permeated her clothes. She couldn't shake it off.

Mitch tucked his arm around her as they exited into the lobby. One of the security guards rested his hand on his gun as he watched them pass. The car was out front, doors open, engine running.

She rolled down her window as soon as they pulled away letting in the frigid night air. Her teeth clattered in her jaw before they even crossed Houston.

"What the hell was that?" Mitch demanded.

"Why didn't you tell me?" It took everything in her to make her voice come out evenly. She was shivering so hard it was impossible to believe she would ever be warm again. Cold was better than what she'd been feeling before, pressed up against Dimitrius' body.

"I didn't know."

"Bullshit."

"I swear it. He only told me about the werewolves, about what he was. Never about you."

"But he knew. This whole time, he's known that I—" She swallowed past the burn in her throat.

"Who do you think funds our little agency?" A muscle in his jaw ticked as he strangled the steering wheel.

"What are you talking about?"

"Dimitrius is the one behind everything we do. If not for him, we're out of a job."

It was something she'd never considered before. The money was there in her bank account every two weeks. She barely had time to spend any of it, let alone wonder where it came from. Now it made sense why Mitch was always on the phone with him.

"Maybe I shouldn't have hit him."

"Probably not." Mitch rolled up her window and turned on the heat. "Why *did* you hit him, anyway?"

"You saw what he did."

"I was there. That doesn't mean I can explain why one second you were standing in front of me and the next you broke his nose."

"He had me pinned against the desk. What was I supposed to do?"

From the look on his face, she could tell he had no idea what she was talking about.

"You seriously didn't see that? It was like… it felt like he was testing me somehow."

"It happened so fast. I don't know what I saw."

Sidney sank back in the seat. "What's happening to me?"

"I think he explained that pretty well."

"No fucking way. I am not some kind of ancient… whatever!"

"You'd rather be a werewolf then? Because if it wasn't for this goddess thing you'd be sprouting claws and fur right now. You get that, right?"

She took a moment to consider his words while they stopped at an intersection.

"I'll take this over claws and fur any day," Mitch said. "It *saved* you. What you are is damn lucky."

The reality of it all sank in. Chills ran over her body at the thought of how narrowly she'd avoided becoming something truly monstrous. "Lucky Thirteen."

He threw her a sideways glance as the streetlight cast a green hue over his face. "Something like that."

The sound of keys hitting the door as Mitch turned the lock to let them into his place was familiar and comforting. It was dark inside except for the ambient city light shining through the sliding glass door that opened onto the balcony. It had been weeks, no, maybe even months since she'd been here last.

It was all the same as she remembered. The decorator had chosen a clean, modern style for the fully-furnished condo. Gray accent wall. Shelves and cabinets stained espresso. The dark teal couch was the only splash of bright color in the place.

Sidney stood there and listened to Mitch lock up again, then pause at the front closet to take off his shoes. It felt like she was back from a long vacation. She wondered if she'd made a serious mistake, maintaining that wall of professionalism between them. How different would her life be if she packed up her things and made a home here with Mitch?

"Sid?"

She pulled herself out of her thoughts and took a few steps forward, glancing at him over the breakfast bar that separated the living room from the elevated kitchen area. He pulled a fresh coffee filter from the stack and stood there staring at her. Despite the low light, he must have seen the look on her face.

"It's going to be okay," he said.

"Is it?"

He gave her a strong nod. Normally, she would have felt reassured by his confidence, but not this time. Everything felt off kilter, as if she'd walked into some kind of alternate universe. It was all familiar, but with everything that had happened over the past several days, nothing was the same.

Tears stung her eyes. She went into the bathroom and shut the door.

The big mirror hanging over the double vanity reflected her image. Sidney couldn't look. She already knew what a mess she was on the inside, she didn't need to see what a mess she'd become on the outside, too.

Mitch would be there for her now, like always, and for the first time she thought maybe it wouldn't be so bad to let go and allow him to take care of her. It really would be easier to give in. He cared about her after all, maybe even loved her, but she wasn't sure if that's what she really wanted. If only Mitch would treat her like an equal, instead of running around behind her, expecting her to fall, ready to catch her when she did.

Now there was Dimitrius. Her skin still felt alive where he'd touched her. It was like nothing she'd ever experienced before, as if he'd awakened something within her. The way his hand closed around her wrist, strong, but not overpowering. He wasn't trying to outdo her, simply match her strength. She wondered if it really had been some kind of test. She wondered if she'd passed. All she could think about was that body of his, and how perfectly it fit against hers.

It scared the shit out of her.

She splashed cold water on her face, then pressed a towel over her eyes while she sucked in a few deep breaths. The past few days came rushing back to her; Tom's limp hand, the teeth and claws, so much blood, and then Dimitrius' dark eyes as he leaned into her.

Mitch tapped twice on the door and opened it a crack. "You okay?"

Sidney lifted her face to answer but she crumpled in a sob. "I'm f-fi-ne."

He came in and put his arms around her, held her up.

"Shh. You're safe. I've got you, now."

The room was quiet. The only sounds were his whispering and a small noise coming from the radiator. Except the condo had central air, no radiators. She realized the keening sound was coming from her own body.

"Sid?" He took her face in his hands, pulled her away from his shoulder. "Sidney, you've got to breathe, sweetheart."

But she couldn't. Her lungs collapsed from the inside, forcing every last molecule of oxygen out of her. She clung to his wrists while he held her face.

He shook her. "Breathe."

She swallowed, gulped in air like a fish out of water. Finally, her body worked again. She drew in a long strangled gasp.

"Good, girl. That's good."

The breath came out in a long, ragged scream. She couldn't stop it even if she wanted to. He pulled her face against his chest. She tasted the cotton of his shirt. He held her close while her world crumbled to dust around her.

After a few moments, he ran a clean wash cloth under the cold water in the sink and wiped her face with it, clearing away the tears, and snot, and wet strands of hair.

"Eyes on me, Sidney." Mitch cradled her head in his hand. "Look at my face."

She blinked hard as she tried to focus.

"Watch me. Breathe in." He took in a strong breath through his nose. "Like that."

She curled her fingers into his shirt, trying to copy him. Her nose was so clogged with tears she was drowning. Her struggle only made her more frustrated and the tears came harder.

Mitch leaned in, put his mouth on hers, and everything stopped.

He kissed her hard. The tip of his tongue flicked against her bottom lip. She closed her eyes, forgot to breathe, forgot to move, forgot everything.

After a moment he rested his forehead against hers. His breath was warm and sweet against her wet lips. She pulled in a shuddering gasp as his fingers worked through the tangle of her hair. She was left a shaking, sniffling mess in his arms.

"That's better," he said, and kissed her again. This time more gently. She opened her mouth to him and made a small sound when his tongue slid against hers. He kept kissing her and Sidney reluctantly gave him a nudge when her lungs burned for air.

He pulled back, his breathing almost as ragged as hers. His face was wet. She couldn't tell if it was from her tears or if he was crying too. He held onto her, touching her gingerly as though she might slip through his fingers like a handful of loose sand.

Lips rested against her forehead. He pressed small kisses along her hairline. Sidney closed her eyes, enjoying the closeness. His breath was heavy against her skin.

"Why do you do this to yourself?" He asked the question so quietly, she wasn't sure if she'd even heard it. Before she could open her eyes and process the words, he was back in the kitchen pouring coffee.

Chapter 14

The kiss was still warm on her lips when his phone rang. He took the call in the kitchen while he got the coffee ready, and Sidney stole a minute for her breath to return to normal. It bothered her how good it felt to be taken care of. Everything about her life after her parents died had taught her she was the only person she could depend on. Mitch's overprotectiveness annoyed her because she didn't want to relinquish control. But, maybe that's exactly what she needed. Maybe it was good he had the ability to rein her in when necessary.

Still, it wasn't fair for him to kiss her like that and walk away.

The phone call ended and she marched into the living room as he brought the coffee around. He set the cups down on the table and sank onto the couch.

"That was Banks checking in."

Sidney didn't join him on the couch. "What are we doing, Mitch?"

"Working." He said it with raised his eyebrows as he sipped his coffee, like it was the most obvious thing in the world.

"Two minutes ago you were kissing me."

His expression relaxed. "You were upset."

"What *is* this?" She motioned back and forth between them. "Are we fuck buddies? Is that all that's going on here?"

"Is that all you want us to be?"

"We're not an *us*! This isn't a relationship. Not a real one. Did you think it was? Because I thought we were

114

being 'professional'." She curled her fingers in air quotes on that last word. "You can't kiss me like… like *that*… and then go make coffee like it doesn't mean anything. Does it mean something to you or not?"

"Of course it means something to me." Scooting forward on the couch, he returned his mug to the table, then rested his elbows on his knees.

"Then what are we doing?"

He rubbed his hand over his bare head and looked up at her. "Do you think my head looks like this by choice? I'm old, Sidney. I've done the marriage thing. My chance at having kids has come and gone. Sticking with me means giving up any possibility of having a family of your own. Why would you even want someone like me?"

"Because——" Sidney sighed and let her arms fall against her legs with a muffled slap. "When I came back from boarding school, my grandfather was involved in his own business. He ignored me completely. Hell, he was a stranger even before my parents died. And that big house never felt like home after what happened, I couldn't go back there. I had no home. No one to call family. I was so angry. So, *so*, alone."

She lifted her gaze to the ceiling to keep fresh tears from welling up and out of her eyes again. He watched her intently, and she gave him an embarrassed smile as she swiped her hand across her cheek.

"You came along when I was at my worst. You picked me up, dusted me off, and gave me a purpose." She sniffled. "You and Williams, the agency, you're my family now."

Mitch watched her, his steamy mug forgotten. His eyes were red rimmed behind his glasses, though she wasn't sure if it was from tears or tiredness.

"So… yeah." She laughed a little and cleared fresh tears away. "I don't care how many candles are on your birthday cake. Your body is amazing. I want to rip your clothes off every time I see you."

He smiled a little, and his neck tinged red.

"But I also want your respect," she continued. "I'm good at this job. I'm smart, and capable, and strong. We should be partners, in every way."

"Okay," the word caught in his throat and came out hoarse.

It was a surprise to hear that word. "Okay, what?"

"If that's what you want, I can do that." He stood and came to her, wrapping his strong arms around her shoulders.

"Sidney, you're an amazing woman. Everything you said about yourself is true. I know that, and I'm sorry if I ever made you feel otherwise. But don't discount my perspective in this. I've got thirty years' worth of experience on you. Maybe it's been awhile, but I do know what it's like to be on your end. I've done it. I was where you are once, eager to get out there and prove myself.

"At the same time, I can't help but feel responsible for you. I can't send you out into dangerous situations with no consideration for the risk. You want my respect, and I want yours. If this is going to work, you've got to promise me you'll trust my judgment."

"Okay." Sidney closed her eyes and memorized his smell, the feel of his skin against her face, the beat of his heart against her chest. She curled her arms around his back, under the edge of his shirt. He tucked his finger under her chin and made her look at him.

"I will," she insisted. "I promise."

He slipped his hand around the back of her neck and kissed her hard. This time he didn't stop. She opened her mouth to him, let him devour her from the inside out. He'd always been an amazing kisser, but this time was different. It was like a weight had been lifted. She was finally able to let go and give him everything she'd held back before.

Sidney leaned into him as her knees went weak. He supported her back with his arm, while she lifted her legs and locked them around his waist. It was nice, having an extra inch on him so she didn't have to tilt her neck so far back to reach. She held his face in her hands as he eased back to the couch. When he sat down, she was already in his lap, straddling him.

He rested his head back and she went to work, kissing a line down his jaw, along his throat, while his hands moved up under her shirt.

"Too many clothes," Sidney murmured.

Shirts came off. Skin met skin.

She could smell the day on him. The soap he used, mixed with the sweetness of his faded cologne and the bitter tang of coffee that he breathed out as she ran her hands down his nicely toned chest.

Maybe he didn't have a visible six-pack, but the muscles were there, just under the surface. His body was definitely nothing to complain about.

The bra joined her shirt on the floor.

His large hands replaced the lacy fabric and Sidney felt his reaction between her legs. She responded with a small movement of her own hips.

The cool air swirled over her body, making her nipples rise. He took his time with each side, sucking, pinching, giving both equal attention.

Instead of moving down her body, like she wanted, he came back up to her lips, slipping his tongue against hers. Her hips moved of their own accord.

"You like that?" he asked.

Her heart thudded behind her breasts, where his hand still did its work.

Sidney nodded.

He drew the tip of his finger up the middle of her back. It tickled, making her shiver. His mouth turned up into a smile against her cheek. Goosebumps raised on her arms.

"I missed this," his voice was low, heady, almost a growl. "Missed you."

He trailed a path of slow, lingering kisses down her neck, darted his tongue out to touch the thrum of her pulse. As he moved to her collarbone, the softness of his lips turned to the scrape of teeth. His tongue was hot and wet as he laved over the spot and bit down again. The low groan that came from the back of his throat sounded too much like a growl.

Before she could stop herself she had him pinned to the couch with both hands closed around his throat.

"It's me," he wheezed. "Sid, let go."

It took her an extra few seconds to convince her brain that this man wasn't the creature she'd encountered in the morgue.

She released him and he leaned forward, red-faced and choking for air. She wrapped her arms around his body, buried her face against him.

"I'm so sorry. I didn't mean it. I'm sorry."

"My fault," he said after he recovered. "I should have known better."

Sidney rested her forehead against his shoulder, arms draped around his back, clinging to him as her body trembled.

"Hey, it's okay." He tried to pry her away, but she hung on even harder. "It's fine, Sid. I'm fine."

She shook her head against him, then sat up. "It's not fine. I don't want to hurt you."

"You're not going to hurt me."

"I just did!" She scrambled off his lap onto the sofa.

He removed the chenille throw from the back of the couch and wrapped it around her shoulders like a cape. "Like I said: my fault. You were attacked and bitten a few days ago. It's a perfectly understandable reaction. Anyone else in your situation would have done the same. I'm sorry."

Sidney considered his words for a moment while he curled her hair behind her ear.

"No more teeth?"

He drew an X across his chest with his finger.

The tension eased out of her shoulders. "Let's go to bed."

"Lead the way," he said.

Chapter 15

It didn't take long for her to relearn the contours of his chest and the way the muscles in his back moved as he climbed onto the bed. They lay lengthwise with him on top, supporting himself on his elbows while they took their time kissing, working back up to where they'd left off.

"Tell me what you want," he said.

"Touch me. Everywhere. I want your hands on me."

He worked her jeans off, but left her pale pink panties on. She wanted them off too, but there was really no reason to rush.

He moved to the inside of her thigh, dropping kisses here and there while he ran his hand up and down her leg. He kneeled on the floor by the bed, throwing her leg over his shoulder, letting her foot rest on his back. With his free hand he eased her other leg to the side, spreading her wide open for him.

Digging in to the duvet, she drew in a sharp breath as he touched his lips to the paper-thin fabric, right over the place she wanted him to touch the most.

"Relax," he said, and placed a kiss where her thigh joined her body.

"I am."

"Why are your knuckles white?" He ran his finger over the back of her hand.

"Are you seriously talking right now?"

It was so hard to form the words for the sentence.

"I want to make sure you're enjoying it."

He lifted his face, gray eyes wide. The corner of his mouth twitched and she knew he was teasing.

"I'd enjoy it a lot more without the underwear."

"All in good time." The words were honey smooth, and made her squirm.

He spent more time with her legs, behind her knees, down her calf muscles, the arch of her feet. Strong hands massaged, while his tongue heated her flesh. When he came back up, she thought for sure he would free her from the lacy prison of her underwear, but he didn't.

It made her crazy when he rubbed his thumb along her most sensitive area, through the fabric. She may as well have been locked inside a chastity belt for all the good it did her. The smell of desire on their skin mixed and mingled between them.

It was too much.

"Please," she begged. "I need more."

He gave her what she asked for. After her panties came off, it wasn't long before she writhed beneath him. He worked her core like he kissed her mouth, long strokes of his tongue sliding against her. Together with his fingers, he knew all the right places to touch, and exactly how to draw out the most obscene sounds from deep within her.

"If you don't stop, I'm going to come." She inhaled deeply and squeezed her eyes shut, trying to hold back, wanting to wait for him so they could come together.

"Who says you only get one turn?"

The bed sank under his weight, then his mouth was on her breast, sucking hard. At the same time his fingers slipped inside, touching that place deep within her. She lost the last of her control.

Sidney dug her nails into his shoulder while her body clenched around him.

"That's my girl. Let go." He kissed the side of her face, then moved his fingers more, drawing out her pleasure again and again, until she'd given everything she could.

"Feel better?" He spoke into her hair while he smoothed his hand up and down the gentle curve of her hip.

"Mm hmm."

When she recovered a bit, she sat at the edge of the bed and removed the rest of Mitch's clothes. Then, they threw back the duvet and climbed between the sheets. His eyes were the darkest gray she'd ever seen them. He lay next to her, with his head propped up on his hand. He pushed her hair off her shoulder so he could see all of her, while she gave him a mischievous little smile and wrapped her hand around him.

Mitch wasn't the first man she'd ever been with, but he was definitely the one she'd been with the most. It made her happy that she knew his secrets. She knew that when she wrapped her fist around him and rubbed her thumb in that one little spot, he would shut his eyes and grow in her hand. She grinned wide when he reacted, then she did it again.

She nudged him onto his back and he stretched out, closing his eyes while she took her turn with him. It had been awhile, but she found her rhythm quickly enough. She gave as good as she got. Taking him into her mouth, swirling her tongue around his head, squeezing her hand around his base. His hips took up a gentle rhythm beneath her while she worked.

After a few moments, he tugged her hair and she lifted her head.

His chest rose and fell heavily with short breaths. She grinned and gave his cock one more kiss, then moved up beside him. Just as she was about to ask who should be on top, he was there hovering over her, the tip of his head at her opening.

As earlier, he took it slow, teasing her. He rubbed against her outside, parting her ever so slightly, and the ache of desire filled her again. She kept her eyes locked on his while he toyed with her.

"Talk about a cock tease," her voice shook.

He dipped his head inside her and held still.

She lifted her hips, drawing him in a little further. He was definitely harder than she ever remembered.

"You okay?" she whispered while she drew wide slow circles on his back.

"You feel so good. Too good."

Sidney grinned. Her body ached for him to go all the way, to be complete and full. But she wasn't ready for it to be over yet. "Take your time."

After a few moments, he opened his eyes and asked her the silent question. She nodded, pulling her knees up, opening herself to him. He kissed her as he drove into her, up to the hilt, with one stroke.

It had definitely been awhile, he was big and she was tight. He held still for a moment until her body eased around him. When he did move, it was hard for her to maintain control. She shut her eyes and enjoyed the feel of him inside her. She traced the curve of his neck, and memorized the way his arms tightened as he held himself above her, and how his hips moved as he drove himself in and out of her body. His breath came faster and his stomach tightened, goosebumps rose across his chest, and she knew he was close.

She matched the rhythm of his hips, stroke for stroke, as their bodies came together again and again. It didn't take long for her to throw her head back and cry out. A few seconds later he joined her with a groan, and they rode out the wave with each other until they were completely sated and collapsed in a tangle of limbs neither of them cared to unravel.

Chapter 16

The night was quiet and Sidney couldn't be sure if the echo of a scream she'd heard was real. The shadows in her parents' room were deep and dark. She opened her mouth to call out, but no sound came, no matter how hard she tried.

Something moved.

The massive wardrobe stood solid against her back as she squinted into the darkness. A breeze caught the curtains at the French doors to the terrace, making them billow out into the room like ghostly fingers reaching for her. Moonlight flickered across the intricate design of the parquet floors.

The enormous hand carved bed her parents slept in was at the far end of the room, two steps up from the sitting area where she stood. She wanted to jump up on the bed to find solace between her sleeping parents, but something kept her feet stuck to the floor.

A low growl rumbled out from the bed.

The breath left her body like that time she'd fallen out of the tree in the yard and landed flat on her back. Her whole body felt like it was filled with lead.

She felt blindly along the polished mahogany, fumbling for the drawer pull. She was too afraid to turn around, afraid to show her back to whatever made that awful sound.

She'd seen the nature shows. She knew what happened to animals that tried to run.

It chose that moment to pounce.

Teeth, eyes, claws charged at her.

Fear paralyzed her until she felt the breath on her face. It was the last second possible, but she rolled out of the way. The crash it made hitting the wardrobe hurt her ears.

The thing fell to the floor, unmoving.

Her father's gun was in the back of the drawer. She'd have to move the creature to get it. She should run while it was knocked out. But it would come after her. The only way to be sure she was safe was to kill it.

She bit her lip and made her choice. It took all of her weight to move the heavy body enough to open the drawer. She felt around in the back and lifted the lid to a plain box hidden under a sweater. The box was soft inside, red velvet, she knew, from seeing it in the daylight when her father had opened it.

The metal chilled her palm as she traced the tip of her finger over the edge of the barrel and eased the gun out of the box. Her father always kept it loaded. That's why, he told her, she should never, ever touch it.

But this was an emergency.

The thing moved. The drawer closed on her arm. She squeezed her eyes shut against the pain, and bit down hard on her lip to keep her scream from leaking out. It struggled, trying to climb to its huge paws. When Sidney was free, she brought out the gun and aimed it just the way her father had shown her.

The weapon was heavy.

The thing turned on her. It stuck out a long tongue and licked its dripping muzzle, revealing huge, sharp teeth.

Sidney held her ground, not by choice so much as because she was too afraid to move. She knew she wasn't supposed to look an animal straight in the eyes, but she couldn't help it. She was too frightened to turn away.

It lunged.

The gun exploded. She was on her back, its front paws heavy on her shoulders, pinning her to the ground. She turned her head to the side as it opened its huge mouth, ready to crush her skull in its jaws.

127

She squeezed the trigger again. The fur muffled the shots, and she felt the heat of the muzzle through her pajamas, but she didn't stop firing until long after the gun clicked empty.

The thing crushed her under its weight.

Blood.

So much blood.

It leaked out hot and wet all over her.

She kicked and shoved, trying to get out from under it, but the harder she tried, the heavier it became.

❊ ❊ ❊

Sidney opened her eyes to darkness. It felt as if she were being strangled from the inside out. She struggled in the ocean of sheets, like a drowning victim reaching out for anything she could grab onto, coughing and gulping down air, trying to refill her lungs.

"Breathe through your nose, sweetheart." Mitch rolled onto his back. His words were slurred with sleep. "I'll get you some water."

She wanted to tell him he shouldn't get up, but she was nothing but a shaking, gasping mess in the middle of the bed.

The light turned on in the kitchen. The refrigerator door opened and shut. He left the light on when he came back and she was grateful for it. The bed sank with his weight as he crawled in next to her. He pushed her hair to the side and pressed the bottle between her shoulder blades. The shock of cold surprised her enough that she sucked in a deep breath as a reflex.

"Better?"

She nodded.

He opened the bottle and gave it to her. She took it with both hands and still managed to spill some before she got it to her mouth. She drank it down like she'd walked through Death Valley at high noon.

He rubbed his hand up and down her bare back, kissed her shoulder.

"What time is it?" Her throat was raw.

"Nearly four," he yawned.

They'd only been out a few hours.

"Think you can get back to sleep?"

"Not sure I want to." She handed him the water. He took a few gulps, replaced the cap, and set it on the bedside table. He leaned back against the pillows and pulled her into his arms. They were both still naked. Memories of their love-making came back to her, helping to chase away some of the darkness of her nightmare.

"Same as always?" He rested his cheek against her head.

She played with the edge of the duvet. "Worse. I didn't wake up when it pounced on me. It wanted to eat me."

"Your subconscious trying to deal with what happened in the morgue."

"Now you sound like my grandfather."

"I'm not dismissing it, only trying to help you make sense out of this mess." He squeezed her hand and wrapped his arms around her tighter.

She sighed. "You're right. It makes sense. But it seemed so real. I felt the heat from Daddy's gun when I fired it."

Mitch's chest stopped rising and falling against her back. She was ready to turn around to ask if he was okay when he kissed her cheek and scooted them back down in the bed.

"You're safe now." He wrapped his arm around her. "Try to get some sleep."

Chapter 17

Sidney stretched out across the bed and yawned. The smell of fresh coffee and soft sounds from the kitchen let her know Mitch was near. After the dream she'd had, it was nice not to wake up alone.

The pale light of early morning streamed in through the open bedroom door. She wanted nothing more than to stay there, snuggled up in the warmth and comfort of Mitch's scent.

The thought of what they enjoyed together the night before came back to her and she grinned. The hope of more finally drove her out of bed. She grabbed one of his t-shirts and put it on before she went to the kitchen to find him.

He stood at the sink in dark trousers and a fresh undershirt, rinsing something off. She liked that even though they could wear whatever they wanted to work, he still chose his traditional Bureau uniform.

"Morning," he said.

"You're up early."

"I'm always up early."

"Thought maybe I wore you out last night."

Sidney peeked in the sink and picked a fresh strawberry out of the colander. She opened her mouth to take a bite, but he grabbed her wrist and directed it toward his own mouth. He took a bite, then he leaned in and gave her a kiss, leaving a sweet taste on her own lips.

"It was worth it."

He turned away to flip something in the skillet and she couldn't help but stare at his back, grinning like an idiot. He was always in a good mood after a night like they'd had, but this was a whole new level of feisty. It pleased her to be the one who drew out his playful side.

"Something smells good." She nibbled on the rest of the strawberry as she pondered this new man.

"Omelets," he said. "Coffee's ready too."

"Thanks." Sidney helped herself to the milk in the refrigerator. Her favorite mug, the blue one with FBI printed in gold letters, was already sitting out next to the coffee maker. She poured the milk in, returned it to the fridge, then added the coffee.

Leaning against the counter, she sipped and watched him cook. It was a nice way to wake up. A lot better than rushing to throw on some clothes, and grabbing a quick danish on the way to Grand Central to catch a train downtown. She decided she could get used to this after all.

"What?" He noticed her watching.

She wondered if this was what it was like to be happy. As soon as the thought flickered into her mind, she wished it hadn't come. And she certainly wouldn't dare to speak the words aloud. Merely thinking it was enough to tempt Fate.

"I like a man who can cook." She smacked his ass and went back to the sink for more strawberries, hoping he hadn't noticed her pause or the way her smile faltered

Before she could grab another piece of fruit, he turned her around and pressed her up against the counter. She suddenly remembered Dimitrius, the way he'd pinned her against the desk, and stared at her with those hungry eyes, begging her to taste him.

Mitch's mouth was on hers, but instead of enjoying his kiss, the memory of Dimitrius overwhelmed her.

The wide neck of the t-shirt slipped down her shoulder and he dotted a trail of kisses along her exposed skin.

"The eggs are going to burn," Sidney said.

"So?"

She squeezed her eyes shut and pressed her nose against his neck, but he was fresh out of the shower and smelled like soap. She couldn't find that citrusy sweet scent that was so much a part of him. He moved his hand up the back of her thigh and squeezed her bare bottom. His erection grew hard against her abdomen.

"Mitch—" She was about to tell him to stop when the theme song from *Scooby Doo* started playing. "Shit. That's Williams."

"He can wait."

Sidney reached back to the counter behind the sink, but only managed to knock her phone onto the floor on the other side. She didn't really want to talk to him, but it was a good excuse to extricate herself from Mitch's grasp without having to explain herself.

It wasn't until Mitch's phone rang and both tones were going that he gave up. He checked the caller ID and answered.

"Morning, Banks... no, I was just making breakfast."

Sidney used the distraction to slip out of his grasp and went around to get her own phone. Her knees weren't as strong as they should be so she sank down onto one of the barstools and dialed Williams back.

"Top o' the morning, Lake," he answered.

He was buttering her up, but after recalling his words from the night before, she wasn't in the mood. Why couldn't the real world just go away and leave her and Mitch naked in bed?

"What's going on?" She realized her words sounded irritable, and she didn't care.

"Stopped by your place this morning to give you a ride and you weren't there. Thought maybe you were already at work, but nope. Chief's not here either. Matter-of-fact, I'm the only one at the office. It's like the *Twilight Zone* or something. Where is everybody?"

"We were up late. I crashed with the chief." In more ways than one. Lucky for her, it wasn't that unusual for them to be up late working. She also frequented the guest room at the Williams house.

"So, um did you find out any good news from Dimitrius?"

That was the last name she needed to hear at the moment. She was trying to figure out how to answer when Mitch ended his call and came around the bar.

"Get dressed, we've got another body."

"Did he say, 'get dressed?'" Williams said.

"Yeah, you moron, I'm standing here in the chief's apartment, naked." She went heavy on the sarcasm and hoped he wouldn't believe her.

Mitch turned around and gave her a funny look. "Tell him to meet us at the office."

"He's already there."

"Who's there?" Williams asked.

"You." Sidney rolled her eyes. "There's another body. Stay put. We'll meet you at the office."

❊ ❊ ❊

The wind from the East River cut straight through Sidney's gray wool blazer. There was no sun today, only an overcast sky, heavy with the threat of rain. The sunny mood she'd woken up in had faded with the phone calls, and now her emotions were churning and dark just like the river. They were huddled in a little park on the riverfront, directly below the underpass for FDR Drive. The office was only a few blocks away, so the body was practically in their own backyard.

The victim was a match to the previous body found in the subway. The only difference was this one had soggy fur and his limbs remained intact.

"He didn't drown." Banks wrote on his clipboard as he spoke.

"How can you tell?" Sidney asked. She recalled a case they'd had of a homicidal mermaid who enjoyed dragging people into the Hudson. Tom had to get all the bodies back to the morgue and check the lungs to confirm drowning as the cause of death. She swallowed back a knot in her throat when she thought about Tom, stretched out on one of those cold trays back at the morgue instead of alive and well, and doing his job.

Banks pushed hair away from the victim's forehead, revealing a neat little hole. He glanced up at them.

"Oh," Sidney said. The wind picked up and she tucked her arms across her chest and gritted her teeth to keep them from clattering together inside her head.

"What else can you determine?" the chief asked.

"He was in the river awhile, but I need to get him to the lab to figure out a time frame. The gases from the decay would have brought the body to the surface," Banks explained. "Jogger spotted it this morning."

Williams bounced on the balls of his feet next to her. His nervous energy was rubbing off on her, adding to the irritation she already felt about what he'd said to her the night before in the morgue. She could understand his being afraid, but he didn't have to question her humanity like that. He also didn't have to keep glancing back and forth between her and the body like he was expecting her to change any second.

Sidney stared straight forward. "I swear, Williams, if you make a wet dog joke I might have to punch you in the balls."

"What? I wasn't even—"

"I know what you were thinking."

"All right, listen," he leaned in behind her and spoke under his breath, "I shouldn't have said what I said last night. It was out of line."

Sidney dug at the leg of a bench with the tip of her boot. She wanted to let go of her anger towards Williams, but the truth was, it felt a lot easier to be mad at him than afraid of everything else going on.

"I'm sorry. It's just... it freaked me out, because, well... we're partners." Williams nudged her with his elbow. His earnest face melted her a little. He really was sorry, and she couldn't stay mad when he was looking at her like something out of a Norman Rockwell painting.

"Yeah, okay. Forget about it." She elbowed him back. "It's cool."

Sidney tuned back in to what Banks was explaining.

"… small caliber." Banks smoothed the patchy fur out over the sternum. There were two more holes. "Clean. Straight through the heart."

"Execution?" the chief asked.

"A definite possibility. But why?"

She studied the elongated hands with the claws in place of fingernails. The feet were the same as the victim from the subway. The worst of it was the head; it was nearly human. She could see the man the thing used to be. Aside from the long canines protruding from behind his lips, and the fact that he was a corpse, he might have even been good looking.

"What's this?" Sidney leaned in for a closer view of the right shoulder. There was a darkened spot on the skin but it was mostly obscured by the hair grown out over the area.

The men moved in to study what she'd found. Banks used his gloved finger to part the hair.

"Tattoo, I think. These are letters."

The chief squinted as he read the letters out loud. "United States…."

"Army," Banks finished.

"He was in the Army?" Williams asked.

"What about the others?" Mitch asked.

"The two who reverted to human form didn't have any body art," Banks said. "Our Subway Doe had an Army tattoo, but I'll have to double check for similarities."

"Go ahead and get this body back. Let us know what you find out," the chief said. "Williams, see if the design shows up in any database. This might be our connection."

"Lake." The chief nodded his chin in the direction of the office. "Go see what your friend wants."

Sidney turned around. Renny stood on the corner watching them with his hands tucked up inside the sleeves of that grubby track suit.

Williams crossed the street with her, and Renny backed up.

"Hey, Renny. What's up?" Sidney asked.

"Not him. Only you."

"Yeah, yeah. I get it." Williams continued on up the street toward the office.

"How about we get something warm to drink?" Sidney asked.

"That will be good."

She led him to the coffee shop on the next corner. The space hadn't changed much at all from when the European trading ships brought in fish and spices to the historic Fulton Fish Market at the end of the street. The smell of aged oak, sawdust, and roasted coffee made Sidney feel like she was walking through a time-warp whenever she set foot through the door.

The barista glanced up from polishing the original oak counter. "Anywhere you want."

"Go ahead, Renny," Sidney said.

The informant took his time, studying the room in his usual anxious manner, even though the place was completely empty.

"Here is good." Renny chose a table smack in the middle of the room.

"Sure you wouldn't like the corner better?" Sidney knew how he liked the cozier, private spots.

Renny stepped wide around the chair before he sat down. "No. Is too crowded."

Sidney didn't quite know how to interpret that statement. Renny was so odd she chose to ignore it and sat down.

"Coffee?" The barista plunked down two beverage napkins on the table.

"With milk please," Sidney said.

"I like strong," Renny said.

"You want it Irish?" she asked.

"What is this, Irish?"

"Do you want whiskey in it?" Sidney explained.

"Vodka."

The barista laughed. "Hardcore."

She went in the back to make their drinks.

Renny continued gazing wildly around the room as if he were watching a basketball game only he could see.

"Renny?" Sidney spoke softly, hoping not to startle him. "What's up?"

"I came to tell you—" He cut himself off as he leaned to his side.

"You okay?"

"Sorry. Yes." He kept his eyes focused in the corner of the room behind Sidney.

"You came to see me for something?"

"Is important."

She glanced behind her, fully expecting to see someone in the corner, but it was completely empty.

"What are you looking at? Do you see something over there?"

He lowered his chin to his chest so that only the top of his greasy black hair was visible.

"You can tell me. It's okay."

"No one believes me. It makes them afraid of me. My mother, she was afraid. I tell no one in America."

"Renny, do you see ghosts?" She doubted Renny would know what a spectral apparition was. Besides, now was not the time to be politically correct.

He lifted his head. His nod was so slight, she almost missed it.

"It's all right. A lot of people can see them. Do they speak to you?"

"Sometimes," he whispered.

His eyes were more watery than usual. No wonder the poor guy was always so nervous. Sidney had a hard enough time with her own nightmares. She couldn't imagine how startling it must be to wake up in the night and see random spirits hanging around, watching her sleep.

"Is that why you don't like being around Williams?"

"There is mean old woman with him. Always yelling at him. Wants me to tell him he's not good enough for her niece."

Sidney had to stare down at her lap to hide her smile. She'd never met Megan's aunt Rose, but she'd heard stories about the famous concert pianist. Rose Whitmer had been labeled the female Liberace. Williams always joked that the term female Liberace was redundant. It didn't surprise her that the woman didn't approve of him.

"It's okay, Renny. I know some people you could talk to. People who understand what it's like."

The barista brought in heavy mugs and set them on the table. She went back behind the counter and picked up a worn out paperback of Jane Austen's *Sense & Sensibility*.

"I am not a… freak?"

"No. You're just really sensitive. It's nothing to be ashamed of."

He sat there a moment and sipped his drink. She could see him struggling with this new idea. Then he shook his head and focused his black eyes on her. "We must discuss this some other time. Mr. Dimitrius sent me."

Sidney almost choked. It was the last name she'd expected to hear in this conversation.

"I work for him like I work for you. You buy me sandwich or coffee, I give you information."

"What does he give you?"

Renny stuck out his foot and showed off a pair of brand new Converse high tops. It was the first time she'd ever seen him smile, let alone grin. "Is nice, eh?"

"Yeah, real nice. So why did he send you?"

"Mr. Dimitrius is very impressed by you."

"Impressed. I'm sure." Sidney let out a bitter laugh. "What does he want from me?"

"To talk."

Sidney remembered that hungry look in his eyes, the way he'd pressed his rock hard body against hers. That earthy bitter smell. It made her squirm in her seat. "Well, I have no desire to talk to him. Ever."

"You do not understand. He wants to do the talking to you."

"Thanks for passing along the message, Renny." Sidney shook her head. "I'm not interested in doing any listening, either."

"This is not smart. Mr. Dimitrius does not like to be told no."

"Yeah? Well he's going to have to get used to hearing it. At least from me."

"You are making big mistake."

Sidney decided to change the subject. "Renny, the other day you mentioned that there was something the monsters are afraid of. Do you know what it is?"

The man shook his head, but his wide eyes betrayed him. There was something he wasn't saying.

"I need to know. It's important."

"No one knows. Some have gone missing."

"What do you mean?"

"Some creatures, poof! Gone." He glanced around. "If I say too much, maybe I will poof away too."

"If you know something important you have to tell me." Sidney took out a card with her number on it and slid it across the table. "We can help. It's our job to protect you."

"Talk to Mr. Dimitrius. I know nothing."

Renny slid the card into his pocket and walked out before he'd even finished half of his coffee. Sidney stayed and sipped from her mug. It was the first moment she'd had to herself in days, so she wanted to savor it.

She glanced over to the table by the window where she'd sat across from Mitch when he offered her the job with the agency. She'd been living in a haze of loneliness and it was like he'd handed her a beacon of light. It felt like a lifetime had gone by instead of only six years.

Her phone rang and the moment was over. She answered and got up to leave when she saw it was the chief.

"What did Renny have to say?" he asked.

"He said monsters have gone missing lately. He was really spooked about it. Did you know he's a Medium?" She chose to omit the way Renny had begged her to go see Dimitrius. She knew Mitch would tell her to go, and she didn't want to explain why she'd rather avoid him.

"I'll be damned. That explains a lot," he said. "Listen, I want you to go back to the morgue with Banks. It's still his first week. With Tom gone, somebody needs to stick with him, show him the ropes, and you're the one who spent the most time with Tom."

A gust of wind hit her as she stepped outside, throwing her hair into her eyes, and she barely dodged a guy with the red hood of his jacket pulled up over his head. Usually, she jumped at the chance to go to the morgue, but after everything that happened the thought of walking into that room again made her legs feel as squishy as those fish guts she'd rolled in.

"No problem," she said.

"Be careful." His voice was low and rough, reminding her of some of the sounds he'd made the night before. It set things on fire low in her belly and she had to remind herself to take in a breath.

"Aren't I always?" She smiled, hoping he would be able to hear it in her voice, then hung up.

Chapter 18

Sidney headed down to the waterfront to catch a ride with Banks. It would take awhile for Renny to get back to Dimitrius with her thoughts on meeting with him. He hadn't been able to give any definitive answers on what these creatures were. Maybe they weren't the Saxon-wolves, but some kind of hybrid? She hoped that picking Banks' brain on the actual scientific evidence they had would help come up with something more definitive.

Her phone buzzed again and she answered without checking the caller ID.

"What'd you forget?" she asked, thinking it was the chief again.

"Hello, Sidney."

If she'd just walked through the spectral apparition of Megan's aunt, she wouldn't have felt more shocked and cold than she did at that moment. The voice on the other end of the line was the very last she expected to hear.

"Grandfather."

The surprise of it all made the word stick in her throat and she had to pull in a few breaths of chilled air before she could speak again. "If you're calling to wish me a happy birthday it's not until next week. However, something tells me that's not it, seeing as how you've skipped the last… all of them."

Sidney crossed the road and went back to where Banks crouched. She waved to get his attention and pointed to the phone and a nearby bench to show him she'd be talking while she waited for him to finish up.

"Is that why you've been avoiding me? Resentment because I didn't send you a birthday card?"

Sidney envisioned her grandfather sitting behind the sleek black desk in his office overlooking Battery Park and the busy waterway at the lower tip of Manhattan. Or maybe he was at his tailor's getting fitted for a brand new handmade suit. Alexander Lake never bought anything from the rack.

"Me? Avoid you? Funny, I thought it was the other way around."

There was a pause on the other end of the line. "You are too much like your mother."

"I'll take that as a compliment." Sidney resented him bringing her mother into things. He never had cared for her bold, independent streak, just as he had never cared for Sidney's. "Why are you calling?"

"I heard you were in the hospital."

Alexander Lake had a long reach, but he didn't have spies watching her, did he? Instinctively, she narrowed her eyes and scanned her surroundings. There was no one around except that red hoodie loitering up the street, hands tucked deep in the front pockets of his jacket. She decided it would be best to put her childhood issues aside and focus on the conversation they were having now. She chose her words very carefully.

"How exactly did you hear that?"

"I have my sources."

"TMZ or *Page Six*?"

146

"Don't be ridiculous." He actually sounded exasperated. "Tell me what happened."

He hadn't believed her about the werewolves when she was a child; why should he believe her now? There was no way she would tell him the truth. *Actually, grandfather, I was bitten by a Big Bad Wolf, but it's no big deal because we're part of an ancient magical bloodline!* He'd have the men in white coats come snatch her up and send her off to the loony bin before she could blink.

"Nothing happened. I'm fine."

Banks motioned that he was loading up the van and she held up a finger to tell him she'd be a minute.

"Don't forget, I've always been able to detect a lie when I hear one," her grandfather said.

There was no way she was going to tell him anything, especially the truth, so she didn't say anything at all.

"You are aware my labs on Ellis Island house the most renowned medical research facility in the country," he continued. "The doctors and medical engineers whom I employ are at the cutting edge of all pharmacological advancements."

"Yes, I'm fully aware. And no, I'm not available to attend any fundraisers."

"This isn't about fundraisers. I'm offering you the finest medical care available in the world—"

Her phone beeped telling her she had a call waiting on the other line. She checked to see Mitch's name on the ID and wished she were talking to him instead. As much as she wanted to answer, she wanted even more to put things to rest once and for all with her grandfather.

"You want me to be one of your lab rats? No, thanks."

"Despite whatever issues we may have had in the past, you're still my granddaughter. You deserve the best."

Sidney's cheeks burned. "Oh? I deserve to be taken care of because I'm *your* granddaughter? Not because you love me. Not because I'm a human being and it's the right thing to do." Sidney jumped to her feet, pacing back and forth out of frustration. "See? This is exactly why I don't want anything to do with you. It's all about image, what the rest of the world thinks of you. How would it look if Alexander Lake's granddaughter died of some disease that he could have easily cured? You don't care about *me*. You care about losing funding."

There was silence on the other end of the line. It was the only answer she needed.

"Will that be all? Because I've got things to do," she said.

"You're making a terrible mistake."

"The only mistake I made was answering my phone. Have a nice life."

Sidney hung up and got in the van with Banks.

"Everything okay?" he asked.

"Yeah." Sidney buckled her seatbelt. "Actually, no. A lot of stuff fucking sucks right now."

All she wanted was to rewind the day. The morning had started off so perfectly, she wished she could tell her past-self to turn the damn cell phone off. They could have had an entire day filled with sex and strawberries.

Banks scratched his jaw. There was more than a days' worth of stubble on his face, and his hair looked less like a graham cracker and more like a bale of hay sticking out at odd angles.

"Sorry, I didn't mean to unload on you or anything," she apologized.

"Rant away, honey. I know what you mean."

"Seriously, welcome to New York," Sidney said. "Here you go, have a dead boss and some mean ass shapeshifter werewolf things with claws and teeth all in your first week. I wouldn't blame you if you packed up and headed back home. I'm sure you don't have this kind of craziness where you come from."

He flashed her that big white grin.

"Nah, I grew up in Savannah. They do cemetery tours around town in sawed off hearses. It's not any less crazy, just a different brand."

The corners of her own mouth turned up. That smile was contagious.

"I used to sneak out of bed and sit on the stairs to watch my Granny do seances in the parlor," he said. "Growing up with a Necromancer, I've seen my fair share of crazy shit, believe you me."

That got her attention. She'd had him pegged for a biology nerd like Tom. It hadn't even occurred to her that he may have already had plenty of experience with the supernatural. Then, something clicked inside her brain.

"Hang on, are you related to Amelia Banks?" she asked.

His face actually tinged pink. "That's my Granny."

"I didn't even know she had a grandson."

"Yeah, well, I'm not exactly something she likes to advertise. She's convinced I'm *denying my true self*. Not because I prefer the company of other men, but because I chose science over magic."

"Hmm, disapproving grandparents rock, don't they? My grandfather's kind of the opposite. All science, all the time. He thinks I'm delusional."

"I grew up with a giant crystal ball on the coffee table. Just a way of life. I never knew any different."

She'd meant to ask him about the virus he'd found, but the whole necromancer thing was way too interesting.

"Have you ever seen any zombie raisings?"

Great, now she sounded like a total fan girl.

"Witnessed eight. Assisted in two. Attempted one solo."

"Attempted?"

That smile of his faded. "Big mess. I was young. Stupid. Overzealous. Sentimental. Call it whatever you want. It was a mistake."

Her phone buzzed. Unknown number. She sent it to voicemail, afraid it was her grandfather calling back.

It was clear Banks didn't want to continue down that line of questioning, so Sidney didn't pursue it. She watched him while he navigated the thick traffic back to the OCME.

"It's all good though. I chose to focus on med school instead. Now I study evidence and piece together the scientific clues left behind to find out why people died.

Not as fast as bringing them back and asking them myself, but it sure is a lot less trouble."

There was that grin again, complete with dimples this time. He pulled into the gravel lot behind the morgue and backed up to the loading dock.

"Wanna help me unload?"

They hopped out and went around back. Banks pulled out the gurney and Sidney shut the doors behind him. Her phone vibrated again as she followed Banks through the automatic doors. This time it was the chief's name on the ID and she remembered the call she'd missed earlier.

"Hey, what's up?" she answered.

"Are you okay? I've been trying to call. Are you with Banks? He's not picking up either."

"Everything's fine. We just got to the morgue. What's going on?"

"The bodies— Dimitrius is—"

The words garbled and she couldn't understand what he was saying. Then the call failed. Her heart thudded a little faster when she remembered the other failed calls right before the shifters had attacked her in this very hallway. She had to remind herself she couldn't keep thinking like that, not if she wanted to stay sane and continue doing her job.

"Dammit. Do you have a signal in here?" she asked Banks. Her hands trembled.

He took his phone out, but shook his head. "I forgot my charger. It's deader than… well, this guy. Let's drop him off in the cooler and you can use the landline in my office."

151

"Sounds good." It was much more preferable to standing out in the cold wind, trying to pin down a signal. Sidney held her breath and checked down the hallway toward the elevator. She blew out slowly when she saw it was clear. No wolves.

Banks opened the door to the refrigerated room where the bodies were stored and pulled the gurney inside. Some of the empty shelves put a scowl on his face.

"That's weird," he said.

"What's wrong?"

"The other bodies are gone." He went back outside and examined a clipboard hanging on the wall outside the door. "No record of them being moved. They're just… not here."

The hairs on the back of Sidney's neck raised when she remembered the way that creature had recovered and reanimated even after she'd stabbed it with the scissors.

"It's not like they could re-grow an entire head and walk out." She rubbed her clammy palms on her jeans. "Could they?"

Banks stared at her. "There's got to be a logical explanation."

Sidney nodded vigorously, trying to stave off a panic attack. The idea that those things could be up and walking around again was too terrifying to contemplate. She hoped Banks would attribute her sudden shivering to the cold of the refrigerated room and not the fact that she was scared out of her mind.

"Let's call the chief back," she said.

"Good idea."

Banks' office had only a few days ago belonged to Tom. Everything was still the same as he'd left it, the photo of his wife Carla, the baseball bat signed by Derek Jeter Sidney had bought at an auction for his birthday. The only thing different was that plant he always forgot to water looked surprisingly perky.

She smiled while Banks tossed his keys on the desk. He picked up the phone and dialed the chief's number from a business card.

A thud came from back in the autopsy suite.

Her mind jumped to the sound she'd heard right before Tom's body had fallen to the floor. The brief smile was wiped off her face. This wasn't the same, but it drew her attention.

"Did you hear that?" she asked.

Banks shook his head slightly and shrugged. "Hello, chief? Banks, here."

Sidney was already on edge enough as it was. There was no way she'd be caught without a weapon again. She dried her sweaty palms on her jeans and snatched up the baseball bat.

She tossed a glance at Banks' back and headed out to the lab to investigate.

Chapter 19

"Watch it, you big oaf!" A gruff Highland brogue scratched out.

"Can't help it. It's a bit awkward innit?" A second, less gravelly voice spoke up.

Sidney peeked into the lab to see two men with a body bag between them. She thought of the two men who'd killed Tom. The ones in front of her now were bulkier, red-headed, and dressed casually. They didn't fire off her instincts like the others, but they were leaving the freezer with their last bit of evidence.

"Oh, hell no…." Sidney pushed through door to the lab. "Not this again."

The men were three times her size, but this time she had a weapon. This time she was ready for them to change. She'd killed two others, and somehow survived. She'd do it again if she had to, but there was no way she was going to let them get out that door.

She came at them so fast, they didn't have time to react. She swung the bat and whacked the one closest to her in the back of the knees.

"What the bloody hell?" He hit the floor, dropping his end of the bag.

Now that Sidney saw them closer they looked like they could be twins, except the one on the floor had a full-beard and the other only had a goatee.

"Hey, there. Wait a second—" the one with the goatee said. With the bearded man on his knees, his head was at the perfect height for her to knock it off his shoulders.

Sidney swung again.

The other wrapped his hand around the bat before it connected. Sidney yanked.

"Let go." She struggled in a tug-of-war with him for a second. He was strong, but she gave a good yank and pulled him forward.

His thick eyebrows drew together in a scowl. "What are you playing at, lass?"

He gave another tug and Sidney let go. He fell back, tripping over the other man. He sat up and rubbed his head, then nudged his friend and pointed to her.

"Argus, don't she look like…?"

The one called Argus looked back at her and gave a nod. "Aye, spittin' image."

"Amazing, innit?"

She didn't wait to figure out what was so amazing about her appearance. Instead, she stomped hard on Argus' insole and placed a well-aimed elbow directly into his kidney. He arched back with a roar.

The man with the goatee opened his mouth to speak, but she punched him before he could get a word out.

"Banks, they're stealing the body!" she yelled.

"Agh!" The man doubled over and spit blood on the ground. "She split me lip."

Argus climbed to his feet, and his words came out more like a wheeze. "If you'll just listen a second—"

She turned and kneed him in the groin, wondering why it was taking them so long to shift form. The others had changed immediately.

Banks came in just as she got yanked back by the collar of her shirt.

"All right, Lass. That's enough." Argus wrapped his enormous arms around her, pinning her arms against her sides. He didn't squeeze tight, just enough to keep her under control. She couldn't move her upper body at all, but she kicked her legs out, accidentally catching Banks in the jaw.

"Shit!"

Banks collapsed on the floor, out cold.

The man with the goatee wiped his mouth with the back of his hand. He'd already stopped bleeding. "Honestly, woman. Settle down."

Sidney sank her teeth into the man's meaty arm at the same time he spoke, "Dimitrius—OW!"

She let her body go limp, her dead weight pulled her right through his hands, and she scooted out of his reach.

Sidney crawled over to the wall by the cooler to catch her breath, and the words hit her.

"Wait, what did you say?"

"Argus, no!" The man with the goatee grabbed Argus and held him back as he yelled all sorts of things Sidney had never heard. She wasn't even sure if they were English, but they seemed like some sort of cursing.

"Malcolm, let me go, or so help me, we're not brothers anymore!"

"It'll do no good. You can't do anything."

"She *bit* me!"

Malcolm shrugged and let go. "Suit yourself."

Sidney jumped to her feet as he dove at her. He stopped, inches from her face as if he'd smacked into a glass wall. The man fell back, banging into one of the exam tables before he went down with a thud.

Malcolm put his fists on his hips and took in the scene.

"Well, this is a right mess, innit?"

Sidney stared up at the man. He looked like he'd just climbed down from a beanstalk. If the next words out of his mouth were *Fee, Fie, Fo, Fum,* she'd go for the fire extinguisher again.

"Malcolm, at your service." Her hand disappeared inside his. "You must be Ms. Lake."

"How did you know that?" She tried to pull away, but he hung on. His goatee scratched the back of her hand when he kissed it, and then let go.

"Um, what's going on exactly?" She rubbed her hand on her jeans.

"Dimitrius sent us to bring the body back to his place for safekeeping. I take it you dinna get the message?"

"How did he know the other bodies were missing?"

He shrugged and scratched his goatee. "How does he know anything? I quit tryin' to figure that out a long time ago. Not worth the headache, I promise you that."

Banks groaned on the floor.

"That was a mighty kick you gave this one. Like a damned centaur." Malcolm's eyes grew wide suddenly. "Oh, but I mean that as a compliment."

"Thanks." It was a dubious compliment, but she accepted it anyway. "Help me get him back to the office?"

"Aye." The man hefted Banks up like he was a rock and this was the Highland Games. He followed Sidney to the office and put him down on the small love-seat crammed in behind the door.

"I should get back before Argus wakes up. Don't worry, I'll tell him you're gone. He doesn't take too kindly to being outdone by anyone, let alone a wee little lass like yourself. No offense, of course. That was quite impressive."

"I didn't even touch him. He sort of just... fell over." Sidney stared up at the man, in the same way he regarded her. She was fairly certain neither of them quite knew what to make of the other.

"Part of the deal. Sulis made us what we are. It's impossible for us to touch the bloodline with intent to harm."

"Wait, you're supernatural super-soldiers, like Dimitrius?"

He quirked his head a little at her description. "Aye. There's another, Tyran. I'm sure you'll meet him soon enough. If you don't mind, my lady, my brother will be waking up soon."

"Right. Go... um, take care of him."

The huge man bowed to her in a surprisingly graceful manner and ducked through the doorway.

Banks covered his eyes with his hand and mumbled, "Who were those guys?"

"Long story."

Sidney picked up the phone and called the chief to explain the situation.

"I thought we talked about this, Lake? You know, trusting my judgment, not running off half-cocked, or did you forget already?"

She winced and held the phone away from her ear. His voice came through loud and clear.

"Stay there. Take care of Banks. Don't move. Don't even blink your eyes until I get there. I mean it!"

"Yes, sir."

Lasagna night at *Chez Williams* was always a group event, so Mitch and Williams swung by the morgue to pick up Sidney and Banks on their way to the Upper West Side. He didn't lecture her in front of the others, but she got enough jaw-ticks and worried side-glances that let her know he was simultaneously angry and concerned she'd put her life at risk again so soon. She fought the urge to slip her hand into his, to give him a reassuring squeeze to let him know she was all right.

Thundering feet and high-pitched screams erupted inside as the group made their way up the front steps of the four story townhouse left to Megan by Aunt Rose. The door flew open before Williams could even bother with his keys and two fairy princesses burst out.

"Aunt Sidney!" Rachel threw her arms around Sidney's leg. Williams' older daughter had the same wild mane as her father.

"Hey there, Snow White," Sidney said. The last time she visited, Rachel was going through a Snow White phase and wouldn't go near any apples.

The little girl put her hand on her hip, and modeled her sparkling wings. "I'm not Snow White. I'm Tinkerbell! See?"

"Oh, right. Tinkerbell, you are fabulous." Sidney smiled.

Williams' looks. Megan's personality.

"Mr. Mitch! Up. Up. Up. Up!" Caroline threw herself at the chief. She was the mirror image of Megan, with her mother's strawberry-blonde ringlets, but she'd inherited her father's carefree spirit. Mitch swung her up and Sidney got a waft of marshmallow scent.

Having only turned three, Caroline was right on the bridge between baby and little girl. Sidney didn't miss how Mitch's face brightened when those chubby arms went around his neck for a hug.

He'd never had his own kids, and Sidney wasn't even sure he wanted any. The idea of having children of her own terrified her. It wasn't that she didn't like kids, they were just way too much responsibility. Plus, her job was dangerous, and she knew how it felt to grow up without a mother. It was better to play with someone else's kids and then give them back.

"Get over here, you little monkey." Williams grabbed Caroline and blew a raspberry on her tummy.

She screamed and laughed. "I'm not a monkey. I'm Tinkerbell!"

"No, I'M Tinkerbell." Rachel stomped her foot. "ME!"

"You're both monkeys, maybe I'll send you to the zoo." Williams scooped up Rachel in his other arm like a sack of flour, then swept everyone inside and kicked the door shut.

"Who are you?" Caroline asked when she noticed Banks.

Megan came in from the kitchen, barefoot with a tea towel thrown over her shoulder. Even in jeans and a t-shirt, she could be a supermodel. She paused to greet her husband with a lingering kiss.

"Eww! No, mommy, you'll get cooties!" Rachel yelled.

"Cooties? What is this cootie business?" Williams asked.

"Dinner's ready. Go get them washed up while I say hello to everybody," she said to her husband.

"I'll give you monkey cooties." Williams made monkey noises while he carried the girls into the kitchen. Megan watched them for a second.

"And no wings at the table," she called out.

"It's like having three kids," Mitch said.

"They're a mess." She shook her head, grinning.

"How are you?" Megan gave Sidney a good squeeze. She smelled like fresh lemons and verbena.

"Fine." If she ever had a sister, Megan would be the one she would have picked out.

Sidney was definitely not the domestic type, so she admired her greatly for the way she managed her home. It carried over into the rest of her life as well. Megan was a mother to everyone. Sometimes it was unnerving the way she could take one glance at her and know something was wrong. She stared at Sidney for a second and then gave her another squeeze before she planted a quick kiss on Mitch's cheek.

"Good to see you," she said. "I'm glad you all came."

"Thanks for having us." Mitch stepped aside to introduce Banks. "This is our new Medical Examiner Dr. Jackson Banks."

"Nice to meet you, ma'am." Banks offered his hand.

Megan shook his hand, but held on for a second and squinted. "Are you from Savannah?"

"Yes, ma'am. Born and raised. Did the accent give me away?" Banks showed off his pearly whites.

"Do you happen to have a cousin named Kelli?"

"I do, on my mother's side."

Megan laughed. "She's my sorority sister! Alpha Gamma Delta."

"Go Squirrels!" Banks laughed. "What a small world, we're practically family."

"What happened to your face? Are you okay?" Megan leaned in closer to check Banks' jaw.

"Runaway gurney," Banks said without even blinking. "First and last time I'll forget to set the break on that thing, I swear."

"Oh no! I'll get you an ice pack. Come on in, everybody. The Merlot should be done breathing, and I just pulled out the lasagna. Make yourselves at home."

They followed her through the living room and into the kitchen where the table was already set. Crayon drawings and name tracing sheets fluttered as Megan opened the freezer to grab a princess shaped ice pack. Rachel and Caroline shared a stool to reach the sink, and Williams stood behind them getting more water on the floor than they did.

"Girls, say hello to Dr. Jack." Megan handed the ice pack to him.

"Do you chase monsters out of closets like Daddy and Aunt Sidney?" Caroline asked.

"He's a doctor, honey. He works at the hospital," Megan explained as she transferred Caroline from the stool to her booster seat at the table.

"Do you see people's guts?" Rachel climbed up into her own seat across from Caroline.

"Sometimes," Banks said.

Williams set her plate of lasagna down and put on a goofy voice, "Eat your great big plate of greasy, grimy, gopher guts."

"Gross!" Rachel giggled.

Megan elbowed Sidney and spoke out of the side of her mouth, "He's cute, right?"

She shrugged. "I guess."

"Oh, come on! Didn't Graham mention wanting to go out? I told him to ask you."

Sidney kept her voice down to a low whisper. "*He's the doctor you wanted to set me up with? Trust me, I'm really not his type.*"

"I got that impression." Megan shrugged. "But that doesn't mean we can't still go out!"

Sidney held out her plate while Megan piled it high with pasta. "Not happening."

"Ohh, come on. It could be fun." Megan dragged her to the other end of the counter where she poured the wine.

Sidney glanced over at Mitch as he helped himself to some pasta. His forehead creased slightly as he noticed her stare. She turned back to Megan. "It's just… I'm not looking for anything right now, that's all."

"Why not?" Megan gasped and grabbed Sidney's arm. "Are you seeing somebody?"

"What? I—"

"Who is it? Do I know him?"

"Oh, God. It's not even a thing, okay?"

"What are you girls whispering about over here?" Mitch set his plate on the counter. He turned and rested his hand on Sidney's waist as he reached past her to grab a glass of wine.

"Nothing," Sidney said. Megan's eyes flicked downward to Mitch's hand, and she choked as she took a sip from her own glass. Sidney glared hard at her.

Williams came over and patted his wife on the back. "Glitter Britches, I know you like the Merlot, but take it easy okay?"

The two men took their wine and sat down with Banks at the table.

"You guys get started," Megan said. "I'm going to show Sidney that new, um… dress I bought."

Megan dragged her up the first flight of stairs into a pale pink room with purple wooden letters spelling out C-A-R-O-L-I-N-E over a white wrought iron day bed. Sidney flopped down on the white tufted duvet.

"If you're going to say anything that doesn't pass the Bechdel Test, I don't want to hear it." Sidney told her.

"Please. You don't have kids, neither of us have time for movies, and my book club only gets together for an excuse to day drink and not pass the Bechdel Test. We all know what happens at your day job stays at your day job. So, spill." Megan paced in front of her on the faded pink rug. "What's going on with you and Mitch?"

Sidney grabbed a squishy pink elephant from the bed and tried to hide her smile.

Megan's eyes rounded. "Are you in loooove?"

"No! I... don't know." She hugged the elephant. "Maybe?"

"You so are! How did this happen?"

Sidney hitched her shoulder up and let it drop. "We've been keeping things casual, but I think last night it finally got serious."

It fluttered her insides to even speak the words.

"How could you not tell me this?"

"We work together. It's complicated."

"And now it's a thing?"

"I think so, yeah."

Megan sat down next to her. For a second, Sidney felt like she was back in boarding school telling her roommate how she'd lost her virginity to a boy called Theodore Hutchings, III.

"What changed?"

"We talked about what we both wanted. We went to bed. He made me breakfast."

"Why this face then?" Megan put her hand on Sidney's knee. "You look like you're stuck in the middle of a crosswalk with the business end of a cab heading for you. People in love are supposed to smile."

Sidney took Megan's place pacing on the rug.

"This is the first time I've ever said anything about it out loud." She sighed. "I haven't been this close with anyone since my parents were killed. Mitch is different. He takes care of me—he made me omelets for fuck's sake. But he's also our boss. What if things get weird? What if it doesn't work? What if it *does* work? What if… what if I love him and something awful happens? It'll be all my fault."

"Because you loved him?"

Sidney strangled the elephant and nodded.

"Oh, honey. I can't pretend to know what it feels like to lose your parents like that. I hate that it happened to you. But I do know what it's like to be afraid of losing the person you love. Every time Graham walks out that door, I say a prayer he'll walk back through it just one more time."

Sidney gnawed on her bottom lip while she considered her friend's words. Megan got up and hugged her hard.

"The thing is, if you stay focused on the fear, you miss out on all the good times. The end will come, no matter what. It's inevitable. All you can do is take whatever moments you're given together and appreciate them for what they are."

She pulled back and gave Sidney a small shake. "Be happy. God knows, you of all people deserve it."

"Thanks." Sidney gave her a reluctant smile.

"Okay? Good." Megan took the elephant and tossed it back on the bed. "Let's go before dinner gets cold.

Chapter 20

"Ms. Megan, your lasagna is absolutely delicious," Banks said.

"Aww, thanks." Megan placed the dish in the middle of the table. "Feel free to have seconds if you want."

Mitch dished out some more. "Seriously, you could freeze this stuff and sell it."

Sidney sat down across from Mitch and dug into her own plate.

"That's what I keep telling her." Williams spoke with his mouth full. "We'd be billionaires. Forget all that trust fund business from dear Aunt Rosie."

The wine bottle next to his plate tipped over and dropped off the table. It hit the floor with a loud bang, but didn't shatter.

Williams jumped up. "You guys saw that, right? I didn't even touch it. I swear this place is haunted."

Sidney choked on her pasta. He glared at her.

"What?"

She fanned her mouth. "Hot."

"Shh, Graham." Megan smacked his arm, then spoke up in a cheerful voice, "Daddy's just being silly. There are no ghosts in this house."

"Spectral apparitions," Rachel said.

The cheerful tone in Megan's voice didn't match the nasty look she gave her husband. "Tub time, let's go!"

She clapped her hands and chaos erupted momentarily while she cleared the girls' plates and herded them upstairs.

"I'm gonna have to call Peters to come bless this place again." Williams took care of the empty wine bottle and grabbed another one.

Sidney hid her smile behind her napkin. She wasn't ready to reveal to Williams what Renny had said about Aunt Rose. Messing with him was too much fun.

"No more for me, thanks." Mitch waved his hand at his wine glass. "Lake and I have to head out soon."

"Head out where?" Sidney asked.

"I told Dimitrius you'd stop by to apologize."

She scowled. "Apologize for what?"

"You punched him in the face, for one thing. Then, he sent his men over to do us a favor and you beat the shit out of them."

"Hold on, you punched Dimitrius in the face?" Williams gawked.

"There's a chance I may have overreacted to some news." Sidney gulped down the last of her wine.

Williams gave everyone a refill except the chief. "What news?"

Sidney exchanged a desperate look with Mitch. She didn't even know where to begin.

Williams waited for more information, but it didn't come. "Well?"

Sidney took another long sip of her wine and stared into her glass. "Dimitrius says I'm descended from some kind of ancient bloodline or something. I have magical blood, and that's why I didn't change into a werewolf."

"Really," he said. Williams took a moment to study his plate before he got up and took it to the sink.

Sidney picked at the last few bites of her lasagna while she waited for whatever joke she knew was coming. There was no way he would let this one slide.

He came and sat back down. "So, when's your letter from Hogwarts coming?"

"Shut up." She threw her napkin at his head.

"That actually makes some sense," Banks jumped in. "Not the letter from Hogwarts I mean, but the bloodline thing, from a genetic point of view. You could have inherited some type of gene, or mutation in your DNA that would repel this particular virus."

"Like what?" Mitch asked.

"An example is the Delta-32 gene mutation. A virus needs to latch on to a host's cell in order to replicate. Different types of human cells have different shaped receptors. A receptor from a virus would have to match up in order to latch on."

"You can't fit a square peg in a round hole?" Mitch asked.

"Exactly. To use that example, people who have the Delta-32 mutation have round receptor sites while a virus like the Bubonic Plague has square receptors. Therefore, people carrying this gene mutation from both parents are immune to infection by that particular type of virus. It's extremely rare, but it's plausible."

"What if someone has the mutation from only one parent?" Sidney asked.

"Then, they might get infected or become a carrier, but not necessarily die."

"How do you know if someone has this gene?"

"It would show up in a DNA profile." Banks shrugged. "That's not to say there's no magical elements involved in your case. But maybe a little science and magic both?"

Mitch nodded, then turned to Williams. "What did you find out about the tattoos?"

"Do you know how many people out there have Army tattoos? It's ridiculous. If we had a unit number or a special slogan, that would be helpful. The national database came up with thousands of hits. I'll need more specifics or it'll take forever to go through."

"I'm still waiting on the ink results," Banks said. "If they were in the same unit together, it's likely they got them done at the same time, or at least by the same artist. The ink should match."

"The only commonalities are the tattoos and the unusual physiology of the bodies," Sidney said. "The M.O. on how they were killed is completely different."

"I'd like to know why the two guys who killed Tom reverted to human form after death, while the Doe from the subway and the one from this morning maintained their animal form. Are we dealing with two different species?" the chief asked.

"It's more likely a different form of the pathogen." Banks sat back in his chair, using his hands to help demonstrate his point. "Once a virus latches on to a host cell, it injects its own DNA into the cell's nucleus and reprograms it to behave differently. Viruses change and adapt all the time to survive. It's why there's a new flu shot every year. Maybe this virus mutated from the time it infected one set of bodies to the next?"

170

"Like in *Outbreak*," Williams said.

They all turned to stare at him. "The virus in *Outbreak* that killed Patrick Dempsey and his girlfriend wasn't airborne. But the one the pet shop dude got when that monkey bit him in Cedar Creek *was* airborne, which is why you should always, *always*, get the hell out if anybody starts coughing in a movie theater."

Banks nodded. "Something like that, yes."

Mitch's cell phone rang and he checked the ID before he answered. "Hey, Peters."

"Oh, tell him to call me this weekend," Williams said.

Mitch held up a finger and his forehead creased. "Dammit. Yeah, we'll be right down."

He hung up and pushed his chair back.

"What's going on?" Sidney asked.

"The WIF he's been monitoring just disappeared," Mitch said.

"WIF?" Banks asked.

"Wee Irish Fellow," Williams said. "If they hear the word *Leprechaun*, they go nuts, and you don't want to be on the wrong side of that Irish temper. See this scar?"

He pulled up his pant leg and showed off a white mark on the side of his knee. "Those bags of gold hurt like a bitch, man."

"Williams, drop off Banks and see what you can do to help Peters. Lake, I'll drop you by the club."

Sidney opened her mouth to protest, but Mitch cut her off.

"It's not up for discussion."

She pushed back from the table and put her plate in the sink.

"Is his club in that old church over on 6th Avenue?" Williams asked.

"*Bitten*," Mitch said.

Sidney made a face. "Why couldn't he come up with a better name?"

"I know, right?" Williams jumped in. "So cliché."

"Completely unoriginal. Like he can't afford a marketing team? There's a million other things they could have called it."

"Club Emo," Williams said.

A smile twitched on Sidney's mouth. "Therapy."

"Asylum."

"Trauma."

"Bleeding Heart."

Sidney waved her hand like she was motioning to a huge sign in the sky. "POE'S."

Williams lost it as they all made their way to the front door.

Banks turned to the chief. "They always like this?"

"Honey, we gotta go!" Williams called up the stairs.

Megan came down. "So soon?"

"Sorry to eat and run," Mitch said. "We have a situation. Dinner was delicious, though. Thank you."

"My pleasure." She smiled. "You guys be careful, okay?"

"It was nice meeting you, cousin once removed," Banks grinned. "Thanks for the lasagna, and the ice pack. I'm sure we'll see you again soon."

"I'll look forward to it." Megan gave him a hug, then squeezed Sidney tight and spoke quietly in her ear. "Take care of my man."

"Always." Sidney gave her an extra squish back. "Thanks for dinner."

"Don't wait up, my little love bug." Williams grabbed his wife in a bear hug and gave her a sloppy kiss.

"We'll see you guys there," the chief said.

Chapter 21

Mitch double parked around the block from the club and cut off the engine. Sidney didn't move.

"I'm sorry I yelled earlier. I know what it must have been like to walk in on two guys taking another body. Especially after what happened the night Tom was killed," he said. "Just because I don't condone your actions doesn't mean I don't understand them."

"Thanks." Sidney appreciated the apology, but she was too nervous about seeing Dimitrius again to show it.

He reached over and took her hand, kissing the tips of her fingers. It was a small gesture, but it made her feel better.

"Go in, smooth things over, then meet me back at my place. You still have the extra key, right?"

She nodded, but stayed where she was.

"Talk to me, what's bothering you about this?"

"I haven't set foot inside a club in six years."

The streetlight reflected off his lenses as he leveled his gaze on her. "You're not that girl anymore."

She stared at her lap. "Thanks to you."

"What else?" He squeezed her hand like he might pull the words out of her.

"There's something not right about Dimitrius. I feel like he can read my mind or something. He smells… weird."

The streetlight reflected off Mitch's lenses as he leveled his gaze on her. "He smells weird."

"I don't know, maybe the whole rich and powerful thing just reminds me too much of my grandfather."

Mitch rested his head back against the seat.

"Dimitrius is *nothing* like Alexander Lake." He circled his thumb around each of her knuckles. "I know that much, at least."

Sidney scrunched her nose. "Speaking of my grandfather, he called me this morning."

Mitch frowned. "Why?"

"He wanted to know why I was in the hospital."

"How did he find out?"

"No idea."

"What did you tell him?"

"Nothing. He only wants to use me to make himself look better." Sidney nibbled her lower lip. "I mean, how would it seem if I had some disease he could cure and didn't?"

"You didn't say anything about being bitten?" Mitch squeezed her hand so hard it hurt.

"No! Like he'd believe me anyway? He spent a fortune on therapists to convince me my dreams weren't real. We all know how that turned out."

He massaged her knuckles with his thumb and stared out the window as a surge of traffic swooshed by.

"What's wrong?"

"Nothing." He turned back to her and gave her a reassuring smile that didn't quite shine in his eyes. "You should get going."

She pouted.

"You'll be fine." He grabbed her and caught the pout of her lower lip between his own. They kissed long and slow and she forgot all about her grandfather, Dimitrius, everything. They kissed until her body ached and her face stung from the scrape of his five o'clock shadow.

"Call me when you're done," he said.

She ran her hand up his leg, but he caught it and shook his head.

"Quit stalling."

She narrowed her eyes. "You kissed me first."

"Go."

She slid out of the car and checked up and down for traffic before she jogged across the middle of the road. The pavement was wet and shiny from a fresh rain and the long line of patrons waiting outside sent up little puffs of white breath. Sidney combed her fingers through her hair, glad for the cold night air to lower her temperature. It wasn't as good as an icy bath, but it would have to do.

The huge wooden doors stood open and the *thud, thud, thud* of the music leaked out onto 6th Avenue. Some of the people in line moved to the beat, either inspired by the music or simply trying to stay warm.

The crowd eyed her carefully as she approached the huge bouncer. He was taller than the chief and almost as wide around as an Ogre. The circumference of his bicep alone was bigger than Sidney's head. His skin was so dark he was like a huge shadow standing in front of the door.

Despite his massive size, she wasn't intimidated. She'd taken out those two creatures that killed Tom, and that was before she was bitten. Besides that, this man smelled fresh and a little bit sweet, like cucumber-melon. Not scary at all.

As she approached, she realized that if there were any special instructions on how to get inside, she'd missed the memo. There was no way in hell she was standing outside in the cold.

Those waiting in line seemed to hold their breath as she reached the velvet rope, craning their necks to see if she would get in. The last time she'd set foot in a club, not getting in hadn't even crossed her mind. Every bouncer at all the hottest clubs knew her, and a lot of them had probably become more familiar with her than she'd ever admit to or even be able to remember now.

Sidney didn't get a word out before the man unhooked the rope and stepped aside.

"Right this way, Ms. Lake." He hadn't even checked his clipboard.

The patrons at the front of the line groaned and a few people cursed. Most of the girls started chattering behind well-manicured nails, wondering who she was. A few people used their cell phones to snap a quick photo.

"Just like old times," she muttered to herself.

Sidney stepped inside and immediately drowned. The lights, the music, the mix of so many different smells combined into a dizzying assault against her senses, instantly transporting her back in time to her brief stint as a party princess. Almost an entire year after her eighteenth birthday was lost to a hazy blur of pills and enough hard liquor to fill a pool. Merely setting foot inside the place brought back the crushing ache of loneliness she'd tried to fill with friends who weren't friends, and fans who worshipped her just because of the size of her grandfather's bank account.

The Narthex had been turned into the bar area, with the Sanctuary beyond cleared out and used as the main dance floor. The DJ was set up on what had once been the altar, spinning out house music that momentarily cut the bass and sounded like he was taking the listener on a flight through space.

Sidney stood there, barely inside the door, wondering if it was too late to turn and make a run for it.

"Follow me." The booming voice of the bouncer sounded in her ear and she jumped a little.

He cut a swath through the crowd like an air-craft carrier parting the ocean. All she had to do was stay close behind and there was no problem moving through the Narthex towards a blank door at the end of the bar.

The bouncer held the door for her and she blinked as she stepped into a sterile white hallway. The bright fluorescent lighting temporarily blinded her after the darkness of the club. The door clicked shut, canceling out the noise beyond. She could barely hear the *boom, boom, boom* as the beat kicked back in to full swing.

"Some nights are busier than others." The bouncer grinned down at her. His teeth were as bright and straight as the hallway they'd just entered. "My name is Dag, by the way."

Sidney automatically took his hand when he held it out to her. His fingers reached halfway to her elbow.

"Hi." She stared up at him, her mouth wide open. There was no other way to describe it. The guy was huge.

Dag laughed at her reaction. "Come on. I'll take you to Mr. Dimitrius."

They passed a few doors on the way down the hall as plain as the one they'd come through. A waitress exited one and Sidney got a peek at a room swathed in red velvet everything with accents of gold everywhere else. Someone must have hired the same over exuberant decorators as Louis the XIV.

The other doors were marked as restrooms. Sidney didn't get to see inside, but if the previous room was any indication, she guessed the toilets were actual thrones.

Dag reached the end of the hallway and pressed his thumb to a small scanner next to a set of elevator doors. They opened and she followed him in. There was barely enough room for them both, since he took up most of the space and actually had to duck his head a little to fit inside.

It was a short ride, only one level from what Sidney could tell, and they exited out into a small, richly decorated office with a desk and another bouncer. He was a third of the size of her escort, but his muscles told her he could hold his own if needed. Sidney watched herself on a bank of computer monitors by his elbow.

"16 Across: 'The O'Hara Homestead' four letters." *The New York Times* lay open on the desk to the crossword puzzle and the bouncer hunched forward, dark hair falling in his eyes. He smelled like fresh ink and paper.

"Tara," Dag said without blinking. "Hey, Dave. This is Ms. Lake."

Dave jumped to his feet. He glanced up at Dag and then stared at Sidney.

"Nice to meet you," Dave said. He picked up the phone on the desk and punched a number. "She's here."

Dave hung up and pressed a button on the desk. The lock on the door in front of them clicked open. "Go ahead."

"He's been waiting for you," Dag said.

Maybe it was the secured elevator. Maybe it was the two muscled bouncers. Maybe it was that unforgettable smell of moss and steel that suddenly swept into the room. Whatever it was, Sidney felt a lick of panic and seriously doubted whether this was such a good idea.

"Don't worry," Dag laughed. "He doesn't really bite."

Fight or flight. Neither was possible at this point. The only thing she could do was move forward, push that door open, and face Dimitrius.

The man sat behind a huge oak desk to the right, framed from behind by a circular stained glass window. The colors were muted now, but she imagined how beautiful it must be when the sun was out.

A one-way mirror took up the wall to her left, overlooking the dance floor. The sound-proofing in the office was flawless. Not a single beat could be heard from down below, despite the fact she could feel the vibrations through her boots. The patrons danced in silence below, like a television switched to mute.

Sidney took a few steps into the room and froze when the lock on the door clicked behind her. All of her courage fled, leaving her alone under the dark-eyed gaze of this ancient warrior.

"I'm glad you came." Dimitrius stood behind a desk that could have been a twin to the one in his other office. "I wasn't sure you would."

180

"I'm not here because you asked. The chief insisted I apologize in person. Sorry I beat up your guys. It was a misunderstanding." Sidney wished her words had come out stronger. The smoky flavor of campfire, mixed with leather and horses tickled her nose. She motioned to the door. "I'm sure you're busy, so unlock the door and I'll be out of your way."

He stepped around the desk and came toward her, but stopped when she tensed. "You're frightened of me."

She didn't want to lie, but she wouldn't dare admit the truth.

"I have no intention of hurting you," he said.

"I had no intention of breaking your nose."

His eyes were still a little purple underneath, and she was secretly glad.

"You didn't apologize for that."

"I'm not sorry I did it." Sidney gnawed on the inside of her lip.

He smiled.

She was losing her patience. "Renny said you wanted to tell me something?"

"Please, sit down." He motioned to a worn but very comfortable looking couch strewn with faded throw pillows and a knitted blanket.

"No, thanks." Sidney turned to the window. The harder she tried to ignore that scent, the stronger it became. The last thing she wanted to do was get cozy with him on the couch when Mitch's kiss hung fresh on her lips.

Dimitrius grabbed a decanter of amber liquid and two tumblers from a bookshelf. "Would you prefer some fresh air and a drink?"

Sidney nodded. She would have agreed to nearly anything as long as it meant getting out of that room. The door she'd entered through didn't unlock. Instead, he headed in the opposite direction, up a narrow stone stairwell that spiraled deep into the thick wall.

He paused with his foot on the first step, turning to see if she was behind him.

The last thing she wanted to do was allow the dragon to lure her further into his lair. She could fight her way out, use her phone to call for help, or even break off the end of the wooden cross on the bookshelf to use as a steak. All of that required more effort than she was willing to give at the moment. He said he wanted to talk. The sooner she listened to what he had to say, the sooner she could be gone.

Sidney followed him up the stairs.

When they reached the top, she found herself on a wide stone platform with a giant bell hanging in the middle. The carved balustrade overlooked 6th Avenue. Sidney peeked over the edge onto the heads of the patrons below.

Dimitrius moved past the bell and sank into a large upholstered chair as worn as the couch downstairs. Mismatched chairs were scattered around a table barely big enough to hold the decanter and glasses. Sidney had a slatted wooden chair, a modern canvas folding chair, and a three legged stool to choose from.

She remained on her feet, watching Dimitrius pour equal amounts of the gold liquid into both tumblers. He offered one silently to Sidney.

It smelled of something sweet and powerful she didn't recognize.

"Honey mead," he said when she hesitated.

He settled back in his well-worn chair and she watched his neck work as he downed the contents of his glass in two swallows. She knew she wouldn't be able to leave until he said what he wanted to say, or extracted whatever information he wanted from her, so she took her tumbler and did the same.

The liquid tasted sweet like honey with a hint of lavender. It built a warmth deep in her belly.

"I knew a girl once, a long time ago, who was headstrong like you." Dimitrius set his glass on the table. "Beautiful and fierce."

Maybe it was the sting of the liquor, maybe it was something in his voice, but her irritation dissipated. He suddenly seemed sad, lonely.

"What happened to her?"

Dimitrius poured himself another drink. "Grew old. Died."

It occurred to Sidney that if this man was truly what he claimed to be, he must have outlived thousands of people he cared about. She couldn't imagine what it would be like to lose her parents that many times over. To love someone and watch them age, knowing they would fade away into nothingness. To do it over and over again.

"And you didn't," she said.

He rested his fingers on the rim of his glass, balancing it on the armrest. He turned his attention to the enormous bell. If Sidney hadn't been watching so carefully, she would have missed the way he shook his head, 'no.'

The raw pain in his eyes made her heart ache as if the burden were her own.

"Sulis?" she asked.

He raised his glass in a silent salute and drank.

"You loved her."

"Deeply."

Sidney shivered. "I suppose to you, love is a relative term."

"Love is the truest form of magic. It cannot be explained or quantified. It just… is."

Sidney loved Mitch. She knew it that moment in a way she never had before. She couldn't imagine watching him grow old and die, then spending a thousand lifetimes without him. She wouldn't wish that kind of heartache on anyone.

There was no way she could confirm that this man in front of her was what he claimed to be. But, as she stared into the unfathomable depth of his eyes and saw the ancient hurt he carried there, she understood it to be true. The longer she stared, the more she felt as if there was some kind of invisible tether gathering, weaving its way around them, drawing them together.

Sidney shook the feeling off and placed her glass on the table for a refill.

Dimitrius stared at her for a second and then a slow smile spread across his face as he poured. "Argus asked if you were one of Hell's Furies."

"I told you, I'm sorry. I thought they were shifters."

Dimitrius waved his hand in dismissal. "No matter. It was his ego that was wounded, nothing more. To be honest, I was quite impressed with you the other evening, and even more so when I heard the report of what happened at the morgue."

The longer she was near this man, the more familiar he felt. It was as if they'd sat and talked a million times before in exactly this way. Sidney couldn't guess what he was thinking so hard about, but he seemed to be working on something inside his head.

"We've all suffered wounds much more extreme. Argus took an axe to the chest once. Malcolm's been punctured by so many arrows I'm surprised he hasn't sprung a leak," he said. "I was strung up in a tree in a village in Massachusetts. The Age of Reason was hardly all that reasonable. We've all been beaten, hacked, cleaved, drowned, shot… you name it. In all likelihood one or the other of us has survived it."

"Are you immortal?"

"No. Just very hard to kill."

"How do you know for sure? Have you ever—" Sidney couldn't bring herself to say the rest of it.

"Ever tried to kill myself?" Dimitrius shook his head. "There were others. Thirteen of us to begin with. Now only four."

"What happened to them?"

185

"Bullet holes, cuts, broken bones can all be healed with time. We cannot, however, seem to regenerate a head."

Sidney made a face.

"Suffice it to say, we all stayed well clear of Paris during the Revolution." Dimitrius poured himself more mead.

"How do you do it? How do you keep going when everyone you love, everyone you've known is gone?"

"Some days are harder than others. On the bad days…." He tilted his head back and drank.

"What does any of this have to do with me?"

"You're a daughter of Sulis. Her blood runs in your veins."

"You said that before." Sidney shook her head. "I still don't really know what that means other than I won't turn into one of those things that bit me."

"Her blood *is* your blood. You're a direct descendant. The color of your eyes is the color of the waters which gave her power. The red of the iron runs through your hair. Sulis revealed herself to you that day at the Chalice Well because she recognized you as one of her own."

"Am I still human?"

"You're everything you've always been." Dimitrius stared at her, then focused on his glass. "There's something else you need to know. The reason I sent Renny to find you."

Dimitrius stood and circled once around the chairs, as if it would help him figure out what he needed to say.

"As the acting General, it was my responsibility—my duty—to pay homage to the Goddess in order to receive her blessings and protection in battle."

He came over to her and leaned his elbows on the balustrade. "So, we were bound together, even before the predicament with the werewolves, to ensure lasting peace and success among our people."

"Bound together, as in, married?"

"In a marriage, two people are symbolically joined as one." Dimitrius faced her. "Our souls were entwined with one another. Inextricably connected for as long as we lived."

Sidney's breath caught in her chest. "You weren't supposed to live this long."

"No, I wasn't. Magic is unpredictable at best. We didn't realize what the full consequences would be when we performed the ritual on the Tor."

Sidney downed the rest of her drink, as if it would stave off whatever he was about to tell her.

"Sulis was quite a bit more powerful than even she knew." He traced one of the red highlights in her hair with the barest tip of his finger. It sent a shiver through her body. "I believe you are as well."

She shook her head and turned to him. "I'm not."

His eyes were black in the dim light, but she wasn't afraid of him anymore. The longer she stood there with him, the more familiar he became, like a word on the tip of her tongue that she couldn't quite remember.

"I can see you feel the truth. Even if you don't believe it yet." His breath mingled with her own. It went

187

straight to her core, warming her from deep within, intoxicating her faster than the mead.

Sidney didn't know what to believe. What she did know was that she liked the way her hair curled around his finger, almost of its own volition. Their fingertips rested millimeters apart on the balustrade, and a pull tugged between them like two magnets trying to link together. Dimitrius followed her gaze to their hands, his hair fell across his strong, square jawline.

Before she could stop herself, Sidney reached up and ran her fingers through his hair. It really was as soft as it looked. As she pushed his hair back, she saw the faded line running down his neck behind his ear.

Suddenly, she wanted to explore every inch of his skin to see how many scars she could find. She wanted to lay in bed all day and listen to him tell the stories behind each one of them. She wanted to feel his touch on the most intimate places of her own body. His lips were a breath away and she had no idea how he'd gotten so close.

Except, she'd just been in the car with Mitch, wanting to tumble into bed with *him*. Dimitrius was alluring. There was no doubt about that. But, he didn't know her. Not like Mitch knew her.

Sidney was fully aware she had some issues regarding her romantic life, but she was definitely not a hussy.

"I have to go." Her words barely rose above a whisper, as their breath mingled in a white haze and dissipated between them.

She fled to the stairs with Dimitrius close behind. The mead and the twist of the stairwell made her dizzy. She slipped on the well-worn stone, but he reached out and caught her hand before she went down all the way.

His touch burned like fire and lightning.

Sidney pressed her back against the cold stone wall. They stared at each other in stunned silence, but neither could bring themselves to let go. It was painful, yet despite herself, she wanted more. She reached up, traced the line of the scar down his neck, and the wildfire spread.

Dimitrius shut his eyes. His breath came fast and ragged through parted lips. She could hear the thud of his heart in his chest, just like the beat of the music down below. He snaked his hand up the back of her shirt and splayed his fingers across her heated skin.

Sidney tilted her head back, the rest of her body pressed forward against him. He loosed the fingers of his other hand from hers and cupped his palm around the back of her neck. She traced her finger around the coin pendant into the dip of his collarbone.

All she could think about was getting more of him.

As if he could read her thoughts, his mouth came down on hers.

They devoured each other. Lips parted. Tongues explored. Hands grabbed and tugged. The more skin touched skin, the harder it was to pull apart.

The room and all the things around them disappeared. They were caught up together in a fire of bright, burning colors. Heat swirled around them, consuming them both. The more they fed it, the more insatiable it felt. Sidney couldn't think of anything but absorbing him, losing herself in him, making them into one thing and nothing at the same time.

Steel closed around her body, trapping her, and suddenly she tore in two. As if a piece of her was ripped away.

She screamed.

Another roar echoed hers from across the room.

Sidney forced her eyes open and she was back in the office, near the door she'd entered from. Dimitrius lay sprawled out on the bottom step, propped up by the stone wall. His torn shirt revealed long red marks down the front of his sculpted chest.

A sinister laugh echoed throughout the room, so low and frightening Sidney could feel it in her bones.

Chapter 22

"You thought I could be disposed of so easily?"

A thick mass of pure darkness swirled and billowed in the middle of the room, a storm cloud gathering into a tornado. Fear shot through her veins in less than a heartbeat, drawing up the fine hairs on the back of her neck to full attention.

The demon she thought she'd vanquished stilled in front of her. A mouth of familiar, sharpened teeth appeared out of the darkness in a most evil version of the Cheshire Cat. "You still smell delicious. Fear tastes good. I like it."

A thick line of drool oozed out onto Sidney's boots.

"These are my favorite boots," she said. If it was feeding off her fear, she had to calm down. Allowing the fear to overcome her would only make the demon stronger. She touched the cross at her neck.

"I didn't get a chance to taste you earlier," the demon rumbled. "Perhaps I'll start with your toes and work my way up."

The stink of its breath drifted over her and Sidney shuddered.

"Be gone, devil," Dimitrius said.

"Oh? What have we here?" The thing swept a circle around him like he was something new and interesting to be studied.

Dimitrius held completely still, except for his eyes. He glanced at Sidney, then toward the bookcase filled with all the antiquities and carefully extended two fingers by his side.

Sidney followed his gaze and spotted the wooden crucifix on the second shelf. She returned his look with the smallest possible of nods to let him know she understood.

"If you were going to eat me, you would have done it already." Sidney squared her shoulders and walked over to the bookshelf as if it was the most normal thing in the world. "Maybe you're the one who's afraid."

The demon billowed up between her and the bookshelf, blocking her path. Big yellow eyes with vertical pupils stared her down.

Dimitrius said something in a language Sidney couldn't understand. The demon roared, its teeth gnashed right in front of her face and Sidney flinched. He repeated the phrase and it screamed in rage as it flew back to him.

Sidney grabbed the crucifix and held it straight out in front of her.

"You don't belong here," she said, genuinely surprised at how strong her voice sounded. "Get. Out."

The one-way mirror exploded into glittering dust.

Screams erupted from the crowd below. Sidney and Dimitrius ran to the edge of the window to look down on the people. The door swung open and Sidney held out the crucifix as a reflex.

"Are you all right, sir? Ms. Lake?" Dag asked.

"Fine," Sidney said.

Dimitrius ignored them all. He stared intently at the crowd below.

"It's still here," he said. He nodded casually to the people staring up from the dance floor. Sidney scanned the crowd and spotted a man staring up at them with a grotesque grin on his face that was too big to be natural.

"Ten o'clock," Sidney said without pointing. "In the suit jacket."

"I see," Dimitrius said.

"Please tell me you have some holy water."

"No. But, I do have salt and a silver knife."

"Salt and silver?"

He touched the cross at her neck. "Works wonders."

Dimitrius grabbed a beautiful knife with a hand carved ivory handle from the shelf and offered the hilt to Sidney. She wrapped her hand around the smooth ivory. Mitch would have told her to stay where she was. Dimitrius simply traded her for the crucifix with no question.

"Do your best to keep everyone calm and evacuate the building," he ordered Dag and Dave. "Ms. Lake, this way."

Dimitrius took a leather pouch from his desk drawer, then pulled a book on the shelf halfway out. The shelf swung open revealing a narrow staircase similar to the one leading to the bell tower. Sidney felt her way down the pitch black stairwell, hoping she wouldn't accidentally touch Dimitrius again. She had no idea what the demon had interrupted, but her body was still buzzing from it. Normally, she'd attribute it to an adrenaline rush, but adrenaline didn't typically gather between her legs.

Before she knew it they emerged from the back of the coat check closet. Dimitrius held aside a coat and Sidney ducked through. The Narthex was packed with people. She pushed through the crowd, brushing by a girl in a black lace corset, a man in a red hooded jacket.

Dimitrius grabbed her hand causing that same tickle of electricity to shoot up her arm. She didn't have time to protest.

If she freed herself from Dimitrius' grip, the crowd would easily carry her to safety. She heard Mitch inside her head, telling her to get out. But the demon was in the opposite direction.

The thing thought it could nearly rip her arm off, and come back to finish the job? She'd work on her impulse control later. As far as she was concerned, she had a score to settle.

When they got to the main dance floor, the swarm of similarly dressed club goers made it impossible to distinguish the dark suit jacket from the rest of the crowd. The stink of sulfur hit her nose and drew her attention to the left.

"This way," she told Dimitrius.

She followed the awful rotten egg smell toward the back near the DJ stand. A woman's scream directed them to the man in the jacket with the unnaturally large smile plastered across his face. His hand disappeared inside her chest.

As they approached, the young woman's eyes rolled back into her head. She slipped to the ground like a discarded toy.

Blood dripped from his fist. Sidney fought back a gag when she realized he clenched the woman's still beating heart. The man bit into it. Blood oozed through his teeth and dripped down his chin.

Dimitrius threw a handful of salt from the pouch. The man collapsed in an instant. A laugh echoed in Sidney's ear and a woman next to her seized up like she'd been hit with a taser. Her body went stock still for a second. When she turned, Sidney saw those ugly yellow eyes peer out from her face.

Just as quickly as the demon entered the woman, Dimitrius threw more salt and her body went limp. Sidney remained still, watching with her peripheral vision to see if the same thing happened again. It entered a man with spiky purple hair this time.

"Wait." Sidney held her hand out to stop Dimitrius before he threw more salt. "It's going to keep doing that. It wants you to use it all."

Dimitrius' eyes lit up with a spark of admiration. "What do you suggest?"

The question caught Sidney off guard. That was usually something she'd ask Mitch or Peters. She turned the dagger in her hand while she considered her options. Her mind went completely blank. All she could think about was that man's guts spread out on the floor of the mid-town conference room.

"Fuck if I know. Don't you have some kind of ancient incantation or something?"

"I need an old priest and a young priest," Dimitrius deadpanned.

It surprised her how calm he was, as if he'd seen it all before. After two-thousand years, he probably *had* seen it all. "You're kidding. This thing is about to rip our hearts out and you're cracking a joke?"

The purple-haired man in front of them laughed. Sidney felt like she'd been tossed into a snake pit as the sound slithered across her body.

"He thinks it's funny." Dimitrius shrugged and kept his gaze aimed on Sidney. "Though, it's not as funny as what you did with that letter opener."

Sidney sucked in a deep breath to tell Dimitrius exactly what she should have done with that letter opener, but he tilted his head to the side and she understood the hidden meaning of his words.

She secured her grip on the dagger, took one step forward, and drove it up under the man's chin. The demon gushed out of the mouth in a rush of blood and thick, black goop similar to bog sludge.

The force of it all knocked Sidney to the floor. The dark cloud hovered above her, gathering energy. She shut her eyes and covered her face as it came at her. Pricks and slaps hit her body and she wondered if this was what was like to be caught up in a swarm of bats.

It stopped as quickly as it had begun. She found herself cradled in Dimitrius' arms, warm, and safe, and whole. But the demon was still there. The slits in its eyes narrowed at her.

"What are you?" it asked.

Sidney spit out some goop that had managed to get into her mouth. "If you find out, I'd love to know."

The thing choked. "*What are you?*"

Before she could stop herself, words welled up from within her. She knew the meaning, but the language that came out of her mouth wasn't English. It sounded similar to what Dimitrius had spoken upstairs.

"I'm your end."

Sidney grabbed the bag of salt and threw the entire contents at the cloud in front of her.

The air exploded and blackness covered her vision.

Chapter 23

Eyes. Claws. Teeth.

Sidney pressed the barrel of the gun into thick fur and squeezed the trigger. She didn't stop until the clip was empty.

The creature collapsed on top of her.

She was stronger now. Strong enough to shove the thing off.

The hand lay lifeless in the moonlight.

She tried to scream but no sound came.

The fur was gone. Nothing but pale, smooth skin remained.

Gray eyes stared blankly behind familiar gold-rimmed glasses.

"I should have stayed."

Blood.

"It's not your fault, chief."

There was so much blood.

She stood there, frozen, watching the life leak out of his body onto her bare feet.

"She actually is all right, you know," a third voice said from somewhere far away.

A soft touch smoothed the hair out of her face. Sidney gasped and opened her eyes. She squinted against the light. Her mouth was dry, like she'd swallowed sand. Her head throbbed. It was the worst hangover ever.

Those familiar eyes gazed back at her with worried lines tucked behind the edge of the gold-rimmed glasses. She reached out and felt his chest. No blood. No bullet wounds.

"Are you okay?" she rasped.

"I think I should be asking *you* that question," Mitch said. He squeezed her hand. With his other, he rubbed her arm between her wrist and elbow. It wasn't fire and lighting, but it felt good, like a warm blanket fresh out of the dryer.

"What happened?" She touched Mitch's chest again with her free hand, to be sure he was whole.

"The demon came back. Nearly killed you. Again," Mitch said.

"I meant—" Sidney rubbed her face, as if doing so would erase the terrible dream from her brain.

"You spoke in tongues. Then you threw salt. The demon got all splodey," Williams said. "You were badass."

She took a glance around the room to get her bearings. The bookcase of artifacts stood on the other side of the room, and there was the desk in front of the window. The worn couch in Dimitrius' office really was as comfortable as it looked.

"Splodey?" she asked.

Williams shrugged. "Caroline's new word. It feels appropriate in this situation."

"What are you doing here?"

"There was no sign of the WIF so we came back."

"Yeah, just in time to find everyone evacuating," Mitch said.

"And you being a total badass."

Her gaze drifted over to the bottom step of the staircase where Dimitrius sat. He gave her a small nod. His white shirt was torn and splattered with dried blood. A smear of black cut across his jaw and down his muscled forearm.

She remembered talking with him by the bell.

Remembered his skin.

The taste of honey mead on his tongue.

Heat rushed through her body from her scalp to her toenails. She wondered if they could see her blush. She never blushed.

Mitch put his hand behind her back and helped her sit up. The room flip-flopped around her and her stomach roiled.

"We should get you home, and um… cleaned up." Mitch tried to play it cool, but he couldn't hide his disgust. Her hands and face had been wiped off, but she was still mostly covered in blood and that thick goo. It had dried like tar on her skin.

Normally, Sidney would have ignored the shaky feeling in her knees and tried to stand up. She would have made herself go downstairs on her own two feet if it killed her. Except this time she not only felt weak, she felt empty, like a part of her was missing somehow. She wasn't sure she could find the strength to get out of here no matter how bad she wanted to.

Dimitrius stood and watched her carefully.

Mitch waited with his hand offered to help her.

"Why don't you go get the car warmed up? I'll be right behind you," she said.

He hesitated for a second before he nodded. "I'll pull around to the side door."

Mitch left and she turned to Williams. "It's late, you should get home. Megan will be worried."

Her partner hesitated.

"I'll assist Ms. Lake downstairs," Dimitrius said.

Williams waited for approval from Sidney.

"I'm fine, really."

As soon as he left, she melted back onto the couch. It had taken every ounce of her strength just to hold her head up.

"Your life force is water. It was how Sulis gained her energy. A soak in the tub will rejuvenate you." Dimitrius watched her. His eyes were different, like there was a new light in them, a spark she hadn't seen before.

Sidney rubbed her face, trying to scrub away the awfulness of the night. A bath sounded amazing. Trying to figure out what had happened in the stairwell was too much to deal with on top of everything else. All she wanted was to get cleaned up and sleep for a hundred years. Sidney glanced around. "Where are my boots?"

Dimitrius grabbed them from the other end of the couch. He bent to one knee and held the first one out. She slid her foot in, then he slid the zipper up, encasing her leg inside the well-worn leather. For a split-second she felt the sun warm on her head, smelled fresh hay. It was the most natural thing in the world. Then she blinked and it was gone.

Sidney scowled. "I'll do the other one."

She tugged the boot on and zipped, then stood without thinking. The room spun like she was on a carousel and Dimitrius slung his arm around her waist to steady her.

She pressed her palms flat against his chest, which was a mistake, because her hands molded around the contours of his bare skin where the shirt fell open, awakening that lick of fire from earlier. His earthy scent swept over her, filling the empty hole in the pit of her being. The room stilled, and everything felt right again.

"That was… weird."

Sidney lifted her eyes to his. His hand splayed wide on the small of her back. Their fingers twined together so that she couldn't even tell which were her own.

"I'm sorry. It's the bond. Our souls have come to recognize one another."

Sidney shut her eyes and tried to make sense of what he'd said up in the bell tower. "Your soul was magically tied to Sulis. I come from her bloodline. That makes us…."

"Bound together. Inextricably."

"Um. No." Sidney unwound herself from him and ducked under his arm. "You couldn't come up with something a little less like the plot of a bad soap opera or a trashy romance novel?"

Dimitrius glanced up. Sidney covered her face with her hands and shook her head.

"The bloodline thing? That's messed up enough, but this?" She waved her hand back and forth between them. "Not happening."

"It's a great deal to process." Dimitrius sagged and the weight of all those centuries seemed to press down on his broad shoulders. "Please know that I do not wish to interfere in any current… relationship you might have going on. I only told you so that you might be aware of what was happening."

"Mitch is waiting."

"Of course." Dimitrius held her gaze for a second longer before he turned and went back to his desk. He pushed a button on his phone and Dag entered. "Please escort Ms. Lake out."

Chapter 24

Climbing into Mitch's car was like climbing into a sauna. The heat was blasting on full and the seat warmers were set to high. It was wonderful. He always seemed to know exactly what she needed.

She had no idea what to say to Mitch. The last thing she wanted to do was hurt him. Which was the lesser of two evils, telling him she'd kissed Dimitrius or keeping it a secret? She hadn't meant to do it. Hiding it would only make her feel guiltier. She thought about it as they drove the few blocks up to his condo. He pulled into his space in the garage and put the car in park.

"I kissed Dimitrius." She blurted it out before she could stop herself.

Mitch froze where he was, door half-open, keys in hand. "Excuse me?"

"It was an accident."

"Did he force himself on you?" There was a tone in his voice she'd never heard before.

"No! It wasn't like that." Sidney shut her eyes and shook her head, realizing that probably sounded even worse. "I mean, he said we're bound together somehow. I don't know. There's magic involved. It seemed to make sense when he explained it, but now it sounds crazy. It doesn't matter. I told him to take his mystical bond and shove it."

Mitch turned to her then, eyebrow raised.

"Okay, I didn't say it like that. But I made myself clear."

"Did you tell him about us?"

"No, but I got the feeling he already knows."

He tilted his chin, then continued moving out of the car. "Get out, you stink."

As soon as they were upstairs, Mitch went straight into the bathroom and turned on the shower.

It was becoming a routine. She pulled off her clothes. He gathered them to wash. She wasn't quite sure if they could be saved, but she knew he would try. The same as he always tried to save her from whatever mess she'd managed to get herself into. Goddess or not, maybe she did need him, more than she knew.

"Do you love me?" she asked Mitch.

He went completely still. For a moment the only sound and movement was the rush of water from the shower. It swirled around Sidney's feet and disappeared down the drain.

"Do you love *me*?" he asked.

Sidney didn't know how to put voice to it, how to quantify what she felt within the depths of her very soul. Trying to name it with words made it feel tawdry and insignificant, because it was so much greater than both of them.

He must have understood her silence because he put his hand flat across her chest and pushed her against the wall of the shower. Her head hit with a thud and his clothes were soaked through in an instant.

There was no spark of lightning or swirl of colors when his skin touched hers, but it didn't matter. The kiss with Dimitrius had happened so fast, had been so intense, it felt like a dream. Whatever was between her and Mitch was real, and it was good all on its own. They didn't need magic to make it happen.

All thoughts of Dimitrius were chased away as she opened her mouth to Mitch and he kissed her harder than he'd ever kissed her before. She was drowning in the spray of water. Drowning in him.

She gasped.

His shirt came off and hit the tiles with a wet slap.

Sidney concentrated hard, blinking water out of her eyes, as she tried to undo his belt. The wet leather was hard to deal with, but she managed to get to the part that mattered.

She wiped her face and put her arms around his neck. He lifted her under her hips, using the wall of the shower for leverage.

And then he was inside her. Just like that. He filled her full. Made her ache for more.

"Oh my, God." She wasn't sure if she whispered it or screamed it.

He drove into her hard, over and over. It hurt so good she could barely hang on. He sucked the drops of water off her hardened nipples with gathering intensity, until she really did scream. The sound was cut short as he covered her mouth with his own, his tongue invaded her, matched the rhythm of what he was doing below.

There was nothing left but the sound of water and the slap of their bodies as they met each other full on. Without warning he threw his head back and cried out between gritted teeth. His heat flooded into her. He pinned her against the wall, and dragged her over the cliff with him.

When they came to their senses enough to move again, Sidney lowered her feet to the floor. Mitch held onto her, making sure she was stable before he let go.

He pressed a long kiss to her forehead. "You okay?"

"That was amazing." She traced a drop of water down his jaw line.

"Good." He kissed her again, then turned to pick up his shirt.

"Shit. Are *you* okay?" Ten long lines marked his back where she'd dug in her fingernails. Blood mixed with the water running down his skin, painting the waistband of his jeans. She didn't know she'd grabbed on so hard.

"Yeah. Why?"

"You're bleeding." Sidney felt sick, and the dream she'd had came back to her.

"It was worth it." He gave her a half smile, as he worked off his wet jeans.

She shut off the shower and stood there dripping.

Mitch kissed her cheek and wrapped a towel around her shoulders. "It's just a few scratches. No big deal."

He was the man she'd spent the past six years idolizing. She'd looked up to him as the one who was invincible. Now, things were all upside down and backwards. She was the invincible one and he was the one standing there with deep crinkles at the edges of his eyes. What little hair he had left in the back was white and gray. Despite the fact that he was in good shape for his age, he still had thirty years on her. Sidney wasn't sure if she could stand to watch him age and wither away.

He wiped her cheek with the edge of his towel. "Why the tears?"

She sniffled and shook her head. "It's been a long ass week."

"You're telling me." He pulled her in for a hug, and took a moment to comb through her hair with his fingers. "Did you hear? I'm dating a goddess."

Rolled her eyes and made a face.

Mitch kissed the tip of her nose. "Better than dating a werewolf."

She ran her finger next to the marks on his back. "Might be the same thing."

"Not even close."

"You think this means I get a tiara or something?"

He arranged the towel over her shoulder and hid a smile. "How about a toga?"

She grinned and shoved him. He picked her up and tossed her on the bed, then climbed in after her, and showed her exactly how he thought a goddess should be loved.

Chapter 25

The only sound was the rhythmic splash of her arms pulling through the water. No car horns. No businessmen talking to their brokers on cell phones. No whoosh of the subway through an iron grate. Only the sound of her heart and the occasional breath for air. The solitude of the pool helped her concentrate. It was nothing but her, the water, the rhythm of her body, and her thoughts.

Sidney kept waiting to feel the burn in her lungs that always came by the time she hit the half-hour mark. She expected to feel the ache in her legs as she flipped and pushed off the wall and started in on the next lap.

It never came.

This time she felt like she could swim forever without tiring, so she pushed harder, kicked faster.

It shouldn't be that easy to swim so hard for so long. She went another fifty laps in a full out sprint, then grabbed the edge of the pool, gasping for air and ripped off her goggles.

It only proved that she was different. Something within her had changed, and it wasn't the spark of romance between her and Mitch. Despite what Dimitrius said about being a goddess, she couldn't manage to get her partner's words out of her head; *You may not be you anymore*.

Maybe she didn't have to be so afraid of howling at the moon or tearing people to shreds, but the fight against the demon proved she was more powerful than before she was bitten.

And kissing Dimitrius, well, that was a whole other thing entirely.

It had gone better with Mitch than she deserved. He might not have said much about it, but the way he'd fucked her in the shower made it clear how he felt. The hardest part was that she knew he and Dimitrius were friends. They trusted each other deeply, and she didn't want to ruin that.

It would be great if she never had to lay eyes on Dimitrius again. At the same time, she wanted to lay her eyes, hands, mouth, and everything else all over him.

Repeatedly. On all surfaces. In every location.

But, she loved Mitch. She was *in* love with him. No red-blooded female could deny Dimitrius was good looking, sexy, steamy as hell, but she didn't know him at all. He was a virtual stranger. At one point in her life, she wouldn't have had any problem going to a night club to play tonsil-hockey with some random dude. But that wasn't who she was anymore.

Usually swimming helped her sort things out, but now she was at her usual stopping point with more questions and energy than when she'd started.

She showered off, changed, and headed for Williams' house. They were partners. Sorting through information was what they did best together. Maybe she just needed an objective point of view.

Her partner opened the door with a flourish. "To what do I owe this early morning visit?"

"I need your researching skills." She pushed past him and went inside.

"Banks and I were enjoying some fresh donuts." He said, at the same time she spotted the shaggy blond hair. "Care to join?"

She'd completely forgotten about Banks. Even though she wasn't one for make-up and primping every morning, she had her standards. Stopping in on Williams after a swim was typical, and it didn't matter what he thought about her appearance. But Banks was still new, and she wasn't ready for him to see her post-workout worst.

"Morning, Lake. I was just about to head out," Banks said.

It made it worse that he was showered and shaved. He cleaned up nicely, despite the nasty bruise on the side of his face.

"Don't let me chase you off," Sidney said.

"No worries." He flashed those dimples at her. "Wills, thanks for the donuts, man. I'm gonna hold you to that Knicks game."

They did that awkward high-five, bro-hug thing so many of Sidney's boarding school pals did after a rugby match. Williams walked him to the door and let him out. When he shut it and turned around, he was grinning like a little kid.

"Wills?" Sidney raised an eyebrow.

"What? He's cool."

"Just don't forget who your partner is."

"Do I detect a hint of jealousy?" He grabbed her and rubbed his knuckle into her head. "You hate basketball."

"Yeah, okay. If you need a basketball buddy, that's fine." She shoved him away and smoothed down her hair. "Is Megan taking the girls to school?"

"Yeah, what's up?"

Sidney sank down into a chair at the kitchen table. "What the hell happened last night? What was that?"

"No idea." Williams grabbed two mugs out of the cabinet.

"When I swam today, it was different. I was sprinting and couldn't even feel it. Whatever happened when I was in the hospital changed me." Sidney threw up her hands and let them fall back on the table. "I don't know. Maybe you were right. Maybe I'm not me anymore."

Williams poured coffee and brought the mugs over to the table. He sat across from Sidney, then bit into a donut and chewed for a few moments before he put it down and took a sip of coffee.

He placed his mug down and leveled his gaze on her. "Maybe when you get to Hogwarts you could ask Dumbledore about it?"

Sidney threw a piece of donut at his face. "This is serious. I need to know if Sulis Minerva was a real person. Can you wave your magic research wand and dig something up?"

Williams scooted his chair back. "Step into my office."

Sidney followed him into the small room under the stairs where her partner had a desk, a computer and an old recliner he picked up off the curb down near NYU right after spring semester let out.

Williams sat in the desk chair while Sidney took the recliner.

"Okay, how do you spell it?"

Sidney spelled the name and sipped her coffee while his fingers flew over the keyboard of his laptop.

"Hmm, it doesn't look like there's any evidence to suggest that she was an actual person. She was based on a Celtic goddess named *Sul* that was around like ten-thousand years before the Romans even showed up." Williams kept his eyes on the screen as he spoke. "People used to drop coins and pieces of metal in the water with wishes written on them."

"Check this out." He waved her over. Sidney peered over his shoulder at the screen.

"These were excavated from the baths. They're from all different time periods, but the majority of them came from around A.D. 100, when the Roman Empire was in its heyday in that area."

Williams enlarged a photo of one of the coins. It was worn and hard to read, but Sidney could make out the image of a head and some Latin letters. "Look familiar?"

Sidney stared at the coin. It matched the pendant Dimitrius wore around his neck. "Shit."

"The letters are a name," Williams pointed to a line under the photo. "*Dimitrius Arturus*. This says he was a Roman General in the area around that time."

"Wow. He really wasn't joking," Sidney said.

"If he was the guy in charge, it would make sense his picture would be on the money."

Williams scrolled through more pictures.

"Hang on, go back." She shooed his hand from the mouse and scrolled back up, then stopped on a photo of a sword. It wasn't exactly the same, but it reminded her of the one she'd seen on Dimitrius' wall.

"That looks like the sword on his wall."

"What sword?"

"Dimitrius has a huge sword."

"That's what she said."

Sidney smacked his shoulder.

"Sorry, how could I let that slide?" Williams pointed to the sword on the page. "This is *Caledfwlch.*"

"Cal-eh-what-huh?"

"Cal-ed-*vol*-hagh." Williams repeated slowly. It sounded like he choked up a hairball on the last syllable. "It's the original name for King Arthur's sword, *Excalibur.* Glastonbury is really close to Bath. I'm sort of an Arthurian geek."

"How did I not know this about you?"

Williams shrugged and suddenly found his coffee very interesting. "It was more of a phase I went through in high school. Glastonbury is supposed to be where the land of Avalon was. King Arthur's bones were buried there once, but no one knows what became of them."

"I know. I've been there," Sidney said.

"Wait. *What?*"

"Field trip."

"Right, of course. Me? I went to the Brooklyn Zoo in the fourth grade."

"Yeah, okay," she waved him off. "So, maybe Dimitrius is an Arthurian geek too."

"Actually, the original meaning of *Caledfwlch*, comes from the combination of two Welsh words meaning 'battle' and 'gap or notch', and one of the words in Old Irish for the word 'gap or eye' is *Suil*, sort of similar to Sulis."

Sidney straightened up and frowned. "You think maybe there's a connection between the sword and Sulis?"

"Could be, but what?"

"She was the patron goddess of the baths. Dimitrius said her power came from the water. Wasn't there a Lady of the Lake or something?"

Williams turned in his chair. "In several versions of the legend, the Lady of the Lake did bestow a sword on King Arthur."

"How do swords get their names?"

"It's different for each weapon. Sometimes it could be named after what it looks like, or what it accomplished, or who wielded it."

"Or a local deity?"

"You're suggesting Sulis Minerva is the Lady of the Lake from the King Arthur legend."

"Why not?"

"All right, I can see how a connection between Sulis and the sword might be *plausible*. The Lady of the Lake was supposedly extremely powerful, like a goddess would have been. Maybe over time Sulis might have been replaced with the idea of the Lady, especially with Christian influence over pagan traditions. I mean, the earliest mention of Arthur isn't even until the 5th century when Christianity was—"

"Hey, Wills? Your nerd is showing. Zip it up, buddy."

He snapped his mouth shut.

"If that's true, then how does Dimitrius fit in to all this?" she asked. "Assuming the sword on his wall actually is authentic, and not some showpiece he got at a Renaissance Fair."

Williams stood up and paced back and forth beside his desk. "The guy's wealthy and powerful, and extremely old. There's no telling how he could have acquired it. Inheritance, battle, theft, auction, maybe he saw it saw it stuck in a big rock on the side of the road and thought it was pretty? I don't know."

She studied the photo of the sword on the screen. "What if Sulis gave it to him?"

"What do you mean?"

"His name is Dimitrius *Arturus*."

"But… that would mean… that's impossible…" he sputtered. For a moment, she thought he might start hyperventilating.

"Is it? There's a huge sword over his mantel and he wears that exact coin around his neck. Dimitrius told me Sulis made him what he is. They were in love. What if she gave him a sword as a romantic gesture? That was a common thing back then, wasn't it?"

Williams threw his head back and blew a noisy raspberry at the ceiling. "Please, God, tell me I did not use the word 'splodey' in front of King Arthur."

"At least you didn't make out with him," Sidney muttered.

"Huh?"

"What? Nothing. I'm going to go home and grab some work clothes. I'll meet you at the office and we'll see what the chief thinks."

"I'll see you down there." Williams walked her to the door. He snapped his fingers as she stepped outside. "*Excalibur*! That's what he should have named his club."

Chapter 26

As if the stink of the subway system wasn't bad enough before, it was a thousand times worse with her newly acquired super senses. Even breathing through her mouth couldn't disguise the stench of trash, and rats, and even a tinge of wet dog. It made her think of the shifters, and she clenched her fists automatically, trying to quell the adrenaline that burst into her system.

The tell-tale breeze of the incoming train tossed her hair and blew the scent away. Sidney caught sight of a red hood as she stepped onto the train. Something about the jacket sparked her memory and she stared at the man who sank into the seat at the other end of the car.

That elemental instinct that told her danger was near perked up her senses and her body tingled with the instinct to escape.

The man didn't look at her the entire subway ride. He didn't look at anything but his ratty old boots and the torn hem of his black jeans. It was probably nothing. The call from her grandfather was affecting her mind. He wasn't having her followed. He didn't know what she really was. Still, after working at the agency for so long she'd learned to trust her instincts about things. Usually a creepy feeling indicated something was up.

Sidney dashed out of the train as soon as the doors opened and the red hoodie did too. She merged with the people exiting at Times Square. At the lunch rush, it seemed like everyone in Manhattan was here in this station. She detoured to the platform for the Uptown R train, and then to the Downtown 2 platform, just to throw him off, but when she scanned the crowd again she didn't spot a single flash of red.

When she thought it was safe, she went over to the Shuttle to Grand Central Terminal. The train was already in the station and she jogged on right as the doors closed.

When the train pulled into the station, she blended with the rest of the crowd at Grand Central and stopped glancing over her shoulder every few seconds, even though her heart still banged inside her chest. She told herself it was a coincidence. There were probably thousands of guys in red hoodies all over the city at that exact moment. It didn't mean anything.

"Sidney Lake," a low growl trickled down her spine and a faded red sleeve entered her peripheral vision. She pretended she didn't hear her name and stepped out into the street dodging cabs, cars, and a delivery truck like Frogger across Lexington Avenue.

There was no intention to reach into her pocket, grab her keys and get inside her apartment. She knew she wouldn't make it. Besides, she didn't want this creeper knowing where she lived, in case he didn't already.

As soon as she passed her building, she broke into a run. She only took a few steps before sharp claws dug into her arm and yanked her to a halt. She spun around, ready to plant the heel of her hand in his face, but he blocked her move.

Now that she was close, she could see why he'd kept his hood up this whole time.

"I don't want to hurt you." It was strange hearing actual words come out from between those unnaturally sharp teeth.

Sidney tried not to breathe at all, but her senses were on full alert and she couldn't stop herself from sucking in that smell.

"I only want to talk." That voice was a low rumble.

"Hey, lady." A guy with a messenger bag tossed over one shoulder rode up next to them on a bike. "This guy bothering you?"

The man in the hoodie growled and snapped his jaws. The too-familiar sound made her heart stop.

"Holy fuck!" The bike messenger zipped down the road, nearly splattering into traffic at the bottom of the hill.

Sidney stared at the hybrid man-wolf in front of her. From this distance she could see the similarity between this man and the two John Does they'd found. Only, this guy was alive and breathing. It was like he'd been frozen in the middle of a transformation.

Everything inside her body told her to run, but if there was any chance he could tell her what the hell was going on, give her any clue whatsoever about why these bodies had appeared and who they were, then she would gladly take it.

"You have my attention, but you're going to have to loosen your grip," she said.

"Sorry." He eased his hold on her arm and blood blossomed onto her shirt where his claws had dug in. "Even after all this time, I forget."

"Forget what?" Sidney asked.

"That I'm not human."

"What are you?"

He glanced around, up and down the street. "Not here. Is there some place safe we can talk?"

Sidney weighed the options. It was stupid to bring him up to her apartment, *really* stupid. But they couldn't exactly walk into the coffee shop on the corner, order a cappuccino, and hang out like old friends. Well, they could, but not without sending people out the door screaming.

She shut her eyes and sighed. "My place is right here."

They walked back to her building. She opened the door and nodded him in first, "Third floor."

The creature leaned heavily on the railing, his body not quite moving the way a man's should move to climb the stairs. She sent a text to Mitch: *Earwig*. It was code that he should answer and listen but not speak when she called. They reached her landing and she waved the hybrid inside first, then pointed to the couch.

"Sit down on your... hands. Wait here," she said.

Sidney went back to her bedroom and pulled the gun Mitch had given her out of her bedside table. She checked the clip and made sure it was ready to go. On her way back through the kitchen, she grabbed her biggest chopping knife out of the drawer. It had to be sharp, she never used it. She dialed Mitch and let the phone ring.

Back in the living room, she set her phone on the desk and made no effort to hide her weapons. The man... wolf... thing, sat on the couch exactly as she had instructed. His hood was off his head, revealing his pointy ears and shaggy tangled hair. The eyes and nose were human, but the jawline was off somehow.

It was grotesque, and Sidney wasn't sure what was worse, the fully changed wolves or this other hybrid creature.

"Okay, who are you?" she asked.

"David Anderson, Special Forces, United States Army." He removed his arms from underneath him.

Sidney tightened her grip on the gun. He slowed his motions to let her know he wasn't going to try anything, then pulled up the sleeve of his jacket to reveal a familiar tattoo on his forearm.

"What happened? How did you get to be... like this?"

"We were on a covert operation in Afghanistan back in the '80s, monitoring Soviet action in the mountains. Our squad came under attack one night, only not with firepower. It was something else. Our leader was torn to bits by an animal. We figured it was a mountain lion or a panther." He shoved his disfigured hands in the front pockets of his jacket and kept talking.

"Next night, same thing. Another guy down. Night after that, we were ready, waiting. We opened fire, but it kept coming. I was bitten, so were Knight and Wier. Larsen was scratched all to hell, but we caught the thing. Killed it. It was like nothing I've ever seen in my life before or since."

"Werewolf?" Sidney asked.

He gave a decisive nod. "We were quarantined. Turned into fucking guinea pigs. They told us they were

222

going to find a cure. At first, I could change back. I looked human and nobody could tell the difference. But they kept giving us drugs, said it would fix us—now look at me."

Sidney couldn't help but flinch. Not because of what he was, but what he reminded her of; the body on the platform, the snap of those powerful jaws next to her head, and the scrape of claws across her back. She shivered. It was essential for her to quell her fears and remain focused.

He ran his claws over his head; such a human gesture didn't fit his appearance. Sidney did her best to hide her reaction, but she wasn't very successful.

"See? People are terrified of me. Even you. I can't get a job. Can't have a family. If only they'd left us the hell alone. They ruined us and now they're killing us off, taking care of their mistakes, one by one."

"The body in the subway?"

The thing shook his head. "We were told we were being transferred. They put us on a boat. Once they took out Knight, we realized what was happening. It was an execution. Wier, Larsen, and I overpowered them and escaped. We hid out in the subway a few days, but Wier wanted to get help. Larsen freaked out and killed him. I haven't seen him since."

"Who's 'they'? Who did this to you?" Sidney demanded.

His response was cut off by a loud crash in the back bathroom.

The man launched off the couch. Before she could blink, he had her in his grasp with the gun to her head.

"Don't struggle and they won't hurt you," he growled in her ear. "Just do what they say. They want you alive."

"What is this?" Sidney struggled against his grip, but his strength matched her own. She cursed herself for being so stupid. "What did you do?"

"They said if I got you, they could fix me," he said. "You're the key to all of this."

Two men just like the ones from the morgue barreled through her kitchen door and piled into her living room.

Sidney took a deep slow breath as they blocked both exits. There was no way out.

"You're surrounded. We don't want to hurt you. Come with us quietly and everything will be okay," the first man said.

"It's fine." She forced her body to relax. "I'm not an idiot, I can see when I'm outnumbered."

Her voice was steady and calm, despite how she felt inside. The hybrid's grip on her eased.

Sidney slipped free, grabbing his hand with the gun in it, and squeezed the trigger. The back of the first man's head sprayed across her door.

Chaos erupted. Before he hit the floor, the second man was in motion.

The hybrid's head exploded. Bits of brain matter and bone caught in her hair. Blood splashed across her favorite Waterhouse print. She fired back and hit her target.

At the same time, two more men came through the kitchen door, followed by two fully-changed shifters.

Long snouts caught the scent of carnage in the air and went straight for the fresh bodies. The remaining two in human form came for her.

That was just fine. Humans, she could deal with. She placed a swift kick into the kneecap of the first man to lunge at her. It crunched like a bunch of fresh celery snapping in two. He hit the floor, an unnatural growl emanating from his lips.

The crack and pop of a different kind echoed off her walls as he morphed into a wolf. She fired two bullets into his head and he fell still. After the fight in the morgue, she knew better than to assume he was dead.

Something stung her shoulder. There was a hole in her shirt, and the last man holding a gun grinned in satisfaction. His malicious look melted away when he realized it had no effect. She closed her hand around the knife just as he plowed into her.

She tumbled backwards, ending up on top, knife ready. Her lungs burned from exertion, but she wouldn't dare pause to catch her breath. Mitch yelled, as if he could get to her by sheer will power alone, but his voice was small and ineffectual through the phone.

The intruder roared out in pain as Sidney plunged the blade into his neck. She gagged and twisted the hilt, cutting off the sound of his voice as she slashed the blade under his chin. She shoved him aside and grabbed the gun, glad to have a weapon in each hand.

Heavy paws knocked her into the desk. Stars burst across her vision.

Claws dug into her chest, pinning her to the ground again.

225

Sidney shot the thing. It jerked and rolled to the side. She turned and emptied the clip into it. For an instant she was on the floor in her parents' bedroom, shooting at a different creature. The memory left her dizzy and disoriented.

The door burst open. She threw the knife out of instinct and it lodged in the wall right next to Mitch's head.

"What the fuck?" she yelled.

"Are you okay?" His eyes were wild behind his glasses.

"Are you crazy?" She staggered to her feet. "I could have killed you!"

"Look out—"

He dove at her. She tripped over the chair as she went down. Mitch's weight knocked the breath out of her.

The second shifter pounced on them. Sidney snatched up one of the intruder's guns and put a bullet in the creature's skull.

It collapsed under the table.

She shoved Mitch away, coughing and gasping to get air back into her lungs. When she could breathe again, she pushed up from the floor. There was no reason to rush as she went to the door and tried to yank the knife out of the wall. The hilt slipped through her grasp, covered in blood. She dried her hand on her shirt, and tried again.

Straddling the creature's back, she drove the blade down into the base of its skull, using both hands to twist the knife. A soft sound and loosening of the neck let her know the moment the tendons separated from the spinal column.

She turned and grinned at Mitch.

"That was close, huh?"

Chapter 27

The smile faded from her face when he didn't move, didn't even blink. He just kneeled there, completely frozen.

He said it took more than claws and fur to make a monster. Maybe this is what he'd meant. Maybe she didn't need to change into a wolf to become something that disgusted and frightened him.

"Mitch I—"

"It didn't break the skin." He swallowed hard. Shuddered. "I don't think it broke the skin."

"What?"

He lifted the bottom of his shirt. A red crescent shape marred his abdomen just under his ribs.

Sidney dove for him, ran her fingers over the indention. The marks were red, quickly fading to purple, but the skin wasn't broken. She shook her head.

"It didn't get through." She shut her eyes and leaned her forehead against his shoulder. "It's okay."

He crushed her body against his. It felt like he might break one of her ribs, but she didn't care. She wrapped her arms around his waist and squeezed back just as hard, so relieved he wasn't repulsed by her, that what he'd seen her do hadn't transformed her into a monster in his eyes. He groaned, then pulled back and put his hands on her shoulders.

"Are you okay?" he asked.

"I'm okay." She nodded and put her hand on his cheek, smearing a red handprint across his face.

"What the hell happened?"

They got to their feet and looked around.

"It's like a Tarantino set in here." Sidney couldn't look anymore. She made her way through the kitchen into her bedroom, and he followed. "I think they wanted to kidnap me or something. He said I was the key. What does that even mean?"

The gauzy white curtains in the bathroom caught the breeze from the broken window and billowed out softly. The afternoon sun brightened and warmed the narrow space, almost making it possible to forget the carnage out in her living room.

"If I show up someplace and find you covered in blood one more time, I think I might actually lose my mind."

Sidney turned on the shower to let it heat up. "You and me both."

"You scared the shit out of me." He wrapped his arms around her from behind and she let her head fall back against his chest.

"I didn't know what else to do. He followed me from the subway." She raised her arms up and he pulled her shirt over her head. "Come to think of it, I think he's been following me since yesterday."

"What do you mean?" He pulled off her bra.

"At the crime scene, down by the waterfront, I ran into a guy with a red hoodie, but I wasn't paying attention. I didn't see his face."

"Did you see him anywhere else?"

Sidney kicked off her pants and turned to face him. She thought back, and remembered a flash of red at the club, but she couldn't be sure since she hadn't seen under the hood. It could have been any guy in a red hoodie, or maybe it wasn't even a hoodie.

"I don't remember."

Mitch crossed his arms at his waist and pulled off his shirt. His face crumpled into a cringe when his head emerged.

"Damn, even if it didn't break the skin, it still hurts." He leaned over to push the waistband of his jeans to the floor and Sidney's heart stopped.

Blood smeared his back. A matching crescent marred his skin, and two puncture wounds welled up and over with fresh blood where the animal's canines had sunk into him.

"What's wrong?" he asked.

"It's fine. It'll be fine." She ran into the kitchen, opened the freezer and yanked out the bottle of vodka she kept for the really bad days.

"What the hell?" Mitch stood in the doorway of the bathroom, steam billowing out around him from the forgotten shower.

"Turn around." She shoved him around so fast he had to catch himself on the wall. He stood there like he was ready for a strip search.

"What are you doing? Agh!"

There was at least half a bottle left. She turned the whole thing upside down and let it gush over the wound the same way Peters had dumped the holy water on her arm.

"That's cold! What the hell's the matter with you?"

"We have to disinfect it." Her voice didn't even sound like her own. It was shrill and trembling.

"Disinfect what?" He turned around in a circle, trying to see his back.

"Hold still." She grabbed his arm and shook out the last few ounces. The bottle clattered to the floor. She turned and opened the medicine cabinet behind the mirror. "I swear I had some peroxide or something in here. Where the fuck is it?"

"Stop." He put his hand on hers, but she swatted it away and kept digging through the contents of the cabinet. A rolled up tube of toothpaste fell into the sink. A box of Q-tips scattered everywhere. She found a single alcohol swab in a foil package.

"Come here." It took her a few tries to make her fingers work, but she ripped it open and went for the wounds.

Mitch grabbed both of her wrists. "Stop."

They both stood there for a moment, frozen.

Sidney's face dissolved into a sob. "Why did you do that? Why did you—"

"What the hell was I supposed to do?" He let go of her and she had to take a step back to gain her balance. "I saw that thing come at you, Sidney. *What was I supposed to do?*"

"Not that!" she choked out. "Don't you get it? It didn't even matter if I…."

She couldn't manage to get the rest of the sentence out.

Mitch yelled and smacked the wall. Sidney jumped.

"I'm sorry." He came back to her, gathered her up in his arms. She clung to him, pressed her wet cheek against his chest, and squeezed her eyes shut.

231

"It's going to be fine. I promise." He spoke against her hair, as he ran his hand up and down her back. "It barely broke the skin. There's nothing to worry about. I'll be fine."

Chapter 28

"Look at me. Look at my face." Mitch held her head steady in his hands, but she couldn't meet his eyes. "Whoever did this is going to wonder what went wrong. We need to get out of here. Give me a sign you understand."

Sidney tilted her head up and down the best she could with him holding it.

"Good. Okay, I'm going to call Banks. You need to clean up and get dressed. Fast, Lake, I mean it."

"Yes, sir."

The door closed. Sidney dove for the toilet. Shards of glass and bits of plaster from the broken window dug into her knees as the dregs of donut and coffee she'd had at Williams' that morning came back up. Sitting at his kitchen table felt like a lifetime ago.

The shower scalded her but she didn't care. She scrubbed hard, even after the wound on her arm had disappeared and the water circling the drain was no longer pink with strangers' blood. The curtain slid open and Mitch turned the water off. He rubbed the towel over her, held her hand as she stepped out. She wanted to see the bite again, to make sure it wasn't her imagination, but he swiped her hand away when she reached for his shirt.

"We'll worry about that later," he said. "Your clothes are on the bed. Dimitrius and his men will be here any minute."

The fog of fear cleared from her brain a little.

"Dimitrius is coming here?" She hugged the towel tighter around her body.

"Something about a blood oath." He went to the window and scanned the patio.

"I don't need bodyguards. I can take care of myself."

"Get dressed, Sidney."

She slid on her underwear, then her jeans. "Did you tell him about—you know."

"It doesn't even hurt anymore."

"Maybe he knows what to do. Maybe he can help." Bra, camisole, black sweater over her head. The cashmere warmed her quickly. It was the least practical fabric in her closet, but there was no time to question his choice. Socks and boots on and zipped.

A familiar smell tickled her nose.

"Mitchell? Ms. Lake?"

"Back here," Mitch called out.

Dimitrius was probably the last person she ever expected to see framed in the doorway to her bedroom. His figure looked out of place there, or maybe it was the expression on his face, like a panicked horse that just caught wind of smoke.

He took two quick steps into the room and stopped. Her first instinct was to close the distance, to let him wrap his arms around her, envelop her in that earthy scent and chase away the shadow of fear. But she stiffened, darted a glance toward Mitch, and they both stayed put where they were.

Dimitrius took a moment to study her. His shoulders eased down once he had a chance to see she was still in possession of all her limbs.

"Are you all right?"

Sidney turned her attention to Mitch.

"What happened?" Dimitrius asked.

"She's fine." Mitch gritted his teeth.

"You have to show him." Her voice was barely audible above the deep highland brogues drifting in from the front room.

Dimitrius raised an eyebrow and a bit of that panic came back to his features.

"It's nothing. It barely even broke the skin."

"Show him!"

Mitch squeezed his fists at his side, then turned and lifted his shirt. Even though Sidney was a few feet away, she could see the fine lines of deep purple already creeping away from the tiny puncture wounds. She sank down to the bed and focused on a knot in the hardwood floor.

"We'll discuss this once we get Ms. Lake to safety," Dimitrius said. "Dr. Banks needs assistance with the bodies."

Mitch's heavy footsteps disappeared into the kitchen, but he left the door open.

Dimitrius kneeled at her feet. He didn't touch her, but the bond between them caressed her skin as if he had. She dug her fingers into the quilt and bit down so hard on her lip she tasted blood.

The weight of the silence pressed in and a tear crept onto her cheek.

"I can't lose him. I can't."

"But you will. One day, eventually, he will die and you will go on."

"*Not yet*. Not like this." Her mind went back to the determination on Mitch's face the moment he burst through the door. "He tried to save me. This is my fault."

Dimitrius whispered something under his breath that wasn't English.

"It happened. That is all. No one is to blame."

He curled his hand around the back of her neck, pressed his forehead to hers. She closed her eyes and shivered under his touch. Reaching down the back of his shirt, she splayed her hand out against his skin, tracing the raised line of a scar across his shoulder blade.

With every inch she drew across his skin, the tension within her eased and she felt a little more like herself.

"Do not allow fear to govern your heart." His breath was light and sweet on her lips as he spoke. "He needs you now more than ever."

"Then why am I here with you?" She opened her eyes and tumbled into his dark gaze. For a second she was lost in the depths, but she shook the feeling away. She used her brain to think instead of giving in to that delicious magic swirling around her core. "This really is convenient for you, isn't it? If Mitch is out of the picture, you can have me all to yourself."

"Mitchell is my friend. I care about him a great deal."

"Then why are you here with me?"

He searched the contours of her face and opened his lips to speak, but stopped when a light knock sounded on the door and Mitch stepped in.

"Everything's loaded up."

Sidney pulled back and Dimitrius' hand slipped from her neck as he stood. She couldn't imagine what they must look like to Mitch, but from the thin line his mouth made, it wasn't anything that pleased him. Dimitrius offered a hand to help her up, but she ignored him and followed Mitch out through the front room.

The bodies were gone, but the floor, walls, desk, sofa… everything was splattered with blood. If the scene on the subway platform had been bad, this was six times worse. Sidney faltered when the smell hit her, and Dimitrius pressed his hand into the small of her back to steady her. She focused on that tingling sensation as it traveled up her spine. The distraction helped her move forward through the carnage as she picked her way around the puddles and smears on the floor so as not to track blood out into the hall.

"Once it's safe, the clean-up crew will take care of everything." Mitch shut the door and locked it after they were all out. "You can stay at my place until they're finished."

It was all so natural, Mitch standing there on her doormat, framed by the faded blue entryway as he locked the door. For a split second she forgot about the bite. Then reality crashed in. Staying at his place might not be such a simple solution if he ended up turning furry. She opened her mouth to ask *what if*, but hesitated.

It was only a few days ago that she'd been in his place; terrified about what she might become. Mitch had been confident that everything would be okay then, and he was right. Now, she needed to behave accordingly for him. They didn't know anything yet. The teeth barely broke the skin. He was probably fine.

She snapped her mouth shut. They'd be snuggled up together under his duvet in a few hours, naked and warm. There was nothing to be afraid of.

He seemed to catch that she was holding back, and his expression darkened. He wrapped his arm around her shoulders and swept her toward the staircase.

"Let's go," he said, leaving Dimitrius to follow after them.

Chapter 29

Mitch stared out the window of Dimitrius' car. Sidney held his hand, but his fingers didn't close around hers. Dimitrius sat opposite them in the rear-facing seat. The low afternoon sun lit the golden tones in his dark brown hair. His eyes remained fixed on her.

Sidney lowered her gaze to the back of Mitch's hand. She ran her thumb over the pronounced veins, examined the fine lines in his skin, and his short well-rounded nails. Even though he was fit, his hands showed his age. It wasn't as if they could spend their entire lives together. Mitch had already lived half of his, and hers had only just gotten started. No matter what happened, the harsh mistress of time was already against them.

Dimitrius didn't have an expiration date. He was outside of time altogether. Drifting somehow in a place where age didn't exist. His body didn't wear down. It couldn't.

As far as having someone around forever, he was the safest bet there was. She recalled the look on his face when he mentioned Sulis and how much he'd loved her, how much he missed her. Being with him would mean the constant pain of knowing that he was watching her grow old and die. She wouldn't do that to someone she loved.

Except that she didn't love Dimitrius. She loved Mitch. She *wanted* Mitch. She needed him, and now he needed her too. Even if he was infected, it didn't mean he would die. She had to remind herself of that. The thought of watching him turn into one of those creatures made her stomach churn. Which would be worse? Watching him turn into the Big Bad Wolf occasionally or never seeing him at all?

She squeezed Mitch's hand tighter and rested her cheek on his shoulder.

"Ms. Lake," Dimitrius spoke softly.

She met his gaze.

He tilted his head slightly and his fingers twitched as if he wanted to wrap his hand around hers, but he didn't. As the first shadows of late afternoon passed over his face, she found herself suddenly unsure of what to hope for.

"You're an admirer of Waterhouse?" he asked.

The subject matter was so far away from her thought process, that it took her a moment to work out the question.

"Waterhouse?"

"The artist. I noticed you had a few of his prints in your home," Dimitrius said.

Sidney nodded, understanding now that he was distracting her, offering her an antidote for the worry poisoning her mind. "I like all the pre-Raphaelites, but Waterhouse is my favorite."

Mitch stirred beside her, as if waking from a trance. He paid attention to the conversation even if he didn't join in.

"It's very curious that you should be drawn to the first portrait of *Lamia*," Dimitrius said. "The woman who posed as the model was indeed your great-grandmother."

Sidney frowned and sat up a little. "How did I not know this?"

"She posed for many of his portraits. However, it was not common knowledge. The family had a reputation to uphold."

She rolled her eyes. "How many times have I heard my grandfather say that?"

Dimitrius shrugged. "The times were different back then. I doubt it would have been the scandal she imagined, but we respected her wishes."

"We?"

"John and I."

"You were on a first name basis with John William Waterhouse." Sidney scooted forward in her seat a bit. "For real?"

He gave her a nod. Something about the way the light shaded his eyes seemed familiar. "The knight in that painting is you, isn't it?"

"I allowed him to borrow my likeness, yes."

So many times she'd spent studying that print, the nuances of his hair, the line of his jaw, the way that woman who looked so much like herself gazed up at him with such devotion and longing in her eyes. Sidney loved the way Waterhouse had been able to capture that moment. She'd put herself in Lamia's place so many times when she was younger. She'd thought it was Mitch she was meant to slay those metaphorical dragons with. Now that knight from the painting was flesh and blood, sitting right in front of her.

"Wow," she muttered.

Mitch squeezed her hand. She needed to get out of the car. The smell of them together in such a small space was suffocating.

The dome of Dimitrius' building come into view as they pulled around the corner, and Sidney was actually grateful to see it. Malcolm pulled around to one of the back doors and Mitch slid out before he could even shift the car into park. Dimitrius slipped out after him, but he paused to offer his hand to Sidney.

It felt natural, and she hated herself for thinking that. She hated herself even more for not wanting to let go.

"Lake." Williams power-walked up the sidewalk toward them. "What the hell is going on?"

Her partner made a pointed glance downward, then tilted his head a little and she knew he'd seen. She untangled her fingers from Dimitrius and he went inside.

Williams watched Dimitrius as if he'd just seen the spectral apparition of John Lennon walk by. "Why the heck are you guys holding hands?"

"He was helping me out of the car. It's called manners. You could learn a thing or two."

He lowered his voice to a whisper, "Did you tell the chief about... you know?"

It took her a second to remember what he was talking about, then their conversation from that morning came back to her. King Arthur. The sword. Sulis Minerva.

Sidney shook her head. "I didn't get a chance."

"So, what the hell is going on? Dimitrius called me down here. *He* called *me*."

242

The words just wouldn't come out. How could she break the news about what happened to the chief? In his own way, for his own reasons, Williams cared about Mitch as much as she did. It was probably better for him to know sooner rather than later. Except, if everything was fine, she didn't want to worry him for nothing. Saying it out loud made it real.

"It's bad, isn't it? Just tell me," he said, then his attention diverted to something behind her.

She didn't have to turn around to know it was Malcolm standing there. His shadow completely engulfed her own. She felt him like a mountain at her back. It was reassuring and awkward all at the same time.

"Ms. Lake, Mr. Williams, best you come inside. Quick as you can." His voice rumbled low like thunder over a loch. "Ain't safe out here."

Chapter 30

The blonde assistant led them down a stairwell to the basement of Dimitrius' building. The place had originally been the main police headquarters, and a door halfway down the hall and down a shorter flight of stairs opened into a small tiled morgue with a drain in the middle of the floor.

Banks directed the placement of the bodies into a set of nine stainless steel drawers filling the back wall. It had probably been quite a while since any of them had been occupied let alone nearly filled to capacity. The small room barely held the crowd as Dimitrius, his Highland friends, and a beautiful blonde man Sidney hadn't seen before gathered around an autopsy table.

The assistant paused before heading back upstairs. "Will that be all, sir?"

Dimitrius nodded. "See that we're not disturbed."

Mitch took a spot at the back near the cabinets with his arms tucked across his chest, his gaze fixed squarely on the body bag.

Sidney found a spot near the foot of the table, between Williams and Dimitrius.

"I'm not sure we're all fully acquainted," Dimitrius said. Introductions went around, and when it came time for the blonde man to meet Sidney, he took her hand.

"Tyran, at your service." His eyes sparkled like a glacier in the sun. He was built smaller than Argus and Malcolm, but taller than Dimitrius. His features held an intense and quiet command.

Argus crossed his arms, refusing to look anywhere but the drain in the floor.

Dimitrius cleared his throat and nudged him.

The man with the beard stepped forward. He took her hand and bowed at the waist. She wasn't quite sure how he accomplished it in the small space, but he managed.

In a voice as rough as his calloused palm, he said, "Argus, at your service, my lady."

His beard scratched as he pecked a kiss to her hand.

"Umm… you guys realize this is all super weird, right?" Williams said. "Anybody care to explain what the hell is going on?"

Banks unzipped the body bag to reveal the hybrid in the red hoodie.

"Ohh. Woah. No warning? Just BAM. There it is." Williams glanced up toward the ceiling. He cleared his throat and swallowed hard.

Banks nodded to a jar of ointment on the counter.

"There's menthol rub if you need it," he said.

"I'm cool. Just, maybe a heads up next time?" Williams cleared his throat again.

"Fair enough." Banks nodded.

"All right, what the heck is this thing and why was there a parade of body bags just now?" Williams asked. "And why are you guys making out with Lake's hand?"

This was normally when the chief would step up and use his FBI voice. Sidney waited for it, but it didn't come. He stayed in the back, leaning against the cabinets, his gaze stuck on the body.

"I'm sure there will be a time to explain the answer to your second question, Mr. Williams. But for now, there's the more pressing matter of this body and why it's here, along with the others." He turned to Sidney. "Ms. Lake?"

"This… man followed me to my apartment earlier. He told me the reason he looks this way is because he was bitten by a werewolf, then given an experimental drug to change him back to human. Only, it didn't work."

"Well, that's a giant load of stinkin' horse shit," Argus said.

"Careful, brother," Malcolm soothed.

Sidney glared at him. "I'm just telling you what he told me."

"An' I'm tellin' you there ain't no way this bastard was bitten by a werewolf, because we here killed 'em all." Argus' chest rose and fell like a bellows. "ALL, I say!"

"And what if we didn't?" Tyran asked quietly.

"I'll be damned, if I let one slip through MY fingers!" The small room could barely contain Argus' voice. "Those wiley bastards… we got all of 'em. Every last one, I swear it on the Mother Goddess herself."

"Malcolm," Dimitrius said.

"Aye. Come on, brother." Malcolm urged his brother to the stairwell. "Let's go have a pint or two and see if we can't figure it out."

Dimitrius remained expressionless as the two Highlanders pounded up the stairs. He didn't speak until the door clicked shut behind them. "You'll have to forgive him, please. Argus takes our mission quite personally."

"We all take it personally," Tyran said.

"Of course," Dimitrius said. "Perhaps he's simply the most vocal about it."

Tyran ran his hand through his pale curls. "And how exactly *did* we miss one?"

"What difference does it make?" Sidney asked. "Figuring out how it happened doesn't change the fact that it did. What's important is stopping them now, once and for all."

"Sidney, did he ever say who made the vaccine they tested on him?" Banks asked.

"No, he only said I was the key. He was ready to turn me over in exchange for a cure."

"That's why they wanted to take you?" Dimitrius asked.

"It all happened so fast, I have no idea why they wanted me." Sidney sighed. "But what if he was right? Somebody out there is working on a vaccine for this. What if I can help? What if I can fix this somehow?"

"And do what exactly?" Mitch pushed away from the wall and joined the circle. "Hand yourself over to these guys so they can treat you like a Rhesus monkey? I don't think so."

"But if I can help—"

Mitch cut her off with a shake of his head. "Not like that. It's out of the question."

"If we could at least find out who was working on the cure, that would be something." She pointed at the body on the table. "He knew who was behind this. He knew enough that they killed him before he could say anything else. They never wanted to cure him, they only wanted him dead."

"Too bad we can't just ask him," Williams said.

Sidney stared at Banks. "We could."

"Could what?" Williams said.

"Ask him."

"Dude, he's dead."

"He doesn't have to be," Sidney said.

Banks straightened up from the body and shook his head. "Absolutely not."

"What supplies would you need?" Sidney asked.

"Nothing, because it's not happening."

"Sorry, what the hell are you two talking about?" Williams asked.

"Nothing." Banks shook his head and gave a pointed look to Sidney.

"Banks is a necromancer. He could bring him back and we could ask him."

"Not happening. First of all? I can't. Even if I could, I wouldn't. And even if I would, we don't have what we need. If we had what we needed it still wouldn't work because half his brain is splattered all over your apartment."

"It's our only lead. If we try and it doesn't work, fine. But we have to try."

"Shit." Banks somehow managed to turn the word into two syllables as he stared at the body.

"What do you need?" Dimitrius asked.

"To start with? The four elements: earth, air, fire, water. So, we need some dirt, a candle, holy water… this is way easier in a cemetery."

Sidney hiked her thumb at Dimitrius. "He smells like dirt. Does that count?"

"Dirt?" Dimitrius canted his head.

"It's not a bad thing," Sidney shrugged.

"I don't think that counts," Banks said.

"Are we seriously going to bring this guy back to life?" Williams jumped in. "Like, a werewolf zombie?"

"No, because it's not going to work," Banks said.

"It *will* work," Sidney insisted. She squeezed her eyes shut and concentrated on figuring out a solution. "How about this? I'm a Pisces. Williams is a Leo, and Mitch is a Libra. We just need Earth."

Dimitrius raised his hand. "Virgo."

"This is seriously not even close to how this is supposed to be done, you know that, right?" Banks said.

"We don't have time for a scavenger hunt."

"At the very least, I need some salt," Banks said.

Dimitrius turned to Tyran, but he was already in motion. He disappeared up the stairs just as Williams spoke up again. "You don't need a blood sacrifice or something do you?"

Banks hitched up his shoulder. "Why don't you ask the lady in charge?"

"Do we need to step into the hall for a minute?" she asked.

"Are you gonna hit me?"

"Maybe."

Banks smoothed his expression out and headed up the stairs with Sidney on his heels.

She paced down the hallway, then turned and came back while he leaned against the wall. "Okay, I don't know that much about necromancy, but what I do know is that it runs in your blood. You carry the power within you. The ritual of it all is just to help you get in the right frame of mind. Those objects don't actually mean anything. You can do this, you just have to believe you can."

"You don't know what you're asking me to do, honey." Banks kept his voice low. "Last time I tried this, it was a disaster. Maybe I got the blood, but I don't have the talent. Not by a long shot."

"I know exactly what I'm asking you to do." She stopped in front of him, toe-to-toe. "I'm asking you to do your part to save Mitch."

He narrowed his eyes. "What exactly happened in your apartment today?"

She thought about the answer to that question, and the image of Mitch kneeling on her floor flashed into her mind. Her eyes stung when she remembered how he'd saved her without even thinking about the danger to himself. He would do anything for her, and now she had to do everything she could for him.

"One of those things bit him."

"Good, Lord." He sagged heavily against the wall. "Okay, I'll do it. Just… please don't cry."

"I'm not crying."

"Liar." Banks gave her a half-hearted version of his smile at the same time Tyran returned with the salt.

"This is all I could find."

"That'll do." Banks took the leather pouch, similar to the one at Dimitrius' club, and turned to Sidney. "I sure hope you know what you're doing."

She shuffled down the stairs after them. "It'll work."

He paused with his foot on the bottom step. "But do we really *want* it to?"

Sidney didn't have an answer for him. All she knew was that Mitch was running out of time and this was their best chance to get a lead.

"Okay, you four come over here around the body. One on each side. And make sure fire and water are across from each other, and wind and earth are opposite each other. Not that it matters I guess, but it feels right," Banks said.

They took their places around the table and Sidney stared across at Williams.

"Why do I get the feeling this is going to cause me permanent nightmares?" he asked.

She shrugged. "At least he's not a demon koala."

"Once we begin, everyone should stay inside the circle."

"What happens if we don't?" Williams asked.

"I'm not sure. I've never done it like this before."

"Super."

"Get a grip, Williams."

"What?" He loosened up his shoulders like he was getting ready for a boxing match. "You know I babble when I'm nervous."

Banks reached into the pouch and laid out a thin circle around them. "All right. Everybody take hands. Let's get started."

Chapter 31

"I don't suppose there's any chance you might have caught his name?" Banks asked.

"David Anderson."

"Well, that's something at least."

The bond between her and Dimitrius coiled up and around her forearm like a snake wrapping around a tree branch. She shivered and squeezed Mitch's hand tighter. It was hot and dry, or maybe hers was just cool and clammy. She tried to remain motionless, but it was difficult as the binding worked its way up her right arm and melted into her core.

"How long is this going to take?" she asked.

"It's too late for a bathroom break, if that's what you're asking," Banks said.

Sidney took a peek at Dimitrius to see if he was experiencing the same sensation. He stood still, his eyes focused on the table. She couldn't tell where her hand ended and his began. It felt as if he was an extension of her own body. On her other hand, Mitch's grip was like stone, his fingernails digging sharp into her skin.

"What information do we need?" Banks asked. "The more specific, the better."

"We need to know who told him there was a cure for his condition. What did he mean when he said I was the key? Who tried to kidnap me?"

"Okay, okay, three questions might be pushing it. He only has half a brain anyway. Let's just hope his speech isn't affected."

"Shouldn't we be wearing some kind of protective gear? Those teeth are pretty sharp." Williams edged away.

"Watch out for the salt," Banks said.

"How did I end up this close to his head anyway?"

"Shut up, Williams."

"Okay. Nobody talk. I have to concentrate."

Sidney bowed her head slightly so she didn't have to look at Williams. Silence descended on the room. Banks sucked in a deep breath and blew it out through puckered lips.

Everything settled. The air in the room stilled and grew thick, as if it had substance. Magic licked her skin and raised goosebumps on her arms. It was a different feeling than what passed between her and Dimitrius, different from what she'd felt around the demon.

"We have gathered the elements of the earth together to bring David Anderson back from the realm beyond," Banks said. His voice was a few tones deeper than it had been a moment ago. "David Anderson. I call thee forth. Rise and speak."

The sweet smell of honey and fresh mint leaves filled the room. It was so thick she could almost feel it drizzle across her skin. No one moved or spoke for what felt like an eternity. Sidney held her breath as the mix of two different powers swirled around and through her.

Banks opened his eyes. "I told you—"

"It's working," she insisted. "Call him again."

The necromancer gave her an exasperated sigh, straightened his shoulders and held his palms out toward the body. "I call thee forth, David Anderson. Rise and speak to us."

The hybrid creature on the table jerked once, as if it had been touched by an invisible defibrillator. Williams jumped too.

"Don't!" Banks said at the same time Williams took a step back. The rest of them moved sideways, dragged by his momentum. "I told you not to step outside the salt."

Williams turned and looked at the floor. "Sorry, he moved!"

"That was the point, genius," Sidney said.

"I know, but it's different when it actually happens. Besides, I didn't think it would work."

"It didn't, thanks to you."

"I said, I'm sorry."

"You don't get how important this is. It was our only chance to save the chief."

"Lake," Mitch warned.

"The chief?" Williams frowned. "I thought you were the one they were trying to snatch up. What do they want with him?"

Sidney let her hand drop away from Mitch's and motioned to the hybrid. "This David Anderson guy came to my—"

The body on the table sat straight up, and sucked in a noisy breath. The mouth worked open and closed like a puppet, showing off exactly how long and sharp those canines really were. Eyes rounded open wide, with the bullet hole in his forehead making it look as if he'd blossomed a third.

"Sweet fancy Moses!" Williams yelled.

Sidney took a step to the side, her body lined up with Dimitrius. The bond strengthened between them, spreading down into the very tips of her toes. They were one and the same. A force united. Anything seemed possible in that moment.

"Why did you come to my apartment?" she demanded.

A sound leaked out of the thing's open mouth, something between a growl and a scream. Williams shuddered and shrank against the wall.

"Who sent you?" Sidney asked again.

The thing pivoted its head toward her slowly. That ugly sound grew louder, a continuous groan that didn't seem to end. Her heart thudded in her chest, but she didn't back down.

"Why am I the key?"

The thing lunged at her. Dimitrius grabbed its neck and held it back with one hand as if it was nothing more than a squirming puppy. Claws flailed. Jaws snapped. Tyran stepped forward and twisted the head all the way around with a crack. The body fell limp on the table again, head dangling loosely off the end.

"I should have worn Depends," Williams whispered.

Sidney ripped her hand away from Dimitrius. It stung the same as if his flesh was made of duct tape.

"Ow!" She cradled her arm against her chest. As the bond broke between them, a feeling of emptiness flooded in. It crushed her from the inside, and she felt like she was back in Mitch's bathroom, confused and hopeless, with nothing left to do but scream at the world. "What the hell were you doing?"

"My duty," he said.

"I was fine!" Her hopes of saving Mitch were starting to feel as limp as the dead creature's head dangling off the edge of the table. "What are we supposed to do now?"

"There are six other bodies here," Dimitrius said.

"You told us to sever the heads," Banks said.

"Does that matter?" Sidney asked.

"Just because I can reanimate a body, doesn't mean I can make it functional. There's maybe two people in the world with that kind of power, and I'm definitely not one of them."

"Who? Can we bring them here?"

"They wouldn't make it in time."

"In time for what?" Williams asked.

Mitch put his hands on the corners of the table and leaned heavily against it. "How about Renny? You said he's a medium."

Sidney nodded. The panic threatening to consume her eased back a bit. As long as she had some bit of hope to grasp on to, she could manage. "That's a good idea. We have to find him though."

"I know how to get in touch with him," Dimitrius said. "In the meantime, why don't we remove ourselves to a more comfortable location?"

Chapter 32

The elevator ride upstairs gave Sidney the time she needed to gain a hold of herself and clear her head. The wash of magic had overwhelmed her, and the sudden way it had been interrupted left her feeling drained. But at least there was another option. She had to hope Renny might be able to pick up on something that would help.

It worried her, the way Mitch leaned so heavily against the wall of the elevator. His usually impeccable posture sagged forward slightly, and his knuckles were white where he rested his hands on his thighs. He glanced up at her and the spark in his eyes was faded. The straight line of his lips pressed upward in one corner, as if to reassure her that it would all be fine, but it only added to her worry. She wanted to cross the small space and wrap her arms around him, but somehow she'd ended up on one side, and he was on the other with everyone else in between.

They found Argus and Malcolm in the main room upstairs where Sidney had first met Dimitrius. The two brothers sat at the enormous round table as if they were right at home, with a frosted stein of beer in one fist and a roasted turkey leg in the other. Their hands were so big, they made the huge chunk of meat look like a frog's leg.

With everything that had happened that day, Sidney couldn't find her appetite, so she moved over to the area in front of the fireplace with Mitch, Williams, Banks, and

Tyran. Dimitrius murmured quiet instructions to his assistant, then joined them.

Williams dug his elbow into her side. Sidney glared at him and he gave her a pointed nod toward the sword over the mantelpiece. He arched one eyebrow.

Dimitrius joined them. "Renny should arrive shortly. Would any of you care for dinner while we wait?"

After the episode downstairs, no one else seemed to have an appetite either.

Only Williams spoke up. "I've never seen such a magnificent sword. Not in real life anyway."

"Ah, you're interested in my sword? Many people are fascinated by its enormous size and superior quality." Sidney couldn't be sure, because it happened so fast, but she could have sworn Dimitrius winked at her.

Tyran covered a laugh with a cough and went over to join Argus and Malcolm.

"Oh?" Williams' voice cracked slightly. He pressed his lips together tightly and his eyes watered. It was the perfect opportunity to blurt out *that's what she said*, and Sidney was impressed with his restraint.

"My partner has a thing for big swords. He's quite an aficionado of King Arthur," Sidney said.

"I wouldn't say aficionado. It was more of a phase back in high school, really." Williams scratched the back of his neck as a deep red tinge crept up from his collar into his ears.

"It's not a phase if you know the original word for the sword. What was it? Calla-what?"

"Cal-ed-*vol*-hagh." He reminded her.

"Yeah, that," Sidney said. "*Caledfwlch.*"

The sword jerked from its place on the wall, bounced on the mantel, and fell at Sidney's feet with a loud clang.

Argus, Malcolm, and Tyran all stared.

Sidney didn't dare move an inch.

Dimitrius leaned over slowly to retrieve the weapon. She didn't quite see the moment his hand made contact with the hilt, but she felt it, the very same as if he'd touched her instead.

It was amazing how the steel came to life in his hand. The way man and weapon responded to each other captivated her. Dimitrius' shoulders lowered slightly, his body loosened. He relaxed. It looked as natural as if it was an extension of his own arm, the same as she had felt down in the morgue.

He placed the sword in the middle of the table. It gathered up the light in the room, but instead of devouring it as the demon had, the sword reflected the light in a soft glow. A wave of dizziness overcame her as the pieces of the puzzle fell into place. Sidney reached out and grabbed onto Mitch to keep her balance. It was only a moment before everything cleared again. She wondered if she'd even felt it at all.

"How did you know?" Dimitrius asked.

"We didn't," she said. "It was a wild guess. It just made sense."

"You mean, it's *true*?" Williams asked.

Dimitrius gave a slow and regal bow from the waist.

Sidney shivered as goosebumps rose on her arms.

"I'm still not exactly clear on how everything adds up," she said. "Was Sulis the Lady of the Lake?"

"She was the inspiration, yes," Dimitrius said.

"And the sword?"

"Was given to me as a gift when she tasked us with destroying the werewolves."

"You didn't pull it from a stone?"

Dimitrius gave a slow blink and shook his head. "Dramatic license. Over the centuries the story has evolved in numerous directions as people have added their own take on it. The truth is much simpler, and I'm afraid it might be a little disappointing compared to the legends. Some of the tales are based on rumors I started myself to explain away our longevity and regenerative capabilities."

"Disappearing to Avalon after the fight with Mordred," Williams said. "You were just healing?"

"There were many liberties taken with that story, but yes. That was the idea," Dimitrius said.

"And they never found your bones in that grave in Glastonbury, because, well… you still need them. Obviously." Williams' ears lit up even brighter.

"It was a great deal easier when stories were passed by word of mouth. Before gossip magazines, and paparazzi. Before the invention of internet search engines, where anyone could do a background check or verify someone's identity with a few simple clicks," Tyran added. "People were ready and willing to believe back then. Tales of magic and supernatural valor were not dismissed off-hand the way they are in this age and time."

"What about Merlin? Was he real?" Williams held up crossed fingers. "Please say, yes."

Dimitrius smiled a little. "A descendant of Sulis, yes."

"Guinevere?" Sidney asked.

"Gwenllian was a Daughter of Sulis, just as you are." Dimitrius moved to the table and motioned to the chairs.

They all took a seat. She thought Williams might actually jump out of his skin.

"This table is round. This is *the* Round Table. I'm sitting at the Round Table with King freakin' Arthur," he mumbled under his breath. "Is this heaven? Did I get eaten by the shifter zombie and go to heaven? I think I'm dead. I have to be dead because this is heaven."

"You're not dead," Sidney said. "Be cool."

"Okay." Williams swallowed hard.

"Hold on just a minute here. Is this for real, or are y'all just yanking the new guy's chain? King Arthur. Seriously?" Banks asked. He looked a little pale, wilted even. Sidney felt a tinge of guilt for talking him into the ritual despite his protests.

"Indeed."

"And Lake here is the Lady of the Lake. Go figure. That where your name came from?"

"A poetic coincidence," Dimitrius said.

"Well, that makes a hell of a lot more sense. I mean, with the level of power we had going on down in that room, no wonder we woke that guy up."

"Ms. Lake is quite a bit more powerful than she knows." Dimitrius smiled a little, like there was another secret he was keeping.

"Aye," Malcolm raised his mug. His brother grumbled and gnawed on the turkey bone. Tyran's

262

bright eyes fixed on her like he was waiting for something fun to happen.

Sidney shook her head. "I'm not powerful. I've been lucky. That's all."

"This weapon is imbued with the same power that runs in your veins. You can control it in a way no one else can." Dimitrius motioned toward the middle of the table. "Call the sword."

"Excuse me?"

"Call it."

Sidney sighed.

"Say its name," Dimitrius insisted. "*Caledfwlch.*"

"This is stupid." Sidney crossed her arms.

"*Caledfwlch.*"

The hilt of the sword rose up and the weapon balanced perfectly on its sharpened tip. The electric lights in the room dimmed in comparison to the radiant gleam from the steel.

Sidney jumped up so fast, her chair toppled over.

The sword fell with a clatter.

Seven pairs of stunned eyes focused on Sidney, but it was Mitch's look that was the worst. When she locked eyes with him, she could read the darkness plainly written across his face. The visible weight of dread pulled down the corners of his mouth. It was the look she never wanted to see directed at her.

Fear.

He seemed to realize it, because he rearranged his features, but not fast enough.

Sidney went for the door.

"Wait," Mitch called after her, but she didn't stop. He was on her heels as she stormed down the hallway. "Sidney, wait."

She swatted him away. "Don't touch me."

"Stop!" He grabbed her, wrapped his arms around her whole body, trapping her own arms against her sides.

"Let go."

"No," he said, gently.

"You're afraid of me." She sagged against him.

"Not even close." He squeezed her even tighter. "I'm afraid of what this means for you."

She stopped struggling as she considered his words.

"You're powerful, Sidney. You just proved it. What scares me is that someone out there knows that now and they're after you." He tucked his face against her neck, as he spoke softly into her ear. "What scares me is that I might not be around much longer to protect you. Even worse? You might need protecting from *me.*"

Sidney wrapped her arms around his neck and shook her head against him. "Don't say that. Don't."

Even as she said the words, she could feel that the level of heat radiating from his skin had grown exponentially. His breath fluttered the hair at her ear.

"At some point we have to be honest about this." He pulled back so he could see her eyes. "Remember what you told me in the car? After you were bitten. Remember what you said?"

"I was scared. I didn't mean it."

"You did mean it. And I meant what I said, too. I could never destroy you. But if the time comes, Sid... I need you to be stronger than I am. I need it to be you."

Sidney slapped him hard across his face.

"Don't you dare fucking talk to me like you've already given up."

His surprise faded, and a new sort of resolve steeled itself in his gray eyes as the outline of her hand turned red on his jaw. "You're right. I'm sorry."

"No... I'm sorry." She blew out a heavy breath, then stood on her tiptoes to kiss his cheek. "You're all I have, you know? It scares me when you talk like that."

"What about Dimitrius?"

Her forehead creased. "What about him?"

"You have him, too."

"Are you kidding? He's basically a stranger. He might talk about ancient bloodlines, and bonds, and swords, but he doesn't have the history with me that you do." She reached up and ran her hand over the top of his bald head, but it felt different. A soft layer of peach fuzz covered the smooth surface she was so familiar with. She dropped her hand away and bit her lower lip.

"What is it?"

"Nothing. It's fine." She gave him a small smile, then kissed him.

His wide strong shoulders shuddered under her hands. He tore his lips from hers and she caught a glimpse of his grey eyes for a split second. In that moment, she understood everything as if it was happening in slow motion. They both knew the truth. They both knew, in order to protect each other, they'd play out the lie that everything was fine until it either got back to normal or it went horribly wrong.

"Forget King Arthur." Her lips brushed across the scruff at his jaw. "We'll have our own Camelot."

Mitch bent over double, resting his forehead on her shoulder, leaning his weight almost entirely on her. Sidney staggered back a step, but caught herself and held him up. He groaned in her ear, a strangled cry that was frighteningly similar to the sound that had reverberated against the tiles in the morgue downstairs.

"Not yet," he groaned.

"It's okay. You're okay." Sidney eased him over to the wall. "It's fine."

She leaned him up against the wall and he slid to the floor. His head hung forward, loose on his neck. She lifted his face, but his eyes were closed, jaw slack.

"Mitch?" She shook him. "Mitch? Somebody help! Help!"

Chapter 33

Dimitrius appeared first, followed immediately by Williams and Banks. Tyran and the brothers came into the hall, but kept a distance.

"He just collapsed." Sidney felt of his forehead again as Banks kneeled beside her. "He's burning up."

Banks took Mitch's wrist between his fingers and stared at his watch. "Heart rate is elevated. We need to get him comfortable."

"How can I help?" Williams asked.

Dimitrius stared at Mitch for a few heartbeats before he worked himself into action.

"Wait with Ms. Lake," he said, and motioned Argus and Malcolm over. "We'll take him to the blue room."

Sidney stood and stepped back to give them space. Mitch's head dropped forward as they hefted him up. The tips of his shoes dragged across the carpet between them as they carried him away. A wave of nausea washed over her, and she turned her back so she wouldn't have to see any more.

Everyone disappeared through a door toward the other end of the hall, leaving her alone with her partner.

"Don't look at me like that, Williams."

"Like what?"

"Like I just ran over your fluffy new puppy with a lawn mower."

"Are you going to tell me what happened or stand there and say everything's fine like you always do?"

"One of those things bit him. He came into my apartment to save me and one of those fucking monsters bit him! This is all my fault. Is that what you want to hear? He's going to turn into one of those things because of *me*."

"You could have told me. I thought we were partners. I thought we didn't keep secrets."

"It's not like that." Sidney shook her head. "The teeth barely broke the skin. I thought maybe he'd be okay and you wouldn't even have to know anything happened."

"Yeah? And what about how you guys are sleeping together?"

"I... Megan told you?"

"She didn't have to."

"We were trying to be professional." Sidney frowned. "Why are we even talking about my love life right now? The chief is unconscious...."

"Because you've been living a big fat lie. How am I supposed to trust you now?"

The words stung hard. Sidney squeezed her eyes shut, but not fast enough to stop the tear that escaped down her face.

"I thought we were doing the right thing, trying to keep the job separate. I didn't think it would matter that much."

"It mattered enough to tell Megan."

She wiped her face with the back of her hand and nodded. "I'm sorry. Really."

"What else are you hiding?" He blew out a long breath and shrugged. "Are you some kind of magical unicorn that farts rainbows and butterflies?"

She couldn't help but laugh through her tears.

"Get in here, Lake." He grabbed her and wrapped his arms around her, thumping her hard on the back. "Hug it out."

She leaned into him. "What if he's not fine?"

"Ugh, do you seriously like him like that?" Williams stepped back. "I mean *like* like?"

"If this was middle school, we'd be asking friends to switch so we could be lab partners."

"Intense." Williams scrunched up his nose. "But… he's all *old*."

Sidney shrugged. "Not compared to King Arthur."

"Yeah, okay good point." He leaned in closer and lowered his voice. "Hey, can you do that thing with the sword again?"

She flipped him off.

"Oh, look. Here comes your BFF."

Sidney turned to see Renny following on the assistant's perfectly polished Louboutin heels like he was a garden gnome who'd been tossed into someone else's yard.

"Hey, Renny." She tried for cheerful, but didn't quite make it.

"What in world is going on? The darkness is very angry."

"What do you mean?" Sidney asked.

The man's whole body flinched in his tracksuit. "Is somewhere we can talk? Maybe find more Irish coffee?"

She threw a glance to Dimitrius' assistant, who was standing discreetly off to the side.

"Right this way," she said.

The three of them followed her past the round table into Dimitrius' private study. As soon as the assistant shut the door, Sidney turned to their informant.

"Who's angry, Renny?"

"I don't know what this is. Is not human. Fur and teeth. Very ugly."

"David Anderson?"

"Yes, is him." He bobbed his dark greasy head. "He is not happy with you. He says over and over, 'You should have saved me.'"

"But *how?*"

"You are key."

Dimitrius' assistant tapped softly on the door before entering with a tray of fresh coffee-filled mugs. She placed it gingerly on the table in front of the couch. "May I get you anything else?"

Dimitrius came into the room, followed by everyone else except Banks. His mouth was set in a grim line, and Sidney almost asked how Mitch was doing, except she wasn't sure she wanted the answer.

"How's the chief?" Williams asked.

"Resting," Dimitrius said.

Sidney sank down onto the couch.

"Renaldo, my friend." Dimitrius shook Renny's hand. "I'm glad you're here."

Williams sat down next to Sidney, and cupped his hand on one side of his mouth. He whispered, "No wonder he goes by Renny."

One of the coffee cups jumped off the tray and dumped over on Williams' shoe.

"Ouch, what the… tell me you guys saw that. I swear I didn't touch it."

"Old lady does not like you," Renny said.

"Old lady? What old lady?"

"How should I know? You live in her house. She does not want you there."

"Aunt Rose?"

"Ah, yes. Always saying you are not good enough to marry her niece."

"Is *that* who's haunting me?"

Renny motioned to Sidney, then back to Williams. "Did she not tell you this?"

"You knew?" Williams gaped at her. "When will the secrets end, Lake? Seriously. I don't even know what to do with you."

It was easy to tell by the tone in his voice he was barely serious, and normally she would have appreciated his attempt to lighten the mood. Normally, she would have rolled her eyes and ignored him. Normally, the chief would have been sitting next to her, using his FBI voice to keep her partner in line and direct the conversation back on track.

Only, Mitch wasn't there. He was lying in a bed somewhere, fighting back the monster threatening to take over his body. All Sidney could think about was the way his feet dragged across the carpet.

She leaned in so that her nose was only inches from Williams.

"This isn't about you." She gritted her teeth to keep from screaming at him.

He swallowed hard. "Okay."

271

She stood and turned on Renny next. "What did he mean when he said I'm the key?"

"He… he does not know." The little man cowered.

"How can he not know? He's the one who said it!"

Renny shook his head quickly. "He heard someone else say it. I see white coat. Like doctor wear. This doctor tell him you are key. He say they make him human again if he bring you to them."

Sidney crossed her arms over her chest, if only to hold in the frustration, anger, and fear threatening to burst forth like a dam from within her.

"That's everything we knew before," she said. "Is there anything else you can see? Anything at all to go on. A name tag? Maybe a sign somewhere? A view outside a window?"

The medium shut his eyes and swayed ever so slightly as he concentrated.

"No name. But… there is small picture on coat pocket." Renny opened his eyes. "I draw it."

Dimitrius grabbed a blank sheet of paper and a pen from the desk. Renny stuck the tip of his tongue out as he leaned over the desk and drew the image. Just when the silence was about to explode in her ears, he straightened up.

"Here." Renny set down the pen and held up the paper. "Is this. Snake and sword."

"A Caduceus?" Williams asked. "That could be any doctor."

Sidney buried her face in her palms.

"It's a common misconception, the symbol for the medical profession is a Caduceus," Tyran spoke up. "It's actually based on the Rod of Asclepius. A snake curled around a plain rod. It's evolved over the years to sometimes include a cross. Maybe that's what the sword is supposed to be?"

Sidney lifted her face. "It's not either of those."

The way Dimitrius clenched his fists at his side, she knew he was already thinking the same thing she was.

"That's the featured symbol of the Lake family crest," Sidney explained. "My grandfather used it as the logo for Lake Industries. Whoever told David Anderson they could cure him was working in my grandfather's lab."

Chapter 34

"I need a moment alone with Ms. Lake," Dimitrius said. No one in the room moved. "Everyone leave, now."

The rest of the men filed out of the room leaving them alone with the quiet. They remained still for a few moments as an antique clock on the bookshelf loudly ticked away the seconds.

"Are you all right, Ms. Lake?" he finally asked.

"You had your tongue down my throat last night, you may as well call me Sidney."

At least he had the grace to lower his chin and act embarrassed. "Very well, then."

She sank down onto the couch as he came around the desk. Instead of taking his place in the well-worn chair, he sat beside her. They didn't touch, but he was near enough she could feel the bond flicker to life. Only, instead of creeping across her skin from the outside, it burned from within her. It was comforting and terrifying all at the same time.

"I really hope you didn't know about this already."

"No," he said quietly. "This was something I failed to see coming."

"How? I thought the whole point of your existence was to destroy the werewolves and watch over my family."

"I suppose... I allowed myself to become distracted."

"There's only two of us. What could be distracting enough for you to miss something this huge?"

It took him an extra moment to answer, "You."

His nearness was suddenly too much. Sidney got up and moved over to his chair. Her body molded into the perfectly worn spots as if she'd been sitting there her whole life. The second she realized it, she cursed and got up again.

"My grandfather's company is working on a cure for a werewolf bite. That's just—" Sidney stood there in a daze. "If it's true, then pretty much every single thing I've believed for half my life has been wrong."

"Ms. Lake—" Dimitrius sighed. "Sidney, please forgive me. I should have been more vigilant."

"It's a little late for sorry, don't you think? You were supposed to stop this a long time ago. None of this should have even been possible. Now the only way I can save Mitch is to go to my grandfather and ask him to give me a cure for something he spent a lot of time and money to convince me doesn't exist."

Dimitrius leaned his elbows on his knees and ran his hand through his hair. It flowed through his fingers like liquid silk. Sidney could almost feel the whisper of it on her own hand, and something stirred low in her belly.

"Don't do that."

He paused with his hand on the back of his head. "Sorry."

"Stop apologizing," she snapped.

He arched a dark eyebrow.

The way he sat there, so casual with his knees apart, and the collar of his white shirt unbuttoned and hanging open to reveal his pendant, was such a pleasant diversion. It made her want to climb on top of him and use her tongue to find out just how far down that scar on his neck went. He could be her escape, make her forget everything that was going on, at least for a little while.

"Dammit." She clenched her fists. "Why do you have to be so... *distracting*?"

"This won't get any easier now that the bond has been awakened."

"Wait... what?"

He made a small noise in the back of his throat. "Downstairs, during the ritual with Dr. Banks, the bond had the time and energy to awaken. Every other instance we connected, something has occurred to interrupt it. The salt circle might have had a significant influence as well."

"Why didn't you say something?"

"You seemed so determined the ritual should take place. I didn't want to interfere. I've said before, magic is unpredictable."

Sidney replayed the scene in her head and realized she'd sort of taken over. Maybe Mitch was right to tell her to slow down and think first. It hadn't even occurred to her there could be other consequences to what they'd done.

"Awakened. What exactly does that mean?" she asked.

"Our souls have come to recognize one another."

"Woah. Um, no." Sidney shook her head. "I didn't want this. Undo it."

"What's done is done."

All she had to do was look at his face to know how serious he was. She also knew he wasn't likely to kick the bucket any time in this century, which meant she'd be stuck like this for the rest of her life. "That's just fucking great."

"I'm sorry, Sidney. Truly. I never meant for this to cause you unhappiness. It's supposed to be a good thing."

"Well, it isn't! I love Mitch. *He's* the one I'm supposed to be with."

The silence he left hanging between them spoke volumes. Even as she said the words, she doubted herself. There was no question she loved Mitch, but what if they weren't actually meant to be together? She'd always been so enamored by him in one way or another, she never stopped to wonder if it was right. But wasn't that what true love was supposed to be? An instinct, something undefinable. It didn't have to be right to be real.

"Damn you." She hugged her arms around herself. "Damn you for so many things."

He flinched.

"Mitch. Damn it, what do we even tell him?"

Dimitrius leaned back on the couch. "I do not wish to cause him any undue stress. He's in a very precarious state right now."

"I can't lie to him."

"Don't. All I mean is that perhaps you shouldn't make it a point to tell him yet. When he needs to know, he will know." He stretched his arms out on the back of the couch. His fingertips nearly reached each end. The dip of his collar pulled apart revealing even more of his chest. It made her want to rip open the fabric like he was a gift and this was Christmas morning.

"I mean it when I say you're going to have to stop doing that."

"What?"

"Being... *you*."

He made a gruff sound in the back of his throat that did things inside of her sound should be able to do.

"I will so totally break your nose again." She sighed. "The worst part about this is that it's not even real."

"I'm not sure I understand."

"These feelings I have for you. It's the bond. It's magic. That's the only reason I'm attracted to you."

"Is it?"

"Of course it is."

He licked his lips and her knees went weak. "How did you feel when you first saw me? Before we ever touched."

Sidney thought back to the way the firelight illuminated his hair. The way he moved. The look in his eyes that made chills run down her spine.

He stared at her with a hint of pain and sadness at the edge of his eyes. "That's what's real."

"Shit." She shook her head. "It still doesn't matter. We have to help Mitch. You *do* still want to help him, right?"

"Of course I do."

"All right, then. How do I waltz into my grandfather's office after six years, and ask him for a cure to something he denies exists?"

"That is a very excellent question."

A few quiet taps sounded on the door.

"Yes?" Dimitrius said.

The door opened and his assistant took half a step inside. "Sir, Mr. Harris is awake."

Chapter 35

It was all Sidney could do to keep from tripping over Dimitrius' assistant as she followed her downstairs. Dimitrius trailed right behind her, and Williams brought up the back. About halfway down the hall, the woman stopped and gestured to a door.

Sidney rushed in without bothering to knock. She immediately understood why Dimitrius had called it the blue room. Everything was decorated in shades of pale blue with silver accents. Mitch sat on the edge of the bed with his shirt off while Banks checked his eyes. She stopped short when she saw the dark lines webbing out across his waist and up toward his shoulder blade.

"I told you, I'm fine. It was nothing," he said.

"Losing consciousness is never nothing," Banks said.

Fine gray hair covered the top of Mitch's head, making it nearly impossible to tell he was ever bald. Sidney forced herself into motion again and he turned when she came around the bed. He was younger and older all at the same time.

"Sid, tell him it was nothing."

She covered her surprise with a small shrug. "I'm not telling him anything. He's the doctor."

While she spoke, she pulled the blue silk duvet back and nudged him into bed.

"I'm fine. And I don't need covers, it's burning up in here." He kicked the blankets away and tried to get up, but she pressed him back against the overstuffed pillows.

Banks slipped out into the hall with Dimitrius and Williams. Sidney was fine staying with the chief. She could see what was happening, she didn't need to hear how bad it was.

"You sound like an old codger, you know that? Next thing you know you'll be shaking your cane, yelling at the kids to get off your damn lawn." Sidney sat on the edge of the bed so he couldn't get up again.

"Old codger? I'm barely middle-aged."

"Exactly. Which means you have half your life left, so there's plenty of time to be grouchy later."

Mitch lay back on the pillow and ran his hand over his head. His gray eyes were tired and sad, faded against the rich blue shade of the pillowcase. The well-worn creases along his forehead and the edges of his eyes seemed smoother, or maybe she was just imagining it.

"Do we have to keep this up?" He continued rubbing his head.

"Keep what up?"

"This charade." He sighed and let his eyes drift shut for a moment. "I'm dying, Sidney."

She swallowed hard. "No, you're not."

He sighed a deep breath and shook his head.

"You're not." She took his hand. "You're just… changing."

"Yeah, into one of those monsters."

She smiled, trying to make it look hopeful, but there wasn't much effort behind it. "It takes more than claws and fur to make someone a monster."

He opened his eyes, a hint of amusement sparked somewhere in their depths. "That's the line you're going to throw back at me?"

"It's a good line. You could never be a monster any more than I could."

"Yeah, go ahead and say that when you wake up to a big bad wolf in your bed."

She swallowed hard, past the panic that image conjured up within her. "That's not going to happen."

"Look at me, I'm halfway there already."

She ran her hand up and down his arm slowly. She'd never really appreciated before how nice it felt just to touch him. "Your hunch about Renny was right. He gave us a clue."

"What clue?" He sat up a little straighter.

"The person who called me the key was wearing a lab coat with the Lake Industries logo on it." She rolled her eyes. "The irony is, the one person who doesn't believe in werewolves is the one who might be able to get you the cure you need."

Mitch frowned, then squeezed her hand. "Your grandfather?"

Sidney nodded.

"But, you're not going there. Promise me you won't go to him."

"What? Why not?"

"They tried to take you! For whatever reason, they want you badly enough to send six shifters after you. You'd just be handing yourself over to them. You can't do that. Not for me, not for anyone."

"It's the only way to save you."

"For God's sake, Sidney. One time in your life, please do what I tell you. Stay. Here."

"Oh? This is the time you choose to put your foot down?" She stood up and went to the end of the bed, then turned around. "I'm Alexander Lake's granddaughter. Do you seriously think anybody would have the balls to abduct me and run experiments on me right under his nose?"

"Maybe. They know how powerful you are. If they think it's worth it, there's no telling what they might do."

Sidney crossed her arms. "I think I proved I can handle myself against these guys."

"You won't have to handle anything if you don't go."

"But I...." She gritted her teeth and made a frustrated sound. "How else am I supposed to save you?"

"It's not your job to save me."

"Yes it is. It's what people do when they love each other."

His forehead creased. "You love me?"

"I do," she whispered.

Sidney tucked her lower lip between her teeth to keep it from trembling. She took in a few slow breaths before she spoke. "There was nothing I could do to save my parents. But if there's any chance at all to save you and I don't follow through with it, I'll never forgive myself. I have to know I did *everything* I could."

Mitch dug his fingers into the duvet and grunted as a shadow of pain flickered across his face. "How do you think I feel? I have to do everything *I* can do to keep *you* safe. If you go there and anything happens to you, I'll never forgive myself either, and I don't have the kind of time left to make peace with that."

She shook her head and blinked the tears out of her eyes. "But if I get you the cure, you will have time. That's the whole point."

"What makes you think there even is a cure?"

"The shifter said there was."

"No. He said they could make a cure, if they had you. The key. Whatever vaccine or cure they say exists, doesn't work. You saw what it did to that guy." He leaned forward a little, his shoulders rose and fell heavily with each breath. "Whatever's going on, they're under the impression they need you to fix it. It's not right Sidney. There's something off about this whole thing. I don't like it and I don't want you to go."

"What if Dimitrius comes with me?"

"No."

"But what if—"

"DAMMIT SIDNEY." In a blink he was out of the bed with his hands wrapped around her shoulders. His fingernails dug sharply into her arms and she gasped. He shook her once and bared his teeth; they were longer than before. She shuddered under his grip.

Dimitrius stepped in. Sidney didn't turn her face to look at him, she couldn't take her eyes away from Mitch, but she felt him there, a force by her side.

"Mitchell, let her go," he spoke softly, as someone might try to calm a wild dog.

He loosened his grip from her, one finger at a time until she was free, but she didn't dare move. She couldn't even if she wanted to. The shock of what just happened kept her bones melded into place.

He turned his back to them, fists clenched at his sides. "Get out."

"Mitch," she whispered.

Dimitrius caught her hand. He gave his head the slightest shake, then angled his body between her and Mitch while he eased her out the door. As soon as the latch clicked shut behind them, she fell to her hands and knees in the middle of the hall and wept.

❈ ❈ ❈

"Why can't I stop shaking?" Sidney hugged the blanket around her tighter as if it was the only thing left holding her together. Maybe it was.

"You're in shock." Banks crouched in front of her, his hands on each arm of Dimitrius' chair. "The tea will help, if you can drink it."

"I can't." Another tremor ran its way through her body. She pulled her knees up and wrapped her arms and the blanket around her whole body, curling into a ball.

He put his hand over the blanket where her knee was. His eyes were honey soft, and filled with genuine concern. "I'm going to do everything I can to keep him comfortable. We'll get him through this, okay?"

"It's not over yet. There's still time to change it," she said. "We can't give up on him."

Williams gave her a desolate look from the couch. He hadn't spoken since she'd left Mitch's room. It was so unlike him, it sent another shiver through her body.

"Mitchell is right," Dimitrius said. "These people have proven they'll go to extensive lengths to get their hands on you. It isn't safe."

"But what if I have you? What if your men come? That's your job isn't it, to protect me?"

"Our job is to keep you safe, lass. Not lead you directly into the den of the Devil himself," Malcolm said.

"It's our only chance." Her voice faltered. "Trust me, the last person in the world I want to see is my grandfather, let alone beg him for help. But if there's even the smallest possibility he can save Mitch, I have to do it."

The four ancient warriors exchanged grim looks, but none of them spared a glance in her direction.

Sidney sighed. "You're going to let them get away with this? A werewolf slipped by you once and the wrong person got their hands on it. I've killed eight shifters myself, who knows how many more could be out there? This won't stop with Mitch. Other innocent people could get hurt too. It's your duty to end this, once and for all."

"Aye!" Argus said, and gave her a firm nod.

The others looked to Dimitrius. "I'll take my men and discuss things with Alexander. But you stay here where it's safe."

"You can't go without me," Sidney insisted.

"I trust Mitchell's intuition. If he thinks it's a bad idea, then you're not leaving the premises," Dimitrius said.

Sidney shook her head. "You don't get it. This is Alexander Lake we're talking about, you can't just mosey in there and start asking questions."

Dimitrius squinted as if she'd started speaking a different language. He was so used to getting his way, to having his orders followed, that it seemed foreign for someone to tell him he couldn't do what he set his mind on.

"It doesn't matter if you're King Arthur or the King of the Universe." She shrugged. "He won't see you without an appointment."

Chapter 36

"I'm here to see Alexander Lake," Sidney said. Her voice wavered, and she hated herself for it. She was here for Mitch, she had to remember that. Whatever issues she had about seeing her grandfather after all these years were nothing compared to what would happen if she didn't get the cure in time.

A woman behind the front desk lifted her face. A well-worn line between her eyebrows deepened into a severe crease. She typed on the keyboard, her long manicured fingernails clacking across the keys so fast they almost purred. "It's late. Mr. Lake doesn't usually see people at this hour. What time was your appointment?"

It wasn't too late for her to turn around and leave. She hadn't thought the idea of being in the same room, under that cold gaze would be so hard. Being around her grandfather reminded her of losing her parents. Whoever said time heals all wounds was a liar. In an instant she was a frightened twelve year old, her parents' murder as fresh as though they were still being packed into body bags in the other room.

She squared her shoulders and cleared her throat.

"I'm sure Mr. Lake will make time for his own granddaughter."

The woman looked out from the top of her bifocals. "Sidney Lake?"

She nodded.

The woman craned her neck around Sidney and studied the four men lined up in a row a few feet behind her. "And they are?"

"They're my...." She turned around and stared at her entourage, her guardians, her new friends, the man who called himself her other half. It was all so ridiculous she couldn't find the words to describe them, so she shrugged and said, "People."

Sidney read the nameplate on the desk. Mrs. Wallace touched the tip of her tongue to the top of her teeth and clicked it once. With a small shake of her head, she adjusted the glasses on her nose. Then her lips twisted into a pucker as nails zipped across keys again.

"One moment please." The woman picked up the phone and waited a few breaths, before she murmured something into the mouthpiece. Then she glanced at Sidney, saw her watching, and turned to the side to say, "But sir, they don't have an appointment."

Sidney crossed her arms and raised an I-told-you-so eyebrow at Dimitrius.

Mrs. Wallace stood and came around the desk. "Right this way, Ms. Lake."

The woman smiled warmly and held the door for her. It was like she was an entirely different person. Sidney stepped through the door and her men moved to follow, but Mrs. Wallace held up a hand. Her face was friendlier than the tone behind her words. "The couch behind you is very comfortable, gentlemen."

Dimitrius opened his mouth to protest, but Sidney shook her head. "Relax, I'll be right back."

Sidney followed Mrs. Wallace into Alexander Lake's private office. The back wall was floor-to-ceiling glass. To the right hand side of the room stood a sleek black desk with a matching bookshelf behind it that held various books, mixed in with photos of her grandfather shaking hands of important people from around the world. The current President held the most prominent spot. No photo of Sidney or her parents was among them.

"Mr. Lake will be with you momentarily." The secretary motioned to the black leather couch and matching end chairs placed around a walnut topped coffee table. "Please, make yourself comfortable."

Sidney made her way over to the huge window. The sun had just dipped below the horizon and the buildings at the lower tip of Manhattan twinkled in the false twilight that always hovered around the city. The water in the bay was choppy, and the Staten Island Ferry chugged past, lined with straggling commuters heading home for the night. The Statue of Liberty watched over it all from next door.

"Lovely, isn't it? Mr. Lake is very proud of the view."

There were a few responses that flew through Sidney's head. None of which would be appropriate to say out loud. "I'm sure he is."

And then she smelled it; the scent of aged oak, and Scotch, with a hint of tobacco. Her grandfather was near.

She watched the reflection in the window as the secretary straightened an already perfectly placed frame on the desk. "Are you sure there isn't something I can bring you to drink?"

"I'm sure." Sidney's mouth was dry and she swallowed hard. She hadn't expected to be this scared. There was no reason for it. It was just her grandfather. He was intimidating and influential, but completely harmless. She'd killed eight shifters singlehandedly, surely she could manage one old man.

"No, *thank you*." Alexander Lake's voice froze the blood in her veins. "Forgive me, Mrs. Wallace, but my granddaughter was never very good about remembering her manners. I see things haven't changed much."

Sidney turned from the window and faced her grandfather. He wore a coal black three piece suit paired with a bright red tie. The cloth was so fine, it had a slight shimmer to it.

"It's late, Mrs. Wallace. You should go home." His eyes remained focused on Sidney as he spoke. There was an intensity there she couldn't quite place. She squeezed her hands into fists at her side, almost took a step back, but stopped herself. He may have gotten away with intimidating her as a little girl, but she was a grown woman now.

"Yes, sir," Mrs. Wallace said.

The door shut with a quiet hush and they were alone. Sidney couldn't find the words to begin. All she could think of was this man telling her that she was ridiculous and speaking nonsense. Except that she'd been right. The wolves she'd seen were very real, or at least one of them had been. The one that killed her parents.

Alexander went to a sideboard next to the sitting area and poured himself a drink. A smug smile sat on his face, as if he was quite pleased with himself about something. "I knew you'd come to me eventually. But I must admit, I didn't think it would be with such a... motley crew."

Her grandfather sipped his drink, then canted his head to the side and his thin lips curved into a smile. "How are you feeling, Sidney?"

His word choice hit her like a punch from the fist of a stone gargoyle. It wasn't 'how are you' or 'long time no see', but *how are you feeling.* She eased her head from side to side, swallowing hard, fighting the sensation of being on one of those boats in the rough water outside.

"That's why you called me the other day?" she whispered. "You already *knew*?"

"The incident in the morgue was purely a coincidence. A happy accident. If you hadn't been attacked, I never would have known your capabilities."

"You sent me to all those shrinks when I was a kid. You insisted what I saw wasn't real."

"Sit with me. Have a drink," Alexander said. "Where is your sense of propriety? I thought I raised you better than that."

"You didn't raise me at all." Sidney cursed the tears that burned her eyes. She gritted her teeth to keep them back.

"I provided for you. I gave you a life most people can only dream of. Everything you have and everything you are is because of me. But that's neither here nor there.

"You could have had a very different life, my dear. It wasn't my first choice to ship you off to boarding school. Unfortunately, you were too much like your mother. Always interested in investigating, and sticking your nose into places it didn't belong. I was never able to trust you to keep your mouth shut. You and your little *stories* about the Big Bad Wolf." He sipped his drink again. "Once you started speaking about sharp teeth and glowing eyes to anyone with ears, you left me little choice but to send you away."

"Did you know the truth when you sat there and told me I had a wild imagination?" Sidney struggled to make her voice loud enough, strong enough, through the rage and fear that strangled her. Half of her entire life hinged on his answer. "For once in my life, tell me the truth. *Please.*"

"Are you sure you want to know?" Alexander's thin lips turned up at the edges, but the look in his turquoise eyes made the action into more of a wince than a smile. "It's terribly gruesome."

"Did you know about the vaccine? Did you know your people were creating these shifters?"

"Shifters?" He raised a neatly groomed gray eyebrow.

"Werewolves."

"Ah," Alexander took a slow sip from his crystal tumbler. "Here at the facility, we refer to them as Lycanthropes."

Sidney wanted to throw up. "So you lied to me. You've been lying my whole life."

"Some falsehoods must be told to protect the greater good. White lies." The wrinkles in her grandfather's face deepened as he scowled. "Everything I have done has been for the greater good. Everything."

"What exactly *have* you done?" Sidney didn't make it a habit of asking questions she didn't want the answers to, but the words tumbled from her lips before she could stop them.

"It began before you were even born. A group of soldiers killed a werewolf in Afghanistan. Some of them were bitten. I run the world's leading medical research facility, it was natural the army should approach me for help when their own people couldn't find a cure."

"You sent those men to my apartment to kidnap me?"

Her grandfather eased his eyes shut. "Sidney, I've warned you it's rude to interrupt people."

"It's also rude to send a bunch of monsters to abduct someone."

"Are you interested in the truth, or not?"

Sidney tucked her arms across her chest and closed her mouth.

"Years later, your mother was called to do a special story for *Time* on biological warfare in the Middle East," Alexander explained. "In a twist of fate, the convoy she was riding in was hit with one of the very weapons she was sent to write about. She became very ill."

Sidney stared at her grandfather. "How come I never heard about this?"

"You were so young. It was your parents' wish to protect you. I respected that."

294

Sidney went over and sank into the chair across from him.

"We had already been working on the lycanthropy vaccine for quite some time, though it was still in the testing stages. While we worked on a cure, we were also developing a separate vaccine." He leaned back casually in his chair as if they were old friends meeting for drinks to discuss how the stock market had performed that day.

"Our intention was to extract the healing nature of the lycanthropy virus to cure every disease, whether caused by man or nature. Imagine, a world where disease and illness doesn't exist. The military had a slightly different idea. 4X20 was a drug meant to create a super-soldier with heightened senses, advanced immunity, and the ability to heal rapidly when wounded."

"Wait." Sidney squeezed her eyes shut. "I don't understand what this has to do with my mother."

"Your father came to me for help. All other treatments failed. He knew the drug was still in its testing stages, but he convinced your mother it was her last, best hope. He couldn't stand the thought of losing her."

"You gave my mother an experimental drug and turned her—" Sidney pressed her lips together hard, unable to even finish the sentence.

"Our intention was to extract the elements that gave the werewolf supernatural capabilities, while preventing the transformation into wolf form. The idea is to preserve the human genome, but strengthen it. The military doesn't want a horde of werewolves running around. What kind of story would that make for the evening news?" Alexander chuckled and sipped his scotch again.

"Daddy would never have asked her to do that." Sidney shook her head, her voice small and frightened. "You didn't tell him everything. You couldn't have."

"Despite what you may think of me, Sidney, I am not a monster. I attempted to talk him out of it. He was beside himself with grief. He said if there was any way for her to be cured, he wanted it. She was already dying."

Sidney wiped her face with the edge of her sleeve, angry at herself for letting him see her cry. "What happened?"

"It worked well. Extremely well. We saw great improvements. She was getting better. We were optimistic. We sent her home."

Sidney blinked and tears spilled onto her cheeks.

"However, the virus had caused her DNA to undergo an extreme change. A change we thought had been engineered out of the vaccine. In this version, it took longer to manifest itself. One night, she lost control," Alexander said. "She killed your father and she would have killed you too, if you hadn't shot her first."

Just like that, a lifetime of nightmares suddenly turned into memories. Now she had no idea what was real and what was imagined.

"No. I killed a shifter that night. I felt the teeth, the fur. I saw the hunger in its eyes. That was not my mother, she would never have looked at me the way that thing did," Sidney insisted. "I killed a *monster*."

"Indeed, you did," Alexander said.

Sidney's voice wavered while she choked on hot, angry tears. "You knew this whole time. You've lied to me my whole life, and worse, you paid others to lie, to make me think I was crazy. How do I know you're not lying to me now? How can I possibly trust anything you say?"

A shifter nudged the door open and sauntered over to sit at her grandfather's heel. He scratched behind its ears and patted its head. Sidney tasted the sour acid that rose from her stomach.

"You weren't supposed to be involved in this. Ever," Alexander said. "You wouldn't have been if that damned Mitchell Harris had left you alone. You would never have been in the morgue that night if it wasn't for him bringing you into this mess. You never would have been bitten. And I never would have known you were so valuable."

Alexander leaned in and examined her like one of his test samples under a microscope. The liquor on his breath stung her nose, made her gag. "We captured all sorts of rare creatures, trying to balance out the effects of the lycanthropy virus. None of them worked."

"The missing chimera, the WIF? That was you?"

A slow smile spread across her grandfather's face as he gave her a slow nod. "Imagine my surprise when *you* never changed. The one and only subject to have been bitten and infected with the lycanthropy virus and remain in her original form. My own granddaughter, the key to unlocking the greatest achievement in medical history."

He made it sound like something he was proud of. The first time he'd ever sounded like that in her entire life.

"You're crazy," Sidney said.

"The line between brilliance and madness is very fine."

"You have no idea what's really going on." She shook her head, thinking of how Dimitrius had explained the way the blood of Sulis manifested in the males of the line. Whatever magic Sidney had in her veins, she shared with the man standing before her. It had corrupted him, and she was glad Dimitrius had never told him the truth.

The shifter growled and pointed its snout toward the door a second before it burst open. Several guards shoved Dimitrius and his men into the office.

The first guard said. "What should we do with them?"

Dimitrius captured Sidney's gaze and gave a nearly imperceptible nod. The ropes in her stomach eased as the stink of the shifter was replaced with that now familiar smell of steel and sweet moss. The cool peace Dimitrius brought with him washed over her, giving her new strength. But the feeling was short lived.

"That guy had this on him." The guard shoved Dimitrius with his shoulder as he handed over *Caledfwlch*. Dimitrius didn't even blink as he was manhandled. He kept his eyes fixed on Sidney's.

"My, my." Alexander took the weapon and examined it. "What an antiquity."

A rage boiled up from within Sidney that she'd never come close to feeling before. The longer he had his hands on the steel and leather, the more violated she felt.

"Don't touch that." Her voice barely contained her rage. She planted her feet on the floor and stood, nails digging into her palms.

Alexander stilled before lifting his head. He stared at her, watching her reaction as he ran his thumb over the edge of the steel, and rubbed the tip of his forefinger and thumb together, examining the cut it left. "Yes. I think this would work nicely for my personal collection. Once it's cleaned up a bit."

He tossed it on the desk like it was last week's newspaper. The bang echoed against the windows, and Sidney felt the blow in her bones as if she had been the one tossed aside.

"What should we do with them?" the guard asked.

Alexander shrugged. "Now that we have the key, we need more test subjects. They look strong enough. Lock them up separately. We'll deal with them when the time comes.

"You'd really do this? Experiment on your own granddaughter?" Sidney asked.

Her grandfather pressed his lips together, gave her a look a look that he used before, a look that made the most powerful men in the world cower in their freshly polished shoes. "Think of it as making a sacrifice for the good of all mankind."

"You really are a monster," she whispered.

"I'm sure history will prove me quite the opposite. A hero in fact." He gave her a self-satisfied smile, then turned to his guards. "Take them to Building Four."

"You can't do this!" she shouted. Her whole life, she'd thought he was cold, and calculating, even heartless. Now, she saw him for the monster he truly was.

"My dear granddaughter, what could you possibly do to stop me?"

All of the air left Sidney's lungs. The corner of Dimitrius' mouth turned up slightly, and his dark eyes fixed on hers. It happened without even thinking, as easy as drawing in her next breath.

"*CALEDFWLCH!*"

The sword flew into her grasp and she drove it forward.

Alexander coughed once and blood dripped onto his chin.

His aquamarine eyes widened with surprise. She watched the confusion, denial, and horror run across his face as she held his gaze with eyes the same color. He wheezed. More blood spilled out of his mouth onto his pristine shirt.

The shifter lunged at her, teeth bared. She yanked the sword from her grandfather's chest and flicked her wrist. The shifter's head rolled across the floor.

Dimitrius and his men stared at her.

The guards stared at her.

She swiped the spray of blood off her cheek with the back of her hand.

"Who's next?" she asked.

Bones and muscles popped and twisted, as each of the guards shifted. It was a disgusting sound when one of them did it, but all of them together made her skin crawl.

"Sidney." Dimitrius drew her attention to the binding around his wrists.

"You let them handcuff you?"

He shrugged. "Our little deception had to seem authentic. It worked, didn't it?"

She sliced through the zip-tie, then turned and ran the sword through the shifter closest to him. It fell to the ground, half changed. She cut through the neck as easily as she had the plastic binding.

Dimitrius freed Argus, Malcolm, and Tyran. They worked efficiently as a team, it was more than clear they'd had plenty of practice as every one of the shifter heads rolled across the floor.

Argus shook his arms out. "Aye, that felt good."

"Been a while." Malcolm grinned. "Was worried we'd get a bit rusty. Too bad there's no more, I hardly got warmed up."

Her grandfather gasped for air nearby. Blood bubbled out of his mouth as he struggled to for his next breath. Sidney turned and watched.

"Sidney, please." He tried to smile. His teeth were red with blood. "I'm the only family you have left."

"You're wrong." Sidney glanced around at the men who were ready to fight by her side, to risk their lives to save the man she loved. "They are."

Two shifters pushed casually through the half-open door, sniffing the air. The larger of the two emitted a low growl and snapped at the other one.

Argus took a step forward. Sidney stilled him. "I'll take care of this."

He gave her a confirmation nod to show he understood, then led the others out.

Dimitrius stayed behind.

The shifters circled her grandfather, sniffed the air, inched ever closer. For the first time in her life, she saw fear on her grandfather's face.

"Don't." He coughed and reached out to her. "Don't let them...."

The biggest one lunged first. Alexander let out a strangled cry. The sound was cut short as the shifter clamped down on his throat. Another crunch of bone and cartilage, and his head fell unnaturally to the side.

Sidney couldn't manage to turn away.

She stared in horror and satisfaction as the creatures her grandfather created, tore him apart, one piece at a time.

Chapter 37

Dimitrius' hand overlapped Sidney's, clutching the sword along with her. The intensity of his grasp matched the magnetism of the hilt so that her hand was cradled in power.

"We should find the others," his words fell softly next to her ear, barely a breath.

Sidney nodded. She went over to the shifters, who were so occupied with their quarry they never saw the blade coming.

She took one last look at her grandfather's gaping mouth, the way his right eyelid hung slightly lower than the left over his blank stare, how the blood glistened on the viscera that spilled from his stomach onto the expensive Persian carpet.

She thought she should feel something. Anything.

Dimitrius waited for her by the doorway. She went to him, stepped into his embrace, and wrapped her arm around his neck. Holding the sword in one hand, with Dimitrius pressed against her, she'd never felt more complete, more whole than in that very moment. She expected the ache and ignored it when she pulled away and shoved her doubts and desires to a corner of her mind that was so safe she'd never be able to find them again.

"Mitch was right," she said, and gave him the sword. "There is no cure."

"You had to try."

"What do I do now?" Sidney's face crumpled into a sob. "There's nothing left."

A shout echoed down the hallway. Dimitrius took her face in his hands. "This isn't over yet. Stay calm. Follow me."

He took her hand and sidestepped a pool of blood from the severed head of a guard out in the hallway. The body was a few feet away. They stepped over half-a-dozen other shifter bodies as they made their way down the long hallway that led to the lobby by the elevators.

They finally caught up with the others who were grouped at the front desk around another scene of carnage.

"All right?" Argus grinned.

"What do our exits look like?" Dimitrius asked.

"Crowded," Tyran said.

They both stepped to the window. Sidney wasn't ready to let go of his hand yet, and Dimitrius didn't seem interested in letting go of her either. He laced his fingers with hers as he examined the area below the way he'd scanned the crowd for the demon at his club. The entire courtyard outside was covered with shifters, pacing and running long tongues over sharp teeth.

"There's got to be another way out," she said.

She knew without asking that he was running through all the scenarios, calculating his next move.

"The parking lot is on the other side of that building." He pointed to the structure across the way. "We have a better chance if we stay inside as long as possible."

Dimitrius looked to his men who all nodded in agreement.

"I'll take lead. Argus and Malcolm, you're in charge of Sidney. Tyran bring up the back." Dimitrius made eye contact with each of them as he doled out the assignments. Sidney didn't like that she was assigned protectors when she knew she was strong enough to do the protecting. But now was not the time for arguments.

As if Dimitrius could read her thoughts, he gave her a second glance. "Stay with them."

She nodded and he led the way down the stairwell. There wasn't a sound other than the echo of shuffling feet on concrete steps. It was only three levels and they all paused behind Dimitrius when he reached the ground floor.

He motioned the all clear, and they followed him out the door down another short hallway. A shout was quickly shortened by the ring of steel. A snarl and a thud. Sidney angled herself to see around Malcolm's huge shoulders but she had no idea what was happening until they moved forward again and she had to step over two fresh bodies.

"Hold," Dimitrius said.

They waited for a few moments in silence. Argus breathed heavily behind her.

"The door to the next hall requires an access code. We'll have to use the walkway. It's covered, but still open to the courtyard. Move quickly, and do exactly as you're told. No questions."

They eased outside into the covered walkway that led to the next building. Bits of stone exploded next to her head. Her cheek scraped against the paving stones as a heavy weight crushed her body.

"Ow! What the hell?"

Argus' long beard blocked her view. "We're taking fire, lass. Hold your horses."

She gasped for air, choking on loose mortar and dirt.

"They're coming. Move!" Dimitrius called out.

Argus rolled off her, then Malcolm grabbed the waistband of her jeans and lifted her to her feet with one hand. "This way. Let's go."

It was only two steps before she realized Tyran wasn't with them. "Wait!"

She dug in her heels and turned. Tyran was still on the ground, struggling to get up.

"Dammit woman!" Malcolm grabbed Sidney's wrist.

"We can't leave him." Sidney pulled free and went back.

"Stay with the others." Tyran held his hand to the side of his neck. Blood oozed between his fingers.

"You're bleeding," she said.

"So are you," Tyran said.

Her sweater was torn and a gash opened on her shoulder where a bullet had grazed her. She hadn't even felt it.

"We have to keep moving," Dimitrius said.

Malcolm flew backward into the brick archway. A shifter snarled, teeth snapping. The creatures were on them all at once. Tyran got to his feet, only to be pounced on. They knocked Sidney over, trapping her beneath them in the process.

She twisted around. Malcolm was tangled with his shifter. Dimitrius ran his blade through another one. Argus had one by the scruff of the neck, laughing. The thing wriggled and latched onto his arm. With a roar, the Highlander drew his knife across its neck. It jerked and he tossed the limp body onto the ground.

Tyran wrestled with his shifter and Sidney pulled her leg free as soon as he rolled.

"Argus!" She held her hand out. He tossed her his knife.

The shifter growled, teeth bared, as Tyran pushed its head away. Sidney drove the knife up under its rib cage and turned her wrist hard before yanking it out. The thing sputtered blood, and let out an unearthly sound. Tyran shoved it away. Sidney straddled it and jabbed the knife straight through the top of its skull.

"Well done," Tyran said. The wound on his neck had already stopped bleeding, but he still looked slightly pale.

Sidney couldn't hide her worry. "Thanks."

Argus stood there, hand on hip, watching Malcolm wrestle with the stubborn creature.

"Little help here?" Malcolm grimaced. It sat back on its haunches right on his face. He fussed and spit as the tail whacked him in the nose. "If you got time. Don't want to bother you."

"What do you need me for?" Argus boomed. "Looks like you got the little doggy by its tail."

Caledfwlch sang through the air and the shifter's head rolled off its shoulders.

"Follow me." Dimitrius motioned to Sidney and jumped over the low wall of the walkway. He stopped along the way, grabbing up weapons for each of them as they passed piles of clothes shed by the changed shifters.

Tyran paused and took out a sniper on top of the building.

"Get down!" Someone shoved her. The air hit hard and suddenly all she could hear was a high pitched ringing. She lay there on her back, staring up at the sky, thinking how pretty the smoke looked as it swirled up around a water tower in the middle of the courtyard.

Her eyes stung.

Dimitrius pulled her up. He was in her face, his lips moved but no sound came out.

Suddenly the ringing stopped, replaced with the groan of metal. Whatever had caused the explosion had destroyed the main support for the water tower.

Sidney finally heard Dimitrius' voice.

"Run."

They darted past the tower just as the weight of the water became too much for the reserve supports and it collapsed in on itself. The gush of water rose up to Sidney's knees. It tripped her up and sent her splashing to the ground. Malcolm slid into her, carried by the strength of the water.

Dimitrius never faltered, and never let go of her hand. He helped her to her feet as the water rushed away. Tyran and Argus caught up, wiping their eyes. They helped Malcolm to his feet.

"Everyone here?" Dimitrius asked.

"Aye," Malcolm answered.

Sidney took a step and nearly fell over when a sharp pain ripped across her thigh. She looked down to find a huge bolt jutting out of her leg.

Dimitrius kneeled and examined her leg. "Can you walk?"

She shook her head. "And don't you dare carry me like I'm some kind of damsel in distress."

A smile flickered across his face.

Tyran pointed behind her. "What's that?"

"Where?" She turned to look. "OW!"

Sidney checked her leg where the bolt had been and Tyran tossed aside the chunk of metal. "Old battle trick. You'll be fine.

They made it around the end of the building and through a narrow alleyway before they emerged into the parking lot. There were no street lights and the buildings blocked the ambient glow of the city. She kept her eyes on Tyran's golden halo of hair as they jogged back toward the car.

A pack of shifters tore around on the left from behind a block of garbage-truck-sized air generators. Dimitrius loosed his hand from hers and *Caledflwch* flowed in an arc around his head. He moved to the middle of a small square of grass, directly past the generators. The shifters circled him like hungry sharks.

"Get to the car!" he shouted.

"He can handle this. Let's go," Tyran urged her.

Dimitrius spun around. He kept his chin down as he swirled the sword through the air, removing a shifter's head in one fell swoop. Another creature lunged. He caught its snout and knocked it back. It opened its jaws wide, ready to sink its teeth into his leg, but he plunged the sword straight down its throat and out the back of the skull.

It was effortless, like a well-practiced dance.

Argus and Malcolm came jogging back. "What's the hold up?"

Sidney couldn't take her eyes off Dimitrius' muscles rippling under his shirt as he thrust the blade into another shifter. The steel flowed through the air over his head, giving light to their surroundings with its preternatural gleam. The man and the sword were each amazing on their own, but both together were downright otherworldly.

"Oh, aye, he's real pretty. We know," Argus said. "Now get a move on, there inna much time."

"Much time for what?" Sidney asked.

The men escorted her back to the car, forcing her to keep up with them. Malcolm scratched the thick stubble of his jaw. "Might've arranged a bit of a gas leak."

"Aye, now get in the car and let's get outta here before the whole island blows sky high." Argus shoved her in the back seat, and the rest of them piled in, with Dimitrius bringing up the rear.

The tires spit dirt and gravel as they spun out onto the narrow bridge connecting Ellis Island to New Jersey. The light from the orange fireball behind them lit up Dimitrius' hair, just like the first time she'd seen him. She cringed when the shockwave rattled the car windows like thunder. Instead of turning around to look at the explosion, she kept her eyes on the man in front of her.

He rested his elbows on his knees and leaned forward, took her hands in his. "Are you all right?"

"Can we pull over for a second?"

"Malcolm," Dimitrius said.

The car slowed and stopped. With the park closed, the road was completely desolate. Sidney tumbled out onto the ground, gravel digging into her hands and knees. She heaved, but there was nothing in her stomach to come up.

Dimitrius pulled her hair away from her face, and curled his arm across her chest, supporting her weight while she coughed and gagged in the weeds. She shuddered and sucked in a few deep breaths to get her body under control. He pulled her back against him, and cradled her there in his arms, under the gleaming lights of the New York City skyline.

"I don't want to go back," she whispered, resting her head back against his shoulder. "Can we just stay right here forever?"

Dimitrius sighed into her hair. "If I could, I would make it happen for you."

"What am I supposed to say to him?" The lights blurred together in her vision creating a smear of brightness in front of her. "How do I tell him I failed?"

"Tell him you love him," he said. "That's all he needs to hear."

"Thank you for going with me. For letting me try."

He pressed his cheek to her temple, wetting his face with her tears. The intensity she'd felt in the club melted into something different. It eased her worry and left her feeling stronger.

"What happens now?" she asked.

"We go take care of our friend."

Chapter 38

"How is he doing?" Sidney asked. From the way Williams' hair stood out from his head in tangled tufts, she was pretty sure she knew the answer.

"He'll be great now that you're back." Williams stopped in front of her and gave her an expectant shrug. "Where's the cure?"

Dimitrius slipped past her into Mitch's room, leaving her in the hallway with Williams.

"I...." She sighed. "There wasn't one. It doesn't exist."

"But I thought—" Williams tugged on his hair again. "What happened?"

Sidney let her hands fall loosely at her sides. "I don't even know where to start."

"Well you have to start somewhere. What do we do for the chief? What are our options?"

She shook her head helplessly.

"We have to do *something*. What can we do?" Williams paced across the plush carpet. "You're the key. Did you find out what that meant? Maybe you have magical spit or something."

"Apparently I'm the only person who's been bitten but didn't change. My grandfather was behind this the whole time, knew everything from the beginning. The army wanted him to create a super-soldier. He wanted to create a cure-all for every disease in the world. He was going to keep me, and Dimitrius, and the others to experiment on us."

Williams stared at her, not even bothering to keep his jaw from hanging wide open. "Dude."

"He lied to me about what happened to my parents. He lied to me my whole life."

"Dude."

She straightened her shoulders, steeling her gaze. "He's not going to be lying to anyone anymore."

Williams stared at her, his mouth working, but for once he was at a loss for words.

Banks joined them in the hall. "Mitch is resting. Dimitrius brought me up to speed. I have him on something to keep him comfortable for now, but he's going downhill pretty fast. It would be best to discuss options now so we have a plan."

Sidney leaned back against the wall. "Is he in pain?"

"It comes and goes. Similar to what you went through in the hospital. You were sedated for most of it, so you probably don't remember much. I can do the same for him."

She nodded. "So we keep him comfortable. We keep him safe."

"We let him do his furry thing and then at the full moon or whatever he's back to himself." They both stared at Williams. "I mean, he will change back at some point, right? He can't stay a wolf forever. And in the meantime, Banks, you work on figuring out whatever it is that made Lake immune to changing and then make that for the chief. It'll be like it never even happened."

"Yeah, but… what about what the chief wants?" Sidney asked.

"What do you mean? He wants to live. He won't give up… not that easily. I know him. He won't," her partner insisted.

Even as the words came out of his mouth, she could see he doubted them.

"If there's any possibility he could hurt anyone, or something worse… what would you choose if it was you?"

Williams nodded and tugged his hair again.

Banks sighed deeply. "One option is to gradually up his dosage of Morphine. It'll make him sleep. He'll stop breathing, slip away. It would be peaceful."

"You mean euthanize him," Sidney said. "Like you'd put down a dog?"

"I didn't mean it like that at all."

"I know. I'm sorry. This just—"

"Sucks." Williams sniffed and cleared his throat. "It really fucking sucks."

"It's getting late. Maybe you guys could take a break for a little while? Go get some food or some coffee or something? Dimitrius and I can stay with him."

Williams nodded and pressed his lips together. He met Sidney's eyes as his own spilled over with tears. "If you think you'll be okay for a while, I um… I need to go home and hug my girls."

"Do what you need to do." She nodded her chin toward the elevator. "Give Megan an extra squeeze for me?"

"Sure thing." He gave her a brave but watery smile, and a peck on the cheek before he headed out.

"You gonna be all right?" Banks asked.

She shook her head. "No."

"How can I help make this easier for you?"

"You can't." She crossed her arms and gave a small shrug. "Unless you use your necromancer voodoo and bring him back."

"Aw, honey. We all saw how that turned out downstairs."

"Yeah. I know." Sidney fought back a wave of nausea as the reality of it all began to sink in.

"Y'all really care about him, don't you?" Banks asked.

She gave him a sad smile as she tried to form the right words. "He's… everything."

"Yeah, I get it. I really do." He squeezed her elbow. "If you need anything just holler. I'll be right upstairs."

"Thanks."

The hallway was deserted except for Sidney, but she couldn't bring herself to step inside the room to face Mitch. If walking through that door meant saying goodbye, then she wasn't ready. Dimitrius had experience with this. He'd probably attended thousands of deathbeds, not to mention all the lives he'd ended on the battlefield. She wondered if that made it any easier or not.

She sank down against the wall and sat next to the door. It was open a crack. Now that she was alone and it was quiet, she could hear Mitch and Dimitrius talking.

"It'll be hardest on her." Mitch's voice was different, but she could still tell it was him. "She'll blame herself no matter what you tell her otherwise."

"She possesses a great deal of determination."

"I think you mean she's damn stubborn."

Sidney smiled.

"I wish you could have seen her this evening. She was… incredible."

"She's brave and strong. Stronger than she knows. But you'll have to help her through this. Losing her parents so early took something out of her. She doesn't trust easily. She questions her feelings on everything. You have to be patient. Love her hard."

"I will. This I vow to you." Dimitrius cleared his throat.

Sidney stifled a sob with the edge of her sleeve.

"I'm so very sorry it turned out this way, my friend," Dimitrius continued.

"You're absolutely sure it's eradicated this time?" Mitch asked.

"Any trace of the virus was destroyed in the explosion."

"Then it ends with me."

"Yes."

"Good."

"You should try to rest. I'll send for more ice."

"Dimitrius?"

The door opened a few inches then stopped.

"Love her."

"I already do."

Dimitrius emerged and shut the door behind him. He stepped into the middle of the hallway and pinched the bridge of his nose at the same place Sidney had broken it a few days ago. "Sulis, watch over him."

Sidney covered her mouth with both hands, but couldn't stop the sound as she gasped between sobs. He turned, startled, then relaxed when he saw it was her.

"How much did you hear?" he asked.

The tears streaming down her face was enough of an answer.

"Sidney." He kneeled in front of her, took her hands and peeled them away from her face, then used his thumb to dry her tears. "Go to him."

"I'm not ready for this."

Dimitrius gave her a pained look. "If I knew the secret to stop time, I would have done it long ago. But then I never would have known you."

He rose and pulled her to her feet. "Go."

Sidney cleared her face, took a deep breath, and opened the door.

Mitch lay in the bed, his back propped up with pillows. The dark lines moved all the way across his chest now, snaking down his arms, marring his perfect abdomen.

She stopped at the end of the bed and stared. He held his hand out and she took it without hesitation.

Sidney squeezed his hand in both of hers, but something felt different. His bones felt more pronounced somehow. Usually, her hand fit perfectly in his, but now it didn't. It looked the same as it usually did, but she wasn't sure if there had been that much hair on the back of it before. And his fingernails were much longer. He always kept them so short. Maybe she was looking too hard, trying to see something that wasn't there.

"Is there anything you want to say?" he asked.

317

Sidney traced the deep purplish black lines up his arm with her eyes. What could she say to someone who already knew everything about her? What could she say that she hadn't already said at one time or another under the covers late at night, over countless cups of coffee, or in the car stuck in traffic?

"I'm going to miss you." She stared up at him then and his features blurred.

He pulled her to him. She stretched out on the bed, rested her cheek on his chest. His skin burned like fire compared to the ice packs tucked up against his side. Mitch tilted his head back and let out a groan.

Sidney lifted her head, but he pulled her back down.

"I'm fine." He spoke through his teeth, as his heart pounded against her ear. "This wasn't an easy decision. I want you to know that."

She wet his skin with her tears. "Mitch—"

"Sidney, let me say this. I need to. Please," he said, as he brushed his hand over her hair. "I don't want to leave you. But the idea of waking up one morning and finding pieces of you spread out across the room, knowing that it would be my fault—I can't take that risk. I won't let what happened to your parents happen to us."

He squeezed his hand around her arm and held his breath while his body shuddered against her. It hurt, but she didn't let him know.

"I spoke with Dimitrius. Your grandfather's labs were all destroyed. This all ends here with me. Do you understand what I'm saying?"

"I understand, but I don't have to like it, do I?" Sidney traced her finger across his chest. His body relaxed, but his chest rose and fell fast under her touch.

"Of course you don't have to like it. I hate it. I hate the idea of leaving you, of not being there when you need me." Mitch gritted his teeth together and fought back another groan. "But I also know you'll survive. I know you'll keep going. And we'll be together again. I promise." He nudged her up and touched the silver cross at her neck. "Your mom and dad, all of us."

"Give them a hug for me? Tell them I miss them." Her tears dripped down the back of his hand. "I'll be there before you know it."

He dug his fingernails into her hand. It hurt. Sidney checked, and they were definitely longer, sharper, than they had been a few seconds ago. He tried to say something but his back arched and twisted in a spasm that drew a roar from somewhere deep inside him. She'd never heard him make a sound like that before. It wasn't even human.

"Mitch?" The way he gripped her hand made her scream out too, but there was no way she would let go.

Dimitrius rushed in, she felt him at her side.

"Not yet. Please, not yet." Sidney didn't know who or what she was pleading with, she just wanted this to stop.

"I'll get Banks." Dimitrius left.

"I love you," Mitch gasped.

Sidney cleared away her tears so she could look into his eyes. The color was faded to a pale blue. So unlike

319

his own. But she could still see something left of him in there, deep down, begging her to put an end to this.

The muscles in his arms pulled tight, drawing his fingers into a fist that locked around her hand. There was a *crack* in each one of his ribs, one right after the other. Hard claws pulled at her skin.

Banks came in and grabbed a vial and a syringe from the bedside table.

"Hurry," she yelled at Banks.

Mitch convulsed so hard his back twisted and arched up off the bed.

"Step back over here." Banks directed her out of the way. He got the needle into his arm and pushed down the plunger.

Something cold and hard pressed into her palm. Dimitrius stood at her back. He wrapped her hand around the weapon and fortified her strength with the look he gave her.

Banks saw the gun in her hand. "What are you doing?"

"Get out of the way," Dimitrius said.

The idea of what she was about to do washed over her. When this was over, she could never kiss Mitch again. Never hold his hand. Never hear him say goodnight, or lay awake and listen to him snore. Never make love to him again.

Mitch roared. His back cracked and he shredded the sheets with his claws. "Sidney, please!"

She went to him and rested her forehead against his. He closed his eyes and his body eased down on the mattress.

"You know I love you, right?" she told him. "More than anything."

"I love you too." He lifted his head and kissed her. "You're the best thing that ever happened to me. I will always, *always* be with you."

Sidney gave him one last lingering kiss, then clicked the safety off.

She pressed the barrel to his forehead, turned her face away and squeezed the trigger. Then put another two shots into the center of his chest.

His body went limp.

He shrank back into himself. His hands became the hands she was so familiar with, the ones that had touched her in the most wonderful ways, taken care of her, and dried her tears. His eyes thawed back into gray, but the spark of life was no longer there.

The gun slipped from Sidney's fingers and landed on the floor with a dull thud. She sank to her knees, pressing her cheek against the edge of the mattress. His arm draped lifeless off the side of the bed. She took his hand in her own and kissed it.

It was still warm.

Chapter 39

"It is unfortunate the world has lost such a good man." The priest shuffled his notes at the lectern. "A man who dedicated his life to the benefit of others. A selfless, God-fearing man who used his life and his wealth to make this planet we live on a little bit better, a bit easier for those who needed it most."

The cloying scent of Easter lilies made it hard to take in a breath. The white flowers covered the front altar of St. Patrick's Cathedral, spilling across the top of an elegant, shining black casket. There was nothing left to put inside. It was all for show, just like the rest of her grandfather's life.

"Alexander Lake will be missed by many, but we need not mourn his death. Merely, celebrate a long and wonderful life. For he will live on forever in all of the many, many lives he has touched." The priest gave Sidney a reassuring nod before he stepped away.

A man in a black suit with a Bluetooth headset attached to his ear came over and crouched in front of Sidney. "Ms. Lake, when you're ready, we'll let you out first. The car is waiting. Again, I'm terribly sorry for your loss."

Sidney knew she should respond, but nothing came out. She hadn't been able to say much of anything at all the past week. A numbness had overcome her that she couldn't seem to shake. She went through the motions, first Tom's funeral, now this one.

They were holding a wake for Mitch at the Cowgirl Sea-Horse that night.

It was like walking through a dream. She was there, but she wasn't.

"Thank you," Dimitrius offered on her behalf. He stood and buttoned his suit coat. Tyran, Argus, and Malcolm followed the same motions beside him. Dimitrius held out his hand for Sidney and spoke under his breath. "One more minute. Then it's over with."

Sidney put her hand in his and stood. Over two-thousand pairs of eyes focused on her. She glanced over at Williams and Megan who were seated in the second row. Peters was there with his wife and daughter as well.

Dimitrius kept his hand firmly in place at the small of her back as whispers and furtive glances followed them like a wave out into the open. Yelling and bright camera flashes erupted when they stepped outside. Sidney only caught snippets of words here and there.

"Ms. Lake!" A blonde woman shoved a microphone under Sidney's nose. "How does it feel to suddenly be worth an estimated $43 billion?"

She stopped and stared at the woman. Argus, Malcolm and Tyran pushed back the urgent reporters and paparazzi, so eager for a sound bite.

"The man I loved most in this world is dead," Sidney said. "I'd give every dime of that money to have one more minute with him."

The reporter blinked, seemingly stunned by such honesty, but she recovered quickly. "So the reports that you and your grandfather weren't speaking at the time of his death are unfounded?"

"That's enough." Dimitrius pulled Sidney away.

"Sidney! How long have you and Dimitrius been dating?" another reporter shouted.

Argus held open the door to the limousine. Dimitrius helped Sidney in, then sank onto the seat beside her. The door shut and the screaming reporters were silenced.

Malcolm went around, got in the driver's seat and pulled away, while the others piled into an SUV behind them.

Sidney leaned forward and pressed the heels of her hands to her eyes.

"It's done." Dimitrius placed his hand on her back.

"They think we're dating?"

"The instant the news broke about your grandfather, the paparazzi started following you."

"I don't want to be a *Page Six* Princess again. I already lived that life. I just want to be left alone."

"It'll die down soon enough."

Sidney pulled out her smart phone and checked the images on the website. She found a grainy photo of her and Dimitrius holding hands as they exited the back door at Bitten. She raised an eyebrow at the caption. "New York's new Power Couple?"

Dimitrius shrugged.

Sidney made a disgusted sound in the back of her throat and leaned into the crook of his arm. It eased the nasty feeling in the pit of her stomach whenever the image of the blood splattered pillow flashed into her mind.

"How long does it take to forget?"

"I'm sorry to say, some things you never forget. All you can do is try not to let the bad memories outweigh the good. The good is always there." He twisted the end of her hair around his finger. "Sometimes it's harder to recall, but there's always something."

"Do you think my grandfather was telling the truth about my mother?"

"What do you believe?"

"I don't know what to believe. I didn't get to talk to Mitch about it." She nibbled her lower lip. "I wonder if he suspected the truth somehow, and that's why he never pursued it any further. Some things are just too ugly to know for sure."

"Do you regret the trip to Ellis Island?"

Sidney shook her head. "No."

"Good."

"I do regret calling Mitch when that hybrid came to my apartment. If I hadn't called, he wouldn't have been bitten."

"You can't spend the rest of your life second guessing every choice." He traced the tip of his finger casually around hers, outlining an invisible handprint on the black wool of her dress. She tucked her hand into a fist and shoved it under her other arm.

"Don't." The tone of her voice was harsher than she'd meant for it to be and she threw him an apologetic glance. "Sorry. I'm just... not ready."

Dimitrius bowed his head in that special way of his, the way that twisted her insides and made her forget for a moment why she kept telling him no.

"I can wait, my lady." He turned his attention out the window. "I have all the time in the world."

Chapter 40

"You still haven't told me exactly where we're going," Williams said.

"Turn right at that gate." She hugged the urn with Mitch's ashes so that it wouldn't tip over.

Williams pulled onto the white crushed gravel drive and stopped at a huge iron filigreed gate with two brick columns on either side of the driveway. The fence went down the road for two miles in both directions. It surprised her that after all these years she still remembered that.

There was an aged bronze sign on the right hand column which read: Lakehurst.

Williams rolled down the window and stared at the numbers on a dialing pad. "Do you have the code?"

Sidney pulled out the piece of paper and read off the numbers as Williams punched them in. "10131993."

The gate opened slowly. It gave Sidney just enough time to think about what a mistake this had been. The last time she'd been here was her first Christmas without her parents. It was so miserable, she always made sure to get an invitation to go on a trip somewhere with one of her friends for the holidays. Skiing in the Alps, cruising through the Eastern Caribbean, hiking in Patagonia, she didn't care where it was, so long as it was far away from this place.

The cherry trees lining the drive up to the house were in full bloom, making it impossible to get a view of the house until they were right in front of it.

"Jumpin' jellyfish," Williams said. He followed the drive around the fountain and parked in front of the door. "Lake, I knew you came from money, but… dude. Does it come with valet?"

"Used to."

A small round woman came out and stood on the steps. She squealed when Sidney got out of the car. "Oh, child! I thought for sure I'd never lay eyes on you again."

She threw her arms around Sidney and smooshed her face with a kiss.

"Hi, Mrs. Black."

"Don't be silly, dear, you call me Jane." The woman brushed Sidney off and fixed her hair while she looked her over from head-to-toe. "Look at you, all grown up. I'm so sorry about your poor grandfather. An explosion at the lab! Terrible. Well, if the gas lines had never been replaced, it's no wonder. But, I thought for sure that man would outlive Satan himself. I see you have his ashes. Why don't you come on in and have a snack before you get to all that? I've got tea and crumpets ready on the veranda. It's such a lovely day out. Come on, then, don't be shy."

Sidney didn't have the time to correct the housekeeper on whose ashes she was holding, even if she wanted to. Williams glanced at his partner and raised an eyebrow. "*Veranda?*"

"The back porch." She elbowed him to follow the housekeeper inside.

A man with graying hair clicked his heels and gave a stiff nod as they entered. "Mr. Shaw, at your service. May I take your coats?"

"Mr. Shaw, really, is that necessary?" Mrs. Black shooed him away. "He likes to keep reminding us he was trained at Buckingham."

"Well, I was," Mr. Shaw said.

"It's just Sidney. She doesn't care about all that. She's not like The Mister. Surprises me they're even related. Poor child."

Williams was too busy ogling the grand staircase to watch where he was going, and nearly collided with a suit of armor. Sidney caught his arm and steered him around it. He leaned in and whispered. "Where's the entrance to the Bat Cave?"

"Shut up." She pinched the back of his arm.

Mrs. Black led them through the breakfast room. "When you're finished with tea, I'd be happy to give you a tour to help you get reacquainted with the house."

"Thanks, Mrs. Black. I mean, um, Jane, but that won't be necessary. I'm not staying," Sidney said.

Williams gave her a look that clearly said he thought she was insane for not wanting to live in this house. They followed her outside onto the veranda where a spread was set up with tiny sandwiches, scones, fresh fruit, and cookies. There was another cafe table set up for them to sit and eat at. The centerpiece was a small bouquet of pale pink peonies, her favorite. The white table cloth billowed in the wind.

"I was so looking forward to having you here!"

"It's way too much house for me, and I never felt comfortable here after…."

"Of course, dear." Mrs. Black patted her arm. "You poor thing. I understand completely. Your parents were so kind. It's just awful what happened to them. Haunts me to this day. Such a tragedy. But you didn't come here to think about that, did you now? Here, help yourselves and have a seat. I'll go get the tea."

"I appreciate it, but I think we'd better head down first," Sidney said.

"Right, of course dear." Mrs. Black gave an understanding smile. "You do whatever you like."

Williams looked to Sidney. "Lead the way."

She cut a path through the thick sweeping lawn down towards the edge of the woods. There was a single Oak tree that stood out from the rest of the tree line. It was surrounded on all sides by a short iron fence, about waist high. A bright white gravel path started at the gate and led up to a monument at the base of the tree.

A life-sized stone angel wept over a bright white marble tomb. She stood in front of it, reading the names of her parents and the days of their birth and death over and over. It still didn't feel real, even after all this time.

She stepped forward and placed the urn in the center of the monument, right between her parents' names. She and Williams stood there together, staring at it.

"It's weird not having him around," Williams said. "I keep expecting him to call any minute and say we've got a boggart infestation in a warehouse in Brooklyn or something."

Sidney tried not to laugh but she couldn't help it.

"Should we say something?" Williams asked.

"Like what?"

"I don't know. You didn't bring a poem?" he asked.

Sidney gave him a dubious look, complete with raised eyebrow. "I think he'd be laughing at us right now. Standing here like two dumb asses."

"Hey." Williams elbowed her. "Who you calling a dumb ass?"

A black cat came out from around the tree and wound its way between her ankles, rubbing up against her leg. She leaned over and offered her hand. It blinked up at her with pretty gray eyes, while it sniffed her fingers and rubbed its face against her skin.

"It's going to take some time, but things will be okay again. It won't feel like this forever," Williams said.

"I know. I'll be fine. Eventually." She smiled, but didn't put much effort into it.

"Megan says the guest room is yours for as long as you need."

"Thanks." Sidney stood up again. "But, I'm not going back with you."

"I thought you told the housekeeper you weren't staying."

"I'm not. Not here, anyway. I need time. There's stuff I have to figure out. About myself, about Dimitrius, about a lot of things." The cat meowed at her feet. "Mitch owned a cabin in New Hampshire. We would go up there sometimes and—"

Williams held up his hand. "I do not need to hear the sordid details of your love life."

"That's not what I was going to say."

"Yeah, whatever." He nudged the gravel with the toe of his shoe. "Do what you need to do Lake. I'll hold down the fort."

"Thanks, partner."

"By the way, happy birthday."

"Ugh. Everything bad happens around my birthday. Maybe I'll start celebrating my half-birthday in October."

The cat meowed.

"Kitty approves," Williams said.

Sidney didn't put much effort into her smile, but she attempted one at least. She took one last look at the weeping angel, then followed her partner out and closed the gate. The cat squeezed through the fence and followed at her heels.

The ache in her heart wasn't quite as sharp as she always imagined it would be. Sidney had a feeling it would be sooner than twelve years before she returned.

"We get to stay for the food, right? Because those crumpets looked amazing," Williams said as they trudged up the swath of green lawn.

"Leave it to you to think with your stomach," she said. "Do you even know what a crumpet is?"

"Who cares? I just want it in my mouth."

"That's what she said."

Look for the next book in the
Tides of Darkness series:

DARKNESS RISING

Coming in 2017!

ACKNOWLEDGEMENTS

Bringing this book into the world has been a long, painstaking, exciting, and wonderful journey. There is absolutely no way I could have done it alone, nor would I have wanted to. Over the years, I've collected many people to whom I owe an enormous debt of gratitude. You very simply would not be holding this book in your hands without the following people.

To my husband and children: I'd thank you last as you are the most important, but since you are the first in my life today and always then it is only reasonable you shall be the first on this list. Thank you for putting up with me, and everything that comes along in this little package called Wife and Mother. Thank you for waking up to dirty dishes in the sink, and shoving piles of laundry aside before crawling into bed at night. Thank you for your support and encouragement in spite of and during the pursuit of this lofty dream of mine.

Angi Black: You are my other half. You encourage and inspire me every single day to be a better version of myself, as a writer and a human being. There are a million other things I could say, but we share a brain, so you already know what they are.

My Sareys…

Fox: I very simply and honestly could not get through a single day without you. Whether it's picking me up when I'm down or lifting me up for a celebration, you always know exactly what I need and you're always there by my side. You are the example of what it means to be a friend, and I'm so unbelievably grateful to have you.

Henning: You're my sense and my savior. Thank you for being my objective point of view in writing and life in general. Thank you for your grammar wizardry. Thank you for so very many things. Most especially, Dimitrius would like to thank you for his nickname.

Guillory: Is it secret? Is it safe?

Julie Hutchings: I can't even begin to express what a wonderful stroke of fate it was that you happened to need me at the same time I needed you. Thank you for teaching me so much about my characters and myself as a writer. You truly are the magic in my veins. I could sing your praises forever, but instead I'll just say: Spagett.

Amanda Gardner: Thank you for inviting me to eat hamburgers, and then for tirelessly helping me hone my pitch, my ms— all the things. Thank you for being my biggest cheerleader. Your enthusiasm is my fuel. You're a rockstar. You inspire me every single day, and I'm so happy to have you in my corner.

Josh Hewitt: You are my Zen Master. Thank you for putting up with my twisted way of pantsing out a plot. Thank you for making sense of things when I wasn't able to. Thanks for helping me hike my way up above the trees so that I could finally see the whole forest.

Roy De La Rosa: Thank you for being the first— and for a very long time—the only person to say this book was *something*. Thank you for reading all those words that never even made it into these pages. No one would be holding this book if not for you.

Trisha Leigh: My tree hugging sister-friend, thank you for inspiring me to take this leap of faith called self-publishing. Thank you for giving me that one tiny spark of an idea I needed to see this whole book in a brand new light. Above all, thank you for your patience and kindness. You mean the world to me.

Laura Oliva: I seriously would not have survived California or my first years of motherhood without you. Thank you for holding my hand and answering all my crazy self-pub questions. Thank you for freaking out over my words. Thank you for so many lunches and laughs. Thank you for being an all around badass.

Megan Whitmer and Kelsey Macke: Thank you for being my village. You keep me smiling. I love you forever and always.

Kelli Moore: You helped me give birth to both a book baby and a human baby. Thank you for giving me a place to make words, for encouraging me along this wild ride, for the times you understood me best, and for the times you might not have understood my struggle but you gave me hugs and handed me a glass of wine anyway.

Kali Meister: Thank you for being the first person who understood me as a writer. Your support, and encouragement, and power are still a constant inspiration to me. You helped me find myself and my voice. You gave me the courage I needed to write for myself instead of anyone else, to write the book I wanted to read.

Dawn Bridges: Thank you for being my preschool partner. Thank you for the sweet tea fuel that kept me going. Thank you for the trips to Target. Thank you for not laughing me down the hall when I handed you the first terribly, awful draft of this book.

Mandy Mospan and Martha Peribonio: Thank you for being my first readers, and loving my favorite scene as much as I do.

Pam Wallace, Kim Aina, and Beverly Hitt: Thank you for being my unwavering friends. Your love and support has been invaluable.

Gina Ciocca: Thank you for the donuts, and walking my baby across the floor so I could make words. I'm so happy we're finally close enough to see each other on a regular basis.

Megan Orsini: You're pretty and so are your words. I know this because I'm standing right behind you.

Carey Torgeson: I love you, wifey!

Megan Paasch: We pass the Bechdel Test with flying colors. Thanks for being my soul sister.

Derek Chivers: I really was going to include that Bourbon comment, and I totally lost it. Epic Fail. But know that it is awesome, and so are you!

Dave Lin: Thank you for letting me make your home Sidney's home. And here's to all the fun times we had there!

Lauri Goodling: Thank you for being my awesome writer friend. You challenge me in all the best ways, and inspire me to be better every day.

Britt: Thank you for being my first unsolicited fan.

Brenda Drake: If not for you, I would not have discovered the writing community I so desperately needed. Thanks to your unfailing desire to help others. I have felt loved and supported through this entire process by you and the people you ushered into my life. That experience is invaluable and I can never repay your kindness.

For those who taught me:

Judy Honeycutt and Talli Campbell: I don't know how I would have survived my high school years without you both. Thank you for finding ways to encourage my talent and creativity, and for keeping me focused on the light at the end of the tunnel.

Bill Larsen: Thank you for the constant reminder that conflict is drama. You taught me how to fight for my words, and most importantly, to write words worth fighting for.

Allen Wier and Michael Knight: Thank you for not laughing me out of the Creative Writing department. I know my entertainment fiction was a lot to put up with, but you gave me a solid foundation and I'll be forever grateful.

"Auntie" Liz Gilbert: Thank you for your smile and encouragement, in the classroom and long after it. You are still an inspiration to me. On the days when I'd rather wash a load of laundry, fold it, put it away, and wash it all over again instead of write a single word, I think of you and plow on.

Suzie Townsend: Your patience and willingness to help me dig deep into these characters and this story truly helped shape it into something wonderful. I learned so much from your insight. Thank you, from the bottom of my heart.

For my family:

Uncle Gary: Your quiet support and generous nature made it possible for me to follow my dreams. You have always been the best example of what it means to serve and uplift others in a completely selfless manner.

FayFay: Thank you for being my friend, for teaching me so much, and for taking the time to walk and talk with me. Thank you for letting me read my words to you, and for encouraging me to always do my best no matter what path I'm on.

Mama Carolyn: Thank you for your love and support. Thank you for enjoying the endless hours of grandkid time so that I could sneak away and chase my dreams. Thank you for taking such good care of all of us. None of this would ever have been possible without you.

Rachel Hicks and Emily Blair: Being able to share my love of books and writing with you makes me happier than I could ever express. You both inspire me everyday with your strength and fortitude as women and mothers.

Charlie Blair: Thank you for always being there to geek out with me. I'm so thankful you're my big brother and my friend.

Paul Blair: Thanks for your love and support. And thanks for never letting me win at Pickle. I hated you for it at the time, but now that I've gained perspective, I see you were only teaching me how to never give up on my dreams.

Jane Sherrard-Smith: Thank you for being my friend and surrogate mum. You took me under your wing and fostered my love of your country. Our adventures together were the seeds that grew and blossomed into this story. I can never repay your kindness. All my love, xxx.

To the rest of my community, writing and otherwise: Maureen Ruka Ouellette, Ben Hughes,

Elizabeth Stipek, Jessica Dainty, Summer Heacock, Darci Cole, Erica Chapman, Claire Legrand, Renee Ting, Kristi Wright, Kathy Ellen Davis, Emily Bartnikowski, Heidi Schulz, Ann Marie Walker, Jennifer Freely, Sabaa Tahir, Reneé Ahdieh, Ricki Schultz, Liz Lincoln, Donna Cummings, Jessica Collins, Veronica Bartles, Jessica Sinsheimer, Joy Bailey Chapman, Rebecca Coffindaffer, Tonya Kuper, Chuck Sambuchino, Amy Trueblood, Megan Erickson, Paul Adams, Jackie Case, Steph Funk, Danielle Ellison, Catherine Scully, Jessa Russo, Jenny Kaczorowski, Krista Walsh, Kristen Strassel, Gina Denny, Marieke Nijkamp, Cait Greer, Brooks Sherman, J. Liz Hill, My incredible Street Team, my sisters from Sugar Hill, Hicklebee's Novel Society, The Pride, and so many others, thank you for supporting and uplifting me on this journey.

About the Author

photo by James Hicks

Sarah Lee Blair earned a BA in Creative Writing from the University of Tennessee, Knoxville. While spending a semester abroad at Swansea University in Wales she traveled to nearby Bath and Glastonbury often, drawing inspiration for her writing from the myths and legends surrounding the area. Sarah now resides just north of Atlanta, Georgia with her husband, their two children, and chihuahua. While writing is her first passion, she also enjoys sewing, tater tots, catching up on her teetering TBR pile, and hanging out on her porch drinking sweet tea.

53378095R00209

Made in the USA
Lexington, KY
02 July 2016